T0267602

PRAISE FOR MELANIE DICKERSON

"This second volume in best-seller Dickerson's Dericott Tales series follows two narrators who overcome self-doubt in accepting their physical differences and gain the confidence to love while finding solace in their Christianity . . . Dickerson writes a well-developed and wholesome romance between pleasant characters whose happy ending readers will easily root for."

—*BOOKLIST* ON *CASTLE OF REFUGE*

"Dickerson does a nice job of evoking late-14th-century England and has succeeded in crafting a pair of engaging—if sugary-sweet—characters that romance readers will enjoy following. The Christian flavor of the story feels natural and appropriate to the time period."

—*KIRKUS REVIEWS* ON *CASTLE OF REFUGE*

"*Court of Swans* is a well-crafted escape thriller with plenty of longing glances to break up scenes of sword fighting. Delia is a compelling protagonist because she is able to see the good in people—rarely do you see an obviously wicked stepmother so often given the benefit of the doubt. A perfect pick for fans of period dramas who want a little action mixed into their romance."

—MOLLY HORAN, *BOOKLIST*

"*The Piper's Pursuit* is a lovely tale of adventure, romance, and redemption. Kat and Steffan's righteous quest will have you rooting them on until the very satisfying end!"

—LORIE LANGDON, AUTHOR OF *OLIVIA TWIST* AND THE DOON SERIES

"Christian fiction fans will relish Dickerson's eloquent story."

—*SCHOOL LIBRARY JOURNAL* ON *THE ORPHAN'S WISH*

"Dickerson is a masterful storyteller with a carefully crafted plot, richly drawn characters, and a detailed setting. The reader is easily pulled into the story."

"A terrific YA crossover medieval romance from the author of *The Golden Braid*."

"When it comes to happily-ever-afters, Melanie Dickerson is the undisputed queen of fairy-tale romance, and all I can say is—long live the queen! From start to finish *The Beautiful Pretender* is yet another brilliant gem in her crown, spinning a medieval love story that will steal you away—heart, soul, and sleep!"

"Dickerson breathes life into the age-old story of Rapunzel, blending it seamlessly with the other YA novels she has written in this time and place . . . The character development is solid, and she captures religious medieval life splendidly."

"Readers who love getting lost in a fairy-tale romance will cheer for Rapunzel's courage as she rises above her overwhelming past. The surprising way Dickerson weaves threads of this enchanting companion novel with those of her other Hagenheim stories is simply delightful."

LADY *of* DISGUISE

OTHER BOOKS BY
MELANIE DICKERSON

THE DERICOTT TALES
Court of Swans
Castle of Refuge
Veil of Winter
Fortress of Snow
Cloak of Scarlet
Lady of Disguise

YOUNG ADULT FAIRY TALE ROMANCE SERIES
The Healer's Apprentice
The Merchant's Daughter
The Fairest Beauty
The Captive Maiden
The Princess Spy
The Golden Braid
The Silent Songbird
The Orphan's Wish
The Warrior Maiden
The Piper's Pursuit
The Peasant's Dream

A MEDIEVAL FAIRY TALE SERIES
The Huntress of Thornbeck Forest
The Beautiful Pretender
The Noble Servant

REGENCY SPIES OF LONDON SERIES

A Spy's Devotion
A Viscount's Proposal
A Dangerous Engagement

IMPERILED YOUNG WIDOWS SERIES

A Perilous Plan
A Treacherous Treasure
A Deadly Secret
A Stormy Season

LADY *of* DISGUISE

MELANIE DICKERSON

THOMAS NELSON
Since 1798

Published in Nashville, Tennessee, by Thomas Nelson. Thomas Nelson is a registered trademark of HarperCollins Christian Publishing, Inc.

Thomas Nelson titles may be purchased in bulk for educational, business, fundraising, or sales promotional use. For information, please email SpecialMarkets@ThomasNelson.com.

Publisher's Note: This novel is a work of fiction. Names, characters, places, and incidents are either products of the author's imagination or used fictitiously. All characters are fictional, and any similarity to people living or dead is purely coincidental.

Any internet addresses (websites, blogs, etc.) in this book are offered as a resource. They are not intended in any way to be or imply an endorsement by Thomas Nelson, nor does Thomas Nelson vouch for the content of these sites for the life of this book.

ISBN 978-0-8407-0867-0 (hardcover)
ISBN 978-0-8407-0870-0 (e-book)
ISBN 978-0-8407-0881-6 (downloadable audio)

Library of Congress Cataloging-in-Publication Data

CIP data is available upon request.

Printed in the United States of America

24 25 26 27 28 LBC 6 5 4 3 2

To Aaron
The one I love
The one who loves me

ONE

APRIL 1388

LOUISA SCOOPED UP ANOTHER HALF DOZEN TADPOLES with her pottery cup and dropped them in the bucket.

"I'm hungry." Her younger sister, Margaret, sighed and sat back on her heels in the mud.

"Go to the kitchen and ask for some bread and cheese."

"Aunt Celestria said we couldn't come in until we caught at least a hundred tadpoles."

"I've almost got enough. Go get some food." Louisa continued searching the murky water of the fishpond for tadpoles that would grow up to be the croaking bullfrogs that kept their aunt awake at night.

Margaret gave her a look. "She will scream at me."

"Not if she doesn't see you. She never goes to the kitchen this time of day."

Margaret sighed again. "I can wait." She went back to dragging her little cup through the water.

"Girls!"

Louisa turned her head to see the housekeeper, Nesta, motioning frantically to them. Nine-year-old Bertram was beside her, making faces at them—sticking out his tongue and waving his hands above his head like donkey ears. As the heir, their cousin did only what he pleased.

Margaret jumped to her feet and began to run across the grassy yard toward the house, her feet and skirts slinging mud in all directions. Louisa stayed several feet behind her sister, carrying the bucket of tadpoles.

"Covered from head to toe in mud." Nesta's tense voice matched her face. "Get out of those filthy clothes and clean yourselves up. You have to get into your best dresses. Make haste!"

"Make haste!" Bertram mimicked, pointing at them.

"Why? What's happening?" But as soon as Louisa asked, she knew. "Another man looking for a wife." She let out a noisy breath and rolled her eyes.

"Yes, now hurry," Nesta said. "You know how your aunt and uncle get. And you too," she said to Margaret. "You're invited to the feast as well."

Louisa stopped midstep. "Margaret too? Why?" Margaret ran inside and Louisa waited until she was out of earshot. "He would not marry Margaret off, would he?" She was only twelve.

Nesta's brows went up, wrinkling her forehead. "They don't

tell me anything, but why else would she be invited?" She shook her head as she walked away.

In their bedroom, Louisa's heart was in her throat as she imagined her sister—the person she loved more than anyone else in the world; sweet, innocent Margaret—being married off to a wealthy suitor so she could bear the man's children. How could she endure that?

She and Margaret took off their muddy kirtles and under-dresses and used their basins and a cloth to wash.

How much should Louisa say to her little sister? She wanted to warn her, but she also didn't want to frighten her. "Try not to smile or say anything sweet in front of our guest."

"Are you afraid he will pick me for his bride?" Margaret giggled. "I don't even have my breasts yet." She stuck out her flat chest.

"I'm sure you have nothing to worry about." Louisa tried to smile and lightly pulled her sister's hair, and Margaret responded in kind.

Their former nurse, Hanilda, came in. "Stop that foolishness and finish getting ready." She took the washcloth and started using it on Margaret's cheeks and forehead, making her yelp.

"I can wash my own face!"

Hanilda gave her back the cloth and started picking out their best dresses and laying them on the bed.

Louisa had managed to prevent any suitors from choosing her by behaving badly—scowling at them, crossing her eyes, and generally saying and doing anything that might make a man not choose her for his wife—when her aunt and uncle weren't looking. She'd been lucky. But her luck was sure to run out sooner or later. At eighteen years old, she might be considered by some to be past her prime.

Margaret couldn't bear children yet, but she would be able to soon. If her aunt and uncle were already trying to arrange a marriage for Margaret, not even waiting to find Louisa a husband first, then she had to go now and find the Viking treasure her father had told her about when she was a little girl. Finding that treasure and using it to make a future for herself and Margaret was what she had hoped and dreamed about for years.

After changing into their dresses, they hurried down to the Great Hall. Her aunt and uncle were already sitting at the table with food and drink before them. Next to her aunt was a well-dressed stranger with gray hair, and a boy, obviously his son, sat beside him. He looked a year or two younger than Margaret.

Surely the man would not wish to marry someone who was barely older than his own son. Hope bloomed inside her. But then she saw the man staring at her with a greedy smile and her good mood vanished.

"Ah, here they are." Her uncle swept his arms toward them. "My beautiful nieces, Louisa and Margaret." He didn't bother to introduce their guest to them.

Louisa and Margaret bowed to the man as they had been taught.

The old man stood. "I am honored to meet such lovely young ladies, as fair of character as they are of face."

He stared pointedly at their uncle, as if asking for confirmation.

"They both are well-behaved, I assure you." Uncle Eluard smiled as he told the lie, for even though neither she nor her sister were mean-spirited, Louisa disobeyed when she considered their aunt and uncle's commands to be unreasonable—which was often.

Judging by the look of the would-be suitor's clothing, he was rather wealthy. But would he be willing to pay the price her uncle wanted for her?

Uncle Eluard was from a noble family, though he had no title himself, and so was her aunt, who was Louisa's mother's sister. When Father and Mother died of the same fever five days apart, Uncle Eluard had taken over the lordship of her father's manor house and the land attached to it. Louisa had spent her early childhood at Maydestone Manor before her parents' deaths. Then they had to move to Reedbrake, her uncle's manor house. Along with the land and house, her uncle received rent and taxes from all her father's tenants, as well as his own tenants, so they were not poor. But her uncle was always eager to acquire more, for he dearly loved to spend his days eating and drinking, and her aunt loved buying expensive clothing for herself.

Louisa was directed to sit at the long trestle table across from the gray-haired merchant, who was more than twice Louisa's age. Margaret was next to her.

"Are they not comely girls?" her uncle said, nudging the merchant's shoulder with the back of his wrist and grinning.

Louisa felt sick as their guest gazed first at Louisa, then at Margaret. But then his eyes came back to rest on Louisa, and he seemed to be studying her.

Her uncle was focused on his food and used his fingers to bring a chunk of pheasant to his greasy lips, and while he was not paying attention to her, Louisa scowled her most disdainful and angry scowl at the merchant.

The man stared back, but as she continued to scowl at him, he started to appear ill at ease and looked over at her uncle. Louisa quickly glanced down at her food.

She had been hungry, but now her mind was spinning and her stomach churning. She could barely swallow a bite of pheasant, which was one of her favorite foods.

She kept an eye on Margaret, who had her head down and wasn't speaking at all. The stranger's expression must have made innocent Margaret uncomfortable. Something about the way he looked at them made Louisa's skin feel like bugs were crawling on her.

The feast dragged on, with her uncle talking of food and drink, his two favorite things, and the merchant speaking of the goods he imported and bragging about his ships and his fine house in London. When the last course, a plum pudding, was served, their uncle brought the merchant's attention back to Louisa.

"She's as pure as snow, always having been under my protection, and she might not be smiling much now, but believe me, she is as sweet-tempered as you can imagine, once she knows you better."

As the merchant turned his gaze toward Louisa, her uncle was distracted by giving instructions to one of the servants. Louisa crossed her eyes and let her mouth hang open.

The merchant's son laughed.

Unfortunately, the boy's laugh drew her uncle's notice, and he slammed his fist on the table.

The merchant yelled at his son, "Enough of your noise! Get to your bed!"

Aunt Celestria and Uncle Eluard glared at Louisa.

Her uncle ordered, "Go to your room, both of you."

Louisa and Margaret practically ran. Their aunt followed them up the stairs, hissing, "Selfish girl! If you don't marry soon, we will cast you out, and then you shall have to fend for yourself!" She stood in their bedroom doorway glaring at them. "Ungrateful, that's what you are. You can stay in here until you're ready to do your duty to your uncle." She closed the door.

It hurt that her aunt thought she was selfish and ungrateful. She wasn't selfish—no more than most people, she suspected— and she didn't think she was particularly ungrateful either. She just wanted to protect her sister and save herself.

Louisa and Margaret were getting into the bed they shared with Hanilda, who was still about her duties in the kitchen, when they heard a rustling sound coming from underneath the bed.

"What is that?" Margaret whispered, latching onto Louisa's arm.

"Probably one of the dogs." Louisa tried to sound unafraid so as not to frighten Margaret, but she stared hard into the dark room. Thankfully, she had not yet snuffed out their candle.

"It's me," said a child's voice. The merchant's son stuck his head up as he climbed out from under the bed.

"How did you get in here?" Louisa's heart raced at the horror of a year ago, when one of her uncle's suitors had sneaked into her room and tried to force himself on her. She'd had terrifying nightmares for weeks afterward. That was when she had begun in earnest to plan how to run away to Yorkshire and go after the Vikings' treasure.

"I slipped past the servant who was refilling your water pitcher and hid under the bed just as you were coming in the door," the boy said.

"But why?" Margaret asked.

"I'm hiding from my father. I hate sleeping in the same room with him. He snores and cracks me on the head if I ask for a cup of water. May I stay in here with you?"

"What a dreadful man," Margaret whispered.

Louisa quite agreed. The poor boy.

He seemed harmless enough, so Louisa said, "You may stay, but when our servant Hanilda comes, she will probably put you out."

"I can sleep under the bed and she will never see me," he answered.

Truly, he seemed rather pitiful. "Very well, but you will need a blanket," Louisa said.

Margaret sprang from the bed and fetched a blanket and pillow from the trunk against the wall.

"This pillow is rather flat," Margaret said, "and the dog may have peed on it."

The boy sniffed it.

"If it stinks too bad—"

"It's well enough." The boy hugged it and the wool blanket to his chest. "Do you have a swimming hole nearby?"

"A swimming hole?" Margaret climbed back onto the bed and sat cross-legged beside Louisa.

The boy hopped up onto the foot of the bed and sat facing them. "Where the river runs off to the side and the water is calm. That's where I go swimming."

"We don't know how to swim. How do you do it?" Margaret looked quite animated. She rarely was able to interact with other children her own age. The tenants' children were half-wild and too much in awe of "the lord's children" to play with her.

Louisa interrupted the boy's explanation. "What is your name? What are we to call you?"

"Maury. I'm the youngest, but if Father marries you, I suppose I shall have more brothers and sisters." He nodded at Louisa.

She half expected him to laugh and say he was only in jest. He did not.

"I don't think my sister will be marrying your father." Margaret was starting to smile, but one look at Louisa wiped the smile off her face.

Louisa felt sick again at the thought of marrying that old, disgusting man and bearing his children. Louisa had her own plans, and they didn't include marriage.

Maury continued to talk. After he described a typical day in his village home not far from London, he changed the subject without warning. "Did you know there is a Viking treasure in Yorkshire? It is guarded by a giant who is so big he can kill ten men with a single blow."

"We have heard of this treasure too," Margaret said, whispering excitedly.

Louisa wanted to shush her sister, but it was too late, so she just nudged her shoulder, hoping she would understand that she shouldn't say anything about Louisa's plans.

"The treasure is from a Viking raider who buried his loot on the mountain and never came back for it. They say the giant who guards it also has a goose that lays golden eggs. If a person were to steal the golden goose, they'd have more gold than they would know what to do with, because the goose would just keep laying golden eggs. I reckon the person who owned this goose could build as many castles as he liked and still have money for a hundred horses."

Even though Louisa had never heard about a giant or a golden goose, Maury was obviously talking about the same treasure that had been constantly in Louisa's thoughts.

"I don't know if there is a giant or a golden goose," Margaret said, "but I do believe in the Viking treasure. It's buried among the rocks on a mountain in Yorkshire."

"Of course there is a giant," the boy said. "How else has the treasure never been found? I also heard from a Scotsman I met in London that there are magic beans, and if you plant them at the bottom of the hill, the vines will grow up in one night, all the way to the top of the rocks, and you can climb the magic beanstalk to get to the treasure."

"Magic beanstalk?" Margaret said in an awed whisper, her eyes wide. "How do we get the magic beans?"

"From the magic bean man, of course." The boy laughed.

Louisa wanted to scoff at the thought of magic beans, a giant, and a goose that laid golden eggs. Those had to be made-up stories. But if the boy knew about the Viking treasure, she might learn something from him.

"Who told you about the treasure?" Louisa asked.

"Everybody knows about the Viking treasure. It was left there by Ivar the Boneless, and he died before he could go back and fetch it."

"Then why hasn't someone found it?" Louisa asked.

"Because of the giant. Weren't you listening?"

"I thought it was the treasure of the Viking king, Harald Hardrada," Margaret interjected.

"A couple of knights could easily kill one giant," Louisa said.

"Don't you think knights have better things to do?" Maury tilted his head to one side as he squinted at her. "They're guarding the king and fighting invaders. It would be beneath them to kill a giant to steal treasure."

His reasoning did not seem sound. There were sure to be greedy knights, just as there were greedy lords and greedy villeins. In Louisa's experience, some people were good and some were bad, and you never knew which they were—until they showed their true natures.

Maury went on. "The Scotsman told me the treasure was in Swaledale, in Yorkshire. He said he knew right where it was, could point out the very mountain it was on."

Louisa's heart was beating faster, but she had to be sure not to show her excitement. She didn't want this boy knowing that her secret ambition was to find that treasure and take just enough of it to make sure she and Margaret never had to worry about being cast off to starve, as her uncle and aunt so often threatened, or sold off to marry men who would just use them and not care about them. She didn't want to take anyone's golden goose, and she didn't believe there was a giant guarding it, for surely by now he would have been killed by some knight with a sword and the training to defeat him. But that didn't mean the treasure wasn't still there to be discovered.

Louisa asked, as if doubting it, "Swaledale? What's the nearest village? Did he tell you that?"

Maury shook his head and muttered, "Don't think so. Say, about that swimming hole. Don't you have a river or a pond nearby? I aim to go swimming in the morning."

Louisa's heart sank, wishing Maury knew more, but she wondered if there was any truth to what he'd already said.

Margaret frowned and shook her head. "We have a fishpond, but it's more of a frog pond. You wouldn't want to go swimming in it. It's muddy and full of tadpoles."

Louisa's little sister began to complain to Maury about having to clean out the tadpoles and frogs from the pond, but Louisa's thoughts wandered.

As soon as this merchant and his son were gone, she would do what she had planned in her head a hundred times. She would dress herself as a boy, pack up her things, and set out for Yorkshire and the Viking treasure her father had told her about.

It was the only way she knew to save herself and her sister.

Two

CHARLES COULDN'T REMEMBER THE LAST TIME HE'D HAD
no duty to perform and no destination in mind. He rode his horse
into a village and bought some fresh bread. Several more miles
down the road, he found a nice, quiet spot in the woods to build
a fire and cook the hare he'd killed earlier that day.

He lay back, his head and shoulders propped on his saddle
and bedroll. Feeling well-fed and sleepy, he took a deep breath
and let it out slowly. No place to be, no one to answer to, and
best of all, no woman to lie to him and make him miserable.

Why did his mind always have to bring him back to Lady
Mirabella? He wanted to forget that she had made him believe
that she loved him, made him believe she wanted to marry him,
when she had told three other knights the same thing.

But now that she was marrying a duke's son, she would not
find it so easy to kiss her father's knights and make them think
she was in love with them.

Charles got up and sat on a log in front of the fire, stirring the embers with a stick and adding some more wood. Last week he had turned twenty-one, and even though it had not been his plan to do so, due to his change in circumstances he had decided it was a good time to go out on his own.

His birthday would forever be marred by the memory of Mirabella's father announcing that his daughter was to marry a duke's son in a fortnight. And by making a fool of himself by climbing up to her room that night.

He'd set the ladder against the side of the castle tower just under her bedchamber window, risking a broken neck to climb the rickety ladder and rap on her window.

"Sir Charles!" Her eyes were wide when she opened it.

"May I come in?"

She stepped back. "Quickly, before someone sees you."

He climbed in, entering her bedchamber, something he never would have done had he not been so desperate to see her.

She embraced him and he held her tight. "I will take you away from here. We will marry in Dericott, and I will earn my fortune in Prussia or—"

"What? No." Mirabella stepped away from him, pushing out of his arms.

His heart sank. "But you cannot marry the duke's son when we . . . I have pledged my love for you and only you, Mirabella. Do you not understand?"

Mirabella was frowning at him as she folded her arms across her chest. "You love me, and I am content to receive your love. But you cannot expect me to marry you when Father has betrothed me to Lord Dowdle, who shall be a wealthy duke someday."

His whole body, mind, and spirit went numb. "Have you even met him?"

"I have met him." She just stared at him, the coldest look he'd ever seen on her face. "You are only a knight. You did not actually expect me to marry you, did you?"

The pain was like a dagger in his heart. "You said you loved me." *Be quiet, Charles.* "You kissed me." *Stop embarrassing yourself.* "You said you would be so happy if we were to marry. You cannot love Lord Dowdle."

Every moment he stayed, trying to convince her that she loved him, wishing this was just a nightmare he would soon wake from, he made a bigger fool of himself. But how could he leave? She was all he thought about, dreamed of—everything he wanted. And he had believed she felt the same.

Just then a quiet tapping came at her chamber door. Her expression suddenly changed. "Hide," she said.

Charles stepped behind the door and waited for her to open it. If it was her father, he would beg the man to let him marry his daughter.

She frowned at Charles, no doubt disapproving of his hiding place. She opened the door about a foot, sticking her face in the opening.

"Don't marry Lord Dowdle," a man's voice whispered.

Someone pushed the door wide-open so that Charles could no longer see Mirabella.

Charles stepped out from behind the door and saw a man kissing Mirabella and holding her in his arms. And if he wasn't mistaken, that man was Sir Fordwin.

Mirabella pushed out of his arms, much as she had pushed away from Charles.

Sir Fordwin caught sight of him and his mouth fell open. "Why are you in Lady Mirabella's room?"

"I could ask you the same question." But Charles was beginning to understand.

"You both are noble knights," Lady Mirabella said while calmly looking from one to the other, her hands loosely clasped in front of her. "I will not prevent you from paying courtly love to me. But I'm afraid I cannot kiss you anymore, now that I am to be married to Lord Dowdle. It would be unseemly. Therefore, you must love me from afar."

Sir Fordwin appeared to be as speechless as Charles. Indeed, Charles felt gutted, like a slaughtered animal, but at the same time, he felt sorry for Sir Fordwin; the man must feel as Charles did, discovering that the woman he thought was as devoted to him as he was to her actually felt nothing for him.

She had duped them both.

"How many men have you been kissing?" Sir Fordwin demanded, no longer whispering.

"I do not like your tone," Mirabella said. "You must go now."

"How many?" Charles moved to stand in front of her.

"You are both behaving badly," she said, starting to pout, her bottom lip protruding slightly.

He couldn't believe he'd once thought her pout the most

adorable thing he'd ever seen. Or that he'd once considered her the most lovely and angelic creature in the world.

Sir Fordwin growled as he leaned toward her menacingly, his hands on his hips. "How many?"

"If you must know, there were one or two others of my father's guards who were favorites of mine. Is that so wrong? If you all wish to love me and give me tokens of your love, I will not stop you. I can ask the duke, when he becomes my husband, if he will hire you both to be in his guard."

"You do understand," Charles said, "that your husband will not wish to have men lurking about who are in love with his wife? Not to mention that I do not want to see you married to someone else."

"I don't understand." And truly, Mirabella looked as if she did not.

"You have read too many stories." Charles shook his head, feeling sick, remembering how he had hoped and planned, thinking he might actually have a chance to marry her, and also now realizing he might have made this young, thoughtless creature his wife, which would have been a huge mistake.

Sir Fordwin, with his hands clenched into fists, turned on his heel and strode from the room. But he only made it into the corridor before he came back and pointed his finger at Lady Mirabella's face.

"You will not see me again. Ever." Then he turned and stomped out.

Charles was still stunned by her words and behavior. Finally, he said, "I am sorry you think a man will pine away for you while you are married to another. Certainly, I have no wish to spend my life in love with a married woman."

Part of him wanted to scold and criticize her, accuse her of being unfeeling, and worse. But he held back, as she was quite young and sheltered, and he had loved her—or thought he loved her.

"That is what knights do—they fall in love with an unattainable lady and then send her gifts, poems and flowers and ribbons. You have disappointed me." Again she stuck out her lip and crossed her arms.

Charles could hardly believe he had been so enamored with this woman. Finally, he walked toward the door and gave her one last glance over his shoulder. "Not as much as you have disappointed me."

It was unchivalrous of him, perhaps, but he was beginning to realize, as the numbness wore off, just how bitterly disappointed he was.

Now, as he sat before his own fire in the woods, thinking about how foolhardy he had felt just a few days ago, he said aloud to himself, "I am a noble knight, trained to fight and avowed to uphold what is good and right. I shall not waste my life, but I shall boldly defend the weak, the innocent, the widow, and the orphan. I shall love only what is good, and I shall defeat wickedness wherever I find it."

He would remind himself of who he was and to whom his loyalty belonged now that he had left the service of Lady Mirabella's father. Was it the duty of a noble knight to simply belong to some duke's guard, even if there was no danger to the duke? No, indeed.

Only recently his brother Merek had been sent by King Richard to serve a baron who, he later discovered, was an evil man who mistreated, murdered, and robbed his own people. Truly, in such a wicked world as this, a knight must seek and find his own noble quest. He couldn't even trust that his king would always send him on an honest mission.

It was better this way, finding himself unencumbered by a lady's love. Who needed a wife? Not he.

Charles had seven noble-hearted brothers, if he counted his sister, Delia's, husband. A wife would make it more difficult to see his family as often as he liked, and a wife would make it impossible to do what he was doing now—going about the English countryside seeking wrongs to make right, damsels in distress to rescue, and other good deeds and noble quests.

He would no longer think about any disappointment over Lady Mirabella. That was over and done, and he wouldn't dwell on how duplicitous she had been.

He stretched out on his blanket and closed his eyes, feeling comfortable and drowsy in the heat of his own fire.

Early the next morning, Maury tiptoed out before Hanilda woke up, and Louisa left right behind him. She slipped out of the house and took the steward's breeches and her uncle's shirt that were still hanging on the clothesline. From the trunk of her dead cousin, Gamel—may God rest his soul—she took a liripipe, hose, a hat, shoes, and an extra tunic and cloak. After all, he had no more need of them.

Girls did not wander the roads alone, but a boy could do as he pleased. Which was why she would bind a cloth around her chest and wear her uncle's thick, bulky linen shirt and some loose breeches. No one would be able to tell that she was a girl if she cut her hair and covered her head with a hat or hood like men were wont to do. She could even tell people she was a lad of fourteen, which would explain why there was no beard or moustache growing on her face.

Dressing as a boy was easy, but cutting her hair? That made her want to cry.

In the evening, after everyone was in bed, she found the map of Yorkshire she had copied from a book she'd discovered among her parents' belongings. She stuffed it inside the bag with her clothing. There was just one more thing she had left to do.

Louisa had Margaret hold the looking glass before her face. She felt a physical pain in her chest when she took a small handful of hair and sliced it off with her uncle's razor. The second handful was cut, then the next and the next, as a weight settled in her stomach. But it was only hair. Why was she being so silly about it?

When she was a child, her mother would brush her hair and say, "Your hair is one of the things that makes you a beauty—soft and smooth, with just a touch of chestnut. It reminds me of my mother's hair, may God rest her soul."

And now, just as she'd feared, Louisa felt ugly without her hair.

"I make a clever-looking fourteen-year-old boy, don't you think?" Louisa said, carefully blinking back the tears.

Margaret's expression was a cross between doubt and concern. But she said, "Yes, you do. But you will have to look grumpy, spit through your teeth, and scratch yourself a lot so people don't get suspicious."

Louisa wanted to cover her face and groan.

This was what she wanted. And she was glad she was finally carrying out her plan. Besides, she had to be brave for Margaret's sake. It would be a long time before they would see each other again.

"Don't forget to bury the hair," Louisa said.

"I won't. And you have your purse?"

"Yes, all the coins I've been saving."

"And Father's dagger?"

"Yes." Louisa had taken her father's dagger from his belongings when her uncle confiscated her parents' possessions after they died.

"To pay for your upkeep," her aunt had explained, though they all knew their uncle was wealthy enough on his own without needing their parents' belongings, which rightfully should have been inherited by Louisa and Margaret.

Apparently not only were her aunt and uncle to profit from their parents' death, inheriting the land and manor house since they did not have a male heir, but Margaret and Louisa were also expected to marry well and further contribute to their coffers. When Aunt Celestria lectured them about getting married, she said, "It is your duty to marry as your uncle sees fit, as it is the only way for you to repay us for taking care of you and feeding you and bringing you up in the Church. And it is your duty to God and to your husband to bear children and baptize them."

The way her aunt talked about it made Louisa want to rebel against such "duties." Before her mother and father died, she had wanted to marry, but Aunt Celestria made it seem like marriage was something distasteful that was done out of duty, not a joyful relationship of love and choice.

Men certainly didn't seem to have such distasteful duties. They could marry whomever they pleased, go and do as they pleased, with no one to tell them they owed their lives as a duty to someone else. Although there was, perhaps, one exception. A knight's duty was to his king and country, and his code of chivalry decreed he must fight bravely and with honor and never fail to rescue any lady who was in trouble. At least that's what the stories all said.

When Louisa looked into Margaret's hopeful eyes, a pang of fear stabbed her stomach. Louisa was concerned that her uncle might try to marry Margaret off while she was gone, but it would take at least three weeks to cry the banns, so she should have at least four weeks, which in her estimation was enough time to get to Yorkshire and back.

Still, she had to hurry, and she couldn't fail. But even if she didn't find the treasure, she would figure out another way to rescue them both. She was like a knight on a noble quest, and her quest was to save Margaret—and herself—from having to marry someone they could not love or respect.

"I must go now. When they ask where I am, simply tell them you don't know, which is true, and that I've gone to seek my fortune. They will laugh and send men after me, but you needn't worry. And remember, do not tell them that I've disguised myself as a boy."

Margaret put her hand on her hip and rolled her eyes. "I am not daft. I certainly shall not tell them *that*."

Louisa looked at herself in the mirror again. Did she look like a boy? She pulled on the flat hat she had taken from one of the trunks. Perhaps if she pulled it low over her forehead, no one would notice that her face was softer and curvier than most boys' faces. She supposed it was the delicate look of her eyelashes, the fullness of her lips, and the extra padding around her cheekbones and jawline.

But there was nothing she could do about those things.

"Remember to walk like a boy," Margaret said, handing her the bundle of clothing and food Louisa had packed.

"I will." Louisa hugged her sister, praying silently, *God, help me come back to her with enough money so I can provide for us both.*

Since some of the servants slept on the floor near the front door of the manor house, Louisa opened the bedchamber window and climbed out, purposely not looking back at Margaret. She climbed down the rope she had hung there and jumped the last two feet to the ground. Margaret was to pull the rope back up, but Louisa didn't wait to see if she had. Instead, she hurried away with her bundle under her arm.

THREE

LOUISA HUDDLED UNDER A TREE THE NEXT MORNING IN the dripping rain. Her hood was soaked through, plastering her hair to her scalp as water ran down her face.

She had planned on walking all night, then finding a spot near the road and sleeping when the sun came up. But it had started to rain when she was barely three miles from home, so she had kept moving, the road becoming muddier and muddier. When she had gone about six miles, exhaustion and cold started to weigh her down and she decided to find a place to sleep. In a thickly wooded area, she dug out a spot for herself under the leaves where it was slightly less muddy and wet. Then she lay down, using the leaves to cover herself the best she could.

A sound had awakened her. How long had she been asleep? She wasn't sure, but her heart was pounding as she heard the sound again—a wolf howling in the distance.

She lay as still as she could, listening. The rain was still falling, constantly making tiny sounds as the raindrops landed on leaves above her head on a tree and on the ground around her.

Just as she was starting to drift off to sleep, she heard the howling again, and this time it was closer.

Louisa jumped up and grabbed her pack, but it was so dark she could barely see the road, which was even muddier now. Her shoes stuck in the sticky brown slop, forcing her to have to stop and clean the mud off every few steps. However, she was too afraid not to keep moving, so she trudged on, hanging her head so the rain wouldn't drip into her eyes.

Would the night never end?

Finally, even though the clouds were heavy and the rain continued to fall, she saw the dull gray light that signaled the dawn approaching.

As she stood leaning her shoulder against the tree, she wondered if she would freeze to death, or if she would catch a disease from being cold and wet for too long.

She had hoped to be far away from home by the time it was daylight. Her uncle's household would be starting to wake, which meant soon a servant would notice her absence, probably Hanilda. Her uncle would realize she had run away and would send his men after her, but not because he was concerned for her. She was valuable to him only as a potential wife for some rich merchant or eager baron's son.

Her uncle's men searching for her was just one of the reasons she needed to travel mostly at night. She feared wild animals attacking her in her sleep, and she could fight them off if she was alert and moving, which made traveling in the dark seem wise. However, she wanted to get as far away as soon as possible, so she would have to keep going despite how little she had slept.

The muddy road was just visible through the trees. She had known this would be a difficult journey, but she hadn't realized just how difficult. Already she was so weary her bones ached. Her feet burned, as if in defiance of the cold. Was she too weary to go on? Or too cold and wet to stay still? She had to choose.

After sighing and letting a few tears mingle with the rain on her cheeks, she sank down on the ground where she was, lay with her hand covering her face, and fell asleep.

Louisa slowly awoke to the sound of men's voices and horses' hooves pounding the ground. She sat up and scrambled behind the nearest tree to watch the road.

From her hiding place she observed a group of five men, two on horses and the other three on mules. They rode at a trot—no doubt the fastest they dared move on the slick mud—past her.

Her heart jumped into her throat and she swallowed it down, the pain proving how thirsty she was and how long it had been since she'd taken a drink of water. And though she was still quite wet and even colder than before, it had stopped raining.

She was suddenly grateful for the rain, which would have washed away her footprints and made it hard for her uncle's men to track her.

How humiliating to have them find her now, shivering and

looking half-drowned. *Thank You, God, for the rain. But please help me get dry and warm.*

It must be nearly midmorning, and even though she was afraid her uncle's men would turn around and see her, she started walking again, staying on the grass on the side of the road as much as possible to avoid leaving footprints in the mud.

After a few minutes she came to a village and a large manor house. It was not a village Louisa was very familiar with, not being the village of Maydestone where her father's tenants lived, nor the market village where they bought their goods, but she was fairly sure this manor house was the home of Lord Metcalf, landholder of this demesne.

There was a stable and a couple of barns. Louisa chose the barn that looked the oldest and least used and went inside. A cow lay in the hay in one corner of the building. By the look of her, she was either sick or about to issue forth a calf.

Louisa threw down her pack, which contained her food and extra clothing, took off her soaked outer garment, and walked slowly toward the cow. "Good morning, mama cow," she said softly. "I won't hurt you, but I would like to be your friend."

The cow only stared at her with an unconcerned look in her dark cow eyes.

"May I lie down beside you? Would that be all right?" Louisa got down on her knees and slowly crawled the last few feet toward the cow, who snuffled and stared.

Louisa lay down, sensing the cow's snuffle was a warning. But even two feet away, she could feel the cow's warmth.

Leastways, it was warmer here in the barn in the hay than it was outside. She made a small pile of hay and propped her arm on it, in turn resting her cheek on her arm.

When Louisa peeked at the cow again, she was chewing her cud.

She decided to try again, scooting closer to the cow, who only looked at her. Finally, Louisa put out her hand and rubbed the cow's side, still talking softly. The cow did not seem to mind, so either she was a milk cow who was accustomed to being in close contact with people, or she had been hand-fed as a calf and was practically a pet.

Louisa inched closer and closer until she was lying against the cow's side. Still the cow did not protest, only lay placidly chewing.

Thank You, God. Louisa let her eyes close, the cow's warmth making her drowsy.

"Who are you? What are you doing in here?"

A man was glowering down at her with a pitchfork in his hands.

Louisa jumped to her feet as the cow bellowed—no doubt taking offense at being disturbed, both by Louisa's sudden movement and the man's angry tone.

"Say!" the man ordered, shaking the iron fork, which could have easily impaled her.

"Nothing. I was only taking shelter and I—"

"Where do you belong? Who's your master?"

The man's glower deepened as he no doubt suspected Louisa was a villein who had abandoned her lord, a serious offense.

"I am a free man on my way to visit family," Louisa said, hurrying to grab her discarded clothing and pack, which was still wet and now covered with the hay that stuck to it from the floor.

It was true that she was free, but the rest was a lie that she hoped would be forgiven, since she was only trying to save herself and her sister.

The man did not say anything, but he watched her go.

People were beholden to the lord of the land where they were born and therefore were not free to go elsewhere. So she was glad he must have believed her story. Either that or he just didn't want to bother with trying to find out where she belonged.

Once outside, she felt the chill again, though her clothes were mostly dry. Her bundle was quite damp, but she clutched it to her chest anyway. Finally, when she was out of sight of the village, she heeded her growling stomach and sat down on a fallen tree. She opened her pack to discover all her food was wet. The bread was soaked and crumbling, but she ate it anyway, until the sogginess made her gag.

There was nothing left to do but keep walking, so feeling only slightly less hungry, she got back on the road and continued on her journey.

The wet fabric of the men's hose rubbed against her inner thighs in a way that was extremely irritating and even starting to burn. How did men wear such things? And now she was missing the warmth of the cow and the barn, the cold, damp air chapping her cheeks and lips. Worst of all were her feet. She was unused to so much walking, and her wet shoes were rubbing blisters.

She felt so miserable that she began to think about going home. But the only future that awaited her there was bondage to some old man with a disturbing glint in his eye.

No, she would keep going no matter how miserable she was. At least she was free.

The smell of smoke tickled her nose. Where was it coming from? There didn't appear to be any houses nearby. Then she noticed, just off the road in the trees up ahead, a line of smoke drifting up into the sky.

Smoke meant there were men in the woods. Were they traveling too? Would they be good or bad men? But perhaps they would leave and she could revive their fire.

Desperately cold and wishing for nothing more than to be warm and dry, Louisa left the road and entered the trees, heading toward the smoke.

It was quite early and dark still because of the heavy clouds. Louisa approached cautiously as the smell of smoke grew stronger. Would the men attack her? Steal from her? Would she be left half dead like the man in the story of the Good Samaritan?

Then she saw it—a small fire, and beside it a man stretched out on the ground under a three-sided makeshift shelter of sticks and hemlock branches. He looked comfortable, wrapped in a blanket, while his horse stood several feet away.

Since the man was obviously sleeping, Louisa quietly lay down on a bed of leaves in the clearing, the smoldering fire between her and him. Surely she would awaken if he made any noise and she could run away if he seemed dangerous or threatened her like the man in the barn who shooed her away with a pitchfork.

She said a quick prayer that the man would not harm her and closed her eyes.

Charles rose, checked on his horse, and was fetching the sticks and broken tree limbs he had stacked under his shelter of tree limbs when he suddenly noticed a person lying on the ground only a few feet from his fire. How had he missed that?

He stood holding his firewood in his arms and studying the young man who lay on his side with a thin hood covering his head and most of his face. He used his arm as a pillow, a small bundle resting against his stomach. He looked wet from the rain, and by his heavy breathing and the fact that he hadn't moved, he must be asleep.

Charles couldn't see much of the man's face, but what he did see looked quite young. What was a boy doing sleeping in the woods by himself after a rain shower? Probably an orphan who had run away from his master. Well, he might as well let him sleep. Charles had no place to be, after all, and he might be able to help the lad.

He got a fire started, fed his horse a handful of oats, skinned the pheasant he had killed the day before, and prepared a spit over the fire to roast it on. Once the pheasant was prepared and beginning to cook, he took out some bread rolls and began to toast them over the fire.

The lad stirred with a sharp intake of breath and sat upright. "What?" he said groggily, staring straight at Charles with a fearful expression.

The hood had fallen off when he sat up, and now Charles could see that the "boy" was actually a young woman. Though she wore men's clothes and her hair was short, he was almost certain she was a female.

"Good morning," Charles said.

She scrambled to her feet, snatching up her bundle as she did. "Good morning."

It was almost comical the way she tried to deepen her voice, but the thought that she was in trouble and afraid—going to such lengths to make herself appear to be a boy—sobered him.

"I saw the smoke from your fire and thought I would . . . thought you might not mind if I shared your fire for a few minutes, but I'll be on my way now."

"No need to go. Stay and have a meal with me, if you're hungry."

The way she was staring at the pheasant and bread told him that she was indeed hungry. The food was probably the only thing keeping her from running away.

When he'd toasted the bread, he held out a roll to her. She hesitated, her gaze flickering from his face to the bread, back and forth for several moments, before finally taking it.

"Thank you." She held it as though warming her hands before biting into it.

"It would be better with some butter."

She shook her head. When she swallowed, she said, "It's very good."

"I bought it yesterday from the village just down the road. I figured I would be too lazy to go to the village this morning and buy fresh bread to break my fast. Toasting it makes it nearly as good as when it's fresh."

She nodded, her eyes watching him as though she still wasn't quite sure he wouldn't pounce on her.

"I'm Sir Charles Raynsford of Dericott." He waited for her to say her name.

"I am Lou—Jack. That is, Louis Jack Smith, but everyone calls me Jack." Her cheeks were turning red.

Charles was careful not to react with skepticism. "And where are you going, Jack? I assume you're traveling."

"On my way to Yorkshire. From London," she added, as if it were an afterthought.

He wondered if anything she was saying was true, since every time she spoke, she avoided looking at him. But regardless, he figured he should travel a little way with her, even though he'd be going back the way he'd come, at least until he made sure she wasn't in some kind of danger. However, the only way he could travel with her was if she didn't know that he knew that she was a girl. For he was a knight and she was a young woman, and a very pretty one too, if he was honest. To travel alone with her would be unseemly.

He would have to pretend he didn't see right through her disguise.

Louisa praised God under her breath. She'd been so afraid of the man who seemed eager to share his food with her, but the more she studied his face, the more he seemed kind and good.

What luck to find a noble knight willing to let her eat with him. And he had not batted an eyelash when she told him her name was Jack.

She'd almost given herself away and said her name was Louisa. She'd nearly swallowed her tongue at that slip. That would have been a daft mistake if ever she'd made one. Louis Jack, indeed. Now, as she remembered it, she had to take a deep breath just to calm her breathing.

She and Sir Charles sat quietly, a lull in their conversation, as they waited for the pheasant to cook. It smelled so good, Louisa's mouth watered in anticipation. *Thank You, God, for sending me this knight to make sure I don't starve.*

She tried not to think about it, but he was a very handsome knight too. Tall and square-jawed, with brown hair that fell across his forehead, he had a boyish look about his eyes.

Though she wanted to ask the knight about his life, she bit back her questions, since he might want to ask her about herself as well, and the less false information she gave him, the better. Louisa had never been good at lying. But since she'd already told him where she was going, she felt safe asking him, "Where are you headed?"

Did she sound like a man? She feared her voice would give her away.

"No place in particular," Sir Charles said. "I was lately a guard in the service of a duke in Derbyshire, but now I have no master besides King Richard and God."

Louisa nodded and spit on the ground, as Margaret had advised her. She'd been practicing that. But she couldn't bring herself to scratch the way men were wont to do.

"What will you do now?" she asked, curious what a knight did when he wasn't guarding some nobleman or fighting in a war or going on a crusade.

"I'm in search of good deeds and noble quests, wrongs to right, that sort of thing."

Louisa stared at him. Surely this was a good and noble knight. She even suspected that if he knew she was a woman, he would not mistreat her. Not that she was planning to tell him. It would be embarrassing, at the very least, if he found out now.

The pheasant was finally cooked, and she watched in fascination as Sir Charles removed the skewer from the spit and began separating the meat from the bones and sharing it with her, along with another toasted bread roll.

Louisa's first bite burned her tongue a bit, but it was delicious. She wasn't sure she'd ever tasted anything so good.

"You really should get some waxed wool or oilcloth to keep the rain off your head," he said between bites. "I might have an extra hood I could spare."

"That is very generous of you. I'm afraid I was ill prepared for the weather."

"You also should take off your shoes until they dry. Your feet will not fare well if they stay wet too long. They might get what I've heard called 'foot rot.' It's a putrid infection that is very serious."

Louisa felt slightly sick. As she carefully pulled off her wet shoes, she wondered if her feet would look too feminine. Did men have very different feet from a woman's?

She was staring self-consciously at her feet when Sir Charles came toward her with a blanket.

"This will help keep you warm while your shoes dry." He picked up her shoes and set them by the fire.

She swallowed, humbled by his kindness. What should she say? She knew very well that men were not effusive in their expressions of thanks and rarely showed emotion.

"Thank you," she said, trying to sound gruff.

"My brother lost his arm, but I think it would be much worse to lose a foot."

"He lost his arm?"

"He was wounded in a sword fight. The barber had to take his arm. We feared he'd die from the wound, but he lived."

"Was he a knight too?"

"He's the Earl of Dericott, my oldest brother."

"Oh." She'd heard of that family. The brothers were rather famous, and the older ones had all married well. They were also nearly beheaded by the king after being falsely accused by a relative, but she couldn't remember the details.

"So you are one of the famous Dericott brothers." She immediately regretted her blunt familiarity.

Thankfully, he just smiled.

"I don't know how famous we are. But I suppose my older brothers have had interesting stories to tell in the last several years. And there was the bit of trouble we had when our stepmother had us accused of murder and treason against the king. But we were eventually exonerated."

"Yes, thank goodness the truth came out before . . ." Her cheeks warmed, unsure if he would resent her speaking so freely.

"Before we were beheaded, you mean? Yes, we were all grateful for that." He laughed. "Don't look so sheepish. I don't mind talking about it."

"Oh, well, I . . . You are very valiant, I am sure." It was so difficult trying to figure out if she was talking as a man would.

"Tell me more about yourself, Jack. Why are you traveling to Yorkshire? Do you have family there?"

Her stomach sank. The inevitable questions.

Did she dare trust him?

Louisa was warm and pleasantly full from the food he'd shared with her, and he had such a kind face. She could trust him, couldn't she? Besides, he was a noble knight. He wouldn't do anything dishonorable. So she opened her mouth and began to tell him the truth about everything—except who she really was.

FOUR

CHARLES HAD HEARD OF THE VIKING TREASURE "JACK" WAS talking about, but why was a young woman willing to risk so much to try to find this fabled treasure?

"So you believe the treasure is there, on that mountain, just waiting to be discovered. How do you know you will be able to locate it?"

"I know it sounds strange. But if I am meant to find the treasure, I will."

"I've heard a giant guards the treasure," Charles said. "My father's friend said he saw the giant, knew him from when they were children growing up in the same village. He grew so tall so fast that his legs were crooked and his neck almost couldn't hold up his head."

Jack seemed to ponder this information. "But why is he guarding the treasure? It doesn't belong to him, does it?"

"I'm not sure if my father's friend ever said. It may just be a story. And he told that story ten years ago. Mostly likely either the story isn't true, or the treasure had already been found and absconded with long ago."

Strange tales were common, tales of miracles and fairies and giants, strange beasts and heroic deeds that defied normal abilities of man. But to leave her home and strike out on her own based on one of these stories . . . He hoped to dissuade her and perhaps encourage her to go back home where she'd be safe.

"You probably think I'm foolish, but my father believed in the treasure, and he was a very wise man. And although my quest might be a waste of time, I know if God wants me to find the treasure, then nothing can stop me."

"You said your father *was* a wise man?"

"He died seven years ago, and my mother too."

"I am sorry to hear that. Don't you have any family at all?"

"I have a sister, Margaret. We live with our uncle and aunt."

He waited for her to elaborate, but she pressed her lips together and was silent.

"I have one sister too, Delia."

"I always thought it would be good to have brothers, but my sister is a beautiful soul. She manages to laugh even when things are bad, and she is so unselfish. I love her dearly, and I would do anything to protect her."

"Does your sister need protection? Is she in danger?"

She seemed to consider this carefully before saying, "No, not the kind of protection that . . . that is . . . I just want to make sure she doesn't have to marry someone evil, and my uncle doesn't care about her and will marry her off to anyone who has money." She bit her lip and looked down at the ground.

He felt a pang of sympathy at her pitiful disguise, her desire to protect her sister, and her desperation that was obviously driving her. And though it was probably unwise to help her in such a foolhardy plan, part of him wanted, needed to take care of her and make sure she was safe.

But first he had to make sure that she wasn't better off going home.

"Do you think your uncle and aunt are worried about you?"

"Oh no." She shook her head, but the way she was not looking at him told him she was probably lying.

"No?"

"They know I am a man now, that I must make my own way in the world." She was fidgeting with the blanket.

"And finding this treasure will help you make your way in the world?"

"Yes. With the treasure I can buy back my family's home, which my uncle and aunt are collecting rent on, and I can make sure Margaret doesn't have to marry if she doesn't want to."

So she wanted to take possession of her family's lands and to protect her sister, and the only way she could imagine being able to do that was to chase after an imaginary treasure. Well, Charles would do his best to help her. Perhaps God would lead him to a good solution for Jack and for her sister, or at least make sure she wasn't harassed, starving, or mistreated while in Charles's company.

"You really need a horse."

Louisa was afraid Sir Charles would say that, and he did, as soon as they started down the road toward Yorkshire. "I am a good walker. I can keep up." But she knew she could only keep up if Sir Charles rode his horse at a slow walk.

"The journey will be much easier and faster if we get you a horse."

"As good as that sounds, I'm afraid I don't have money for a horse." She wanted to impress the handsome knight, but she had to admit the truth.

"A decent walking horse can be bought for less than you might expect, as long as you are willing to settle for an older horse."

Older? The horse would have to be nearly dead for her to afford it.

At the first large village, they went to the baker's shop to buy bread. She noticed how much he bought, then bought an equal amount.

"Where might we purchase a horse?" Sir Charles asked.

"There's a horse breeder in the next village on the road north," the baker said.

Louisa's stomach sank as Sir Charles thanked the man and they turned to leave. She couldn't pay for a horse. A mule, perhaps, but only if it were a very old mule. Definitely not a horse. She'd already told him this. Did he not believe her?

They refilled their flasks at the village well and continued down the road. Soon they were entering the next village, which was considerably larger than the previous one.

"Let's get you a horse." Sir Charles charged ahead.

Louisa hurried after him, but he was asking a man where to find the horse breeder before she could catch up to him. The man pointed and said something.

"Wait," Louisa said.

When he turned to face her, she said as forcefully as she could, "I can't buy a horse. I don't have enough money, and I need what coins I have for food."

"I'll pay for it," he said. "You can pay me back later."

Her stomach sank again. She didn't like the idea of owing this man anything. When he found out she was a woman, would he want his payment in something other than money?

She didn't think Sir Charles was that kind of man, but ever since that suitor had tried to force himself on her, she had been distrustful of men. Thankfully, the man was so drunk that she had fought him off, but it had shaken her and taught her to be wary of men.

She also knew how men tried, and often succeeded in, taking advantage of the servant girls. And she may as well be a servant now. She had no status and no family to protect her. She had only her knife and her disguise.

Even if Sir Charles was the kind of knight who would protect her, she had no way of knowing how long he would travel with her, how long it would take him to decide to leave her to her treasure hunt while he went on to seek a nobler quest.

But right now he was bent on getting her a horse, and she could do little more than follow him, trotting to keep up with his longer stride. Soon they were on the outskirts of the large village at a horse farm. An hour after that, she was sitting atop a gentle mare.

She'd never had a horse of her very own before, and even though she still felt uneasy at how much money Sir Charles had paid for it, she decided to enjoy being able to ride instead of walking and, since Sir Charles still behaved as he had before, to push the uneasiness from her mind. Besides, she had a knife in her pocket and she wasn't afraid to use it. And riding up high on the back of a horse would make even the most crowded road or marketplace more bearable. She had to admit she liked having a horse.

She sighed with relief as they rode. They would be in Yorkshire in less than a month at this rate of travel, and she wouldn't have to worry about her shoes wearing out.

The sound of horses' hooves slowly broke into her consciousness. Several horses were bearing down on them as Sir Charles remarked on the crop that was already well up in the field to the left of the road.

"It looks like barley," he said.

"I think it is barley," Louisa agreed. Why did the sound of horses' hooves cause a niggling of caution at the back of her mind?

The men on horseback came into view and she sucked in a loud breath. She recognized them as her uncle's men, and she quickly ducked her head.

Why had she not been more careful? She should have gotten off the road, should have made up an excuse, should have said she needed to relieve herself. Now it was too late.

Her heart pounded as she kept her head down but sat up in the saddle like a man would. They would not be expecting her to be disguised as a man, would they? They were looking for a girl on foot, not a young man on horseback in the company of a knight. With any luck, they would assume she was Sir Charles's squire. But her heart still beat as if it were trying to escape her chest.

"Good day," the man in the lead, Robert Atwater, said.

"Good day," Sir Charles answered.

"We are searching for the runaway niece of our master Eluard, Lord of the Manor of Reedbrake. Have you seen a young woman of eighteen years in the last two days? Her name is Louisa."

She dared to peek over at Sir Charles. His brows were drawn together. "What does she look like?"

"Medium height, for a woman, and long brown hair, somewhat curly."

Sir Charles shook his head. "That could describe many women."

"She is fair of face and well proportioned, if you know what I mean."

That helpful information was provided by James, the son of her uncle's reeve. She didn't look up, but she could imagine his wide grin. He always did pay too much attention to her, especially when no one else was around. Her stomach roiled.

"I have seen no travelers of that description. Why, pray tell, did she run away? Did someone harm her?"

She wished Sir Charles would not ask questions but let them be on their way.

"No one harmed her," Robert said. "She is a rebellious sort, refusing to marry as the master bids her. But when she is returned home, she will be soundly punished for her stubborn rebellion."

"A good flogging would serve her well," said one of the guards.

Louisa's face burned, as much from anger as fear. Sir Charles was silent.

"Her uncle is offering a reward to anyone who returns her," Robert said. "What about this boy here? Has he seen her?"

Louisa shook her head without looking up. "No." She did her best to make her voice sound gruff and masculine.

"Good day," Sir Charles said, abruptly ending the conversation. He touched his heels to his horse's sides and moved forward. Louisa did the same.

They rode through the group of men, and Louisa prayed, *God, let them not recognize me.*

No one stopped them, but Louisa didn't breathe easy until she looked over her shoulder and saw that they were well down the road and nearly out of sight.

Thank You, God.

Charles noticed how Jack reacted to the men who were searching for the runaway young woman. She was the person they were searching for; he was absolutely certain. After all, she had never hung her head like that when the baker or the horse trader had spoken to them. At least now he knew her name: Louisa.

So the story she'd told about trying to protect her sister may or may not have been true, but she'd also been trying to avoid the inevitable—marriage to the man of her uncle's choosing.

Her uncle was obviously a landholder of some means, with men who did his bidding and enough wealth to employ guards.

On the one hand, it seemed as though Louisa was being unreasonable by running away from her home. All young women were expected to marry whomever their father, or in this case, her uncle, deemed best. Besides, it was a dangerous world for a young woman traveling alone. Even so, Charles had bristled when they'd said she would be punished when she was returned, possibly even flogged. No woman, no matter what she did, deserved such treatment.

The likelihood seemed great that she had been abused and mistreated. Yes, that must be the truth of the matter. And she'd decided to believe in the outrageous rumor about treasure in Yorkshire to give herself the courage to leave her home.

Honestly, he didn't know how much of what she'd told him, if any of it, was true. He knew only that her uncle was searching for her and wanted her back badly enough to offer a reward and send out several men who might be working in the fields at this crucial time of planting crops.

As their horses plodded down the road, Louisa was very quiet. He decided to give her a chance to confess, even though he'd already decided he would not give her up to her uncle's men.

"Have you ever heard of a young maiden running away from home simply to avoid getting married? I can hardly believe such a thing."

"No, never." She looked quite sad and troubled.

"Well, I wouldn't give her up, even if I found her."

"There is a reward."

"I don't care about a reward. I'd rather give the maiden a chance to explain herself. And far be it from me to force a young maiden to do anything she didn't wish to do. That would not be very chivalrous, would it?"

"No, that wouldn't be very chivalrous at all." Her face brightened a bit, and she even looked him in the eye for a moment. "You wouldn't take her back to her uncle if you found her?"

"No, I wouldn't," Charles said. "Those men didn't seem very honorable. Besides, she must have a very good reason for doing something so drastic, so dangerous."

"Yes, that is what I think too."

Her smile was rather adorable.

"And even though it is none of my business, I wouldn't allow a young woman's uncle to flog her."

"You wouldn't?"

"Of course not. Such a thing is barbaric."

"Oh yes, barbaric. That is what I think."

"Women should be cherished and protected, not beaten."

The way she looked at him after he said that . . . He wished Lady Mirabella had looked at him that way.

He should stop teasing Louisa. He didn't really want her to confess, as he didn't want to leave her to fend for herself—or to be discovered by her uncle's men and hauled back home to be punished.

No, it was best that he pretend not to know that she was Louisa, the niece of the Lord of Reedbrake Manor, for he was certain it was she.

FIVE

LOUISA'S HEART SKIPPED A BEAT AT HEARING SIR CHARLES say that women should be cherished and protected. He took her breath away with his chivalry and noble-heartedness.

If only her uncle wanted her to marry *him*. She'd go back home this very instant.

That was a strange thought for someone who did not want to marry at all.

Should she tell him the truth? She hated deceiving him. She also wished that he could see her as a woman, that he could see her as pretty and feminine.

That was something she'd never wanted before.

That night they slept under the trees, as they had done several times. But Louisa wasn't nearly as exhausted since she'd been riding a horse—though she was sore in places she'd never been sore before. Eventually, though, she'd get used to being in the saddle for long periods.

As she lay on the blanket she'd bought at the last village, she reflected over the events of the day. She had spoken less, as she felt some awkwardness with Sir Charles that she hadn't felt before he bought her the horse, and since their conversation about a woman running away from home. It was an uncomfortable feeling to owe someone so much money, but then a thought came to her. When she was able to secure the treasure, she could easily pay him back. Indeed, she would also share the treasure with him, since he would, she hoped, be with her when she found it. And she would tell him so the next day.

She suddenly felt much better.

Dawn was just breaking when Louisa opened her eyes and noticed that the spot where Sir Charles had slept was empty. She decided to go check on the horses, not wanting to venture any farther than that lest she surprise the knight while he was relieving himself.

So far she had avoided that, which would have made things so much more awkward.

She found Sir Charles with the horses. "How are they faring?"

"Very well, I think. I inspected all their shoes."

"When you inspect the horses' shoes, what are you looking for?"

"A rock stuck under the iron, a crack in the hoof, or a red or swollen place, which could indicate that something has injured them—a splinter stuck in the flesh, that sort of thing."

"I see." Louisa didn't want to admit it, but she was still a bit afraid of the large animal, though it had been gentle and relatively submissive so far.

"I wanted to let you know that I will pay you back for the horse."

Sir Charles stopped and looked at her. "I have told you not to worry about that."

"I know, but you cannot buy a horse for every traveler you meet. You will run out of money, and someday you will need a fortune so you can get married. Isn't that how it is for knights?"

"I suppose that's usually how it goes."

There was a subtle change in his expression when she spoke of him getting married. Had she brought up a bad memory?

They went in opposite directions to go relieve themselves in the woods.

Later, while they ate a breakfast of bread and cheese, Louisa said, "I would imagine you have already had a chance to marry, a handsome knight like you."

She immediately regretted her statement, as once again his expression clouded over, but this time his cheeks turned a bit red and he stared at the ground.

"There was a woman I had hoped to marry, but it was daft of me to even think of her. For, as you say, a knight must have a fortune if he wants to marry well."

They were silent for a moment, but Louisa thought it might help him if he were to talk about it.

"Who was she, if you will pardon my asking?"

"The daughter of a duke."

Louisa winced. Even she knew that a duke's daughter would be expected to marry someone of higher status than a knight, especially if that knight had no fortune.

"I know it was foolish to think she would marry me, but she led me to believe that she loved me. I was often assigned to accompany her as one of the duke's trusted guards when she went on solitary rides near the castle. And when we were alone together, she would often . . . bestow the kind of small favors on me that a woman would normally only give to the man she intended to marry."

"She kissed you?"

He nodded.

Louisa felt sick, not only out of pity for Sir Charles but also from the thought that Sir Charles had wanted to marry the woman. Had he been in love with her? She wanted to ask but didn't dare. Instead, she waited silently for him to go on.

Sir Charles held a leaf between his fingers, slowly ripping it to shreds.

"It turned out that I was not the only knight who thought she loved him. She bestowed the same favors on at least two other knights. I only discovered this after her father announced that she was betrothed to a duke's son."

"I'm so sorry." Louisa felt the breath leave her as she imagined his pain. What a horrible woman. Louisa wished she could tell her what a discredit she was to all women everywhere.

"Yes, well, it was a lesson learned. It seems she thought it was perfectly right and good for multiple men to pay her tribute and give her gifts, to even kiss them and make them fall in love with her." Abruptly he dropped the leaf shreds to the ground.

"She sounds very shallow and unfeeling." Among other things.

"It makes me wonder if . . ." He shook his head.

"What?"

"Nothing, nothing." He stood to his feet. "We should be going."

"Makes you wonder if all women are like her?"

He gave her a rueful half frown. "Yes."

"Not all women would behave that way. At least, I don't think they would, not from my experience—with my sister and her friends. Not that I have *that* kind of experience." She would give herself away yet if she didn't stop talking.

His frown turned into an amused smile. "No, I don't suppose all women are like that. Certainly, my sister and my brothers' wives are not. She was just a duke's spoiled daughter, accustomed to getting whatever she wanted, with no compassion for others."

His face clouded over again as he spoke. Poor man. And what a terrible young woman, to have treated a noble knight like Sir Charles in such a way! Certainly, if Louisa were the daughter of a duke, and if Sir Charles were in love with her, she would rethink her wish to never marry. She might even beg her father to let her marry Sir Charles. But if the duke were like her uncle, he would refuse and marry her to someone who would give him more money and status. She sighed.

This was exactly why Louisa was on her way to Yorkshire to get the treasure. With that wealth, she and her sister would not have to marry at all. They would never be anyone's pawn, and they could be free and not be used by some man who only cared about having a boy child to carry on his name. And if Margaret decided she wanted to marry, she would be able to marry whomever she wished. No one could tell them what to do, which was a freedom that very few women, even wealthy dukes' daughters, enjoyed.

God, forgive me if I want too much. And help me not to want Sir Charles, for I am not a duke's daughter and I know he is far too much to ask for.

Charles shouldn't speak of Lady Mirabella. It only made him feel worse. The best thing to do was to forget about her and forget the past.

But it did make him smile to hear Louisa defending women, then get nervous that she might have said the wrong thing.

Truly, it was obvious that she was very different from Mirabella. Louisa was not coldhearted. Her character and morality were far superior to Mirabella's, but . . . something in him didn't like accusing Mirabella. He still had not entirely rid himself of his feelings for her.

He was foolish indeed.

As they rode along, he felt a companionable silence between Louisa and him. She wanted to pay him back for the horse. She even thought she would be able to, so she wasn't trying to use him—as Lady Mirabella had used him.

But he wouldn't think about Mirabella.

Louisa was a good soul, wishing to help her sister, and herself, avoid a bad marriage. He couldn't fault her for that.

Down the road a short way was a man dressed in the long brown robe of a Franciscan friar standing beside a donkey. He stood so still, Charles was certain he was praying.

The friar looked up and waited for them to get closer, then said, "Are you a knight?"

"I am. Are you in need of assistance?"

"My donkey has decided he doesn't wish to walk any farther."

Their horses needed a short rest, so Charles dismounted. "Would you like some help?"

"I'm afraid he will only move if he wants to," the friar said. "I am Brother Matthew, on my way back to Yorkshire after a pilgrimage to Rome."

"I am Sir Charles Raynsford of Dericott."

"It is a pleasure to meet one of our king's noble knights. Thank you for stopping to help me, although I don't believe there is anything you can do. This donkey—I call him Judas when I am angry with him, and Friend when he is behaving as he should—he only moves when he wishes to. Many times at home I have left him where he stood, but now he carries my bedding and the holy relics I have brought back for the Mount Grace Priory, which I pledged to do as part of my penance. Since they are too heavy for me to carry, I have no choice but to wait for this beast. How I do miss my old mule, who served me so faithfully, but alas, he died in France of a putrid condition of the mouth, poor creature."

Louisa had approached the donkey while the friar was

talking and was now murmuring soothingly to the animal and rubbing his head. Brother Matthew took notice.

"Do you know any tricks to make a stubborn donkey go?" he asked her.

"The secret, in my experience, is to speak gently, praise them, and offer them a treat when they do take a step. Most of them will do anything for a carrot, a bit of hay, or a kind word."

The friar raised his brows. "I have no carrots or hay, and I cannot praise the animal for standing still, can I?"

"No, but if I can get him to walk even just one step, then you should praise him in your most loving and enthusiastic voice."

The friar looked a bit put upon but said grudgingly, "Very well. But I don't think you will succeed."

She put her shoulder up to the donkey's side and pushed. The donkey let out a startled bray and took two steps as he tried to regain his balance.

"Well done," she cried, rubbing the donkey enthusiastically. "That's it, just keep stepping. Good boy." She waved frantically at the friar, who took the hint.

"Well done, Friend donkey, old boy," the friar said.

The donkey stared at them, his eyes rolling in his head.

"Try it again. He's taking notice," Louisa said, running around to the other side of the donkey. This time Charles helped her, pushing the donkey off-balance and forcing him to take two steps. They immediately praised the donkey.

"Good Friend donkey!"

"Well done!"

"That's the way, come on."

The donkey caught on and took a few more steps, and they all walked along with him, praising him and patting his back as he went.

"I am amazed!" Brother Matthew's eyes were wide as he looked back at Louisa.

She smiled, obviously pleased, but kept praising the donkey, which kept walking.

"I'll get the horses." Charles ran back to retrieve them both by their reins and soon caught up.

When they had moved a short way down the road and the donkey was walking along with them, the friar asked, "How did you know how to do that? You must have learned that trick somewhere."

"I was raised around animals. My sister and I were better acquainted with animals than with people."

"You must have lived in a small village or on a lord's estate. Perhaps your father was the reeve?"

"In a small village on a lord's estate, yes. Good donkey. You are doing very well. I imagine your owner will feed you some carrots as soon as he is able."

Charles noticed how she only half answered the friar's question.

"Tell us about your pilgrimage. What interesting sights did you see?" Louisa's questions would likely keep the friar talking for hours, if he read the man's pleased expression correctly.

Five hours later, when they arrived in another village, the friar was still talking about Rome and all the impressive towns, people, and cathedrals he'd seen. To be fair, she had encouraged him to keep talking, asking a question here or there. She seemed genuinely interested in his descriptions.

Charles, on the other hand, had often shut out the friar's voice. How could Louisa be so attentive for such a long time? But she probably rarely went outside her village.

As they approached the town's cathedral, Brother Matthew started comparing it to a similar church he'd seen in France.

"The eye is drawn upward into heaven by the structure's straight lines, and especially by the tall steeple. The cross at the top draws one's spirit up to God. Do you not feel it?"

"I like the stained glass windows," Louisa said. "I like to see if I can figure out which Bible story each one depicts."

"Yes, the church builders always try to put the important Bible stories in the windows for the uneducated so that they, too, can feel God's presence. The bright colors encourage their notice."

She raised her brows with a slightly sardonic look. Charles guessed that she didn't appreciate his condescension.

As the two of them discussed the meaning of each of the windows, Louisa actually corrected the friar. "I don't think that is the story of Joseph being taken by the slave traders. I think it is Daniel being saved from the lions' den."

The friar squinted and cleared his throat. "Perhaps."

They all went inside and lit a candle and spent some time in prayer before exiting the church.

On the street a little boy, probably about eight years old, with dirt on his thin face, held out his hand to them. "Alms for the poor?" he asked, his eyes hollow but pleading.

The friar gave him a quick look up and down, then turned away. "Beggars. Someone should put this boy to work."

But Louisa stopped and took some coins from her pocket—some pennies, halfpennies, and farthings. She gave two pennies, her largest coins, to the boy. "Where are your mother and father?" she asked him.

"Dead."

The friar turned and came back. "Good honest work is what you need," he said to the boy. "Hire yourself out to the blacksmith or the butcher. They can teach you a skill. Begging is idleness and is of the devil." Then he turned to Louisa. "Don't you know that giving him money will only encourage him to be a beggar and a thief all his life?"

Charles had taken out his own bag of coins and placed a valuable silver noble in the boy's dirty hand. "Do you have a place to sleep?"

The boy nodded. "I sleep in the livery barn in exchange for mucking out the stalls."

"Good boy." Charles squeezed his shoulder.

The friar made a harrumphing sound as the boy ran off down the street. "No doubt he is up to no good. Probably going to share with his thieving parents who are alive and well and put him up to . . ."

The friar's voice trailed off as they watched the boy approach a little girl in a tattered dress who was squatting beside another small child wrapped in a blanket on the ground. When the little boy showed them the coins, they all three stood with serious but purposeful looks and walked a short way down the street, holding each other's hands, then went into a baker's shop.

Louisa was still staring after them, her chin starting to quiver as tears sparkled in her eyes. She took a deep breath and blinked.

"Well, let us hope they don't turn to thievery," the friar said.

The three children emerged from the baker's shop and ran the opposite way down the street, each clutching a loaf of bread.

"They are only children and were obviously hungry," Louisa said to Brother Matthew.

"It is when they are children that they learn bad habits, and idleness and begging are poor teachers for anyone." The friar was staring hard at Louisa now. Was he realizing she was a woman? Had her compassion and tears given her away? But the friar said nothing.

They continued down the street, but the way Louisa had reacted to those young children stayed with Charles. He could not get the look in her eyes out of his mind. Certainly Lady Mirabella had never looked at anyone the way Louisa had looked at those children.

What had he seen in Lady Mirabella that made him think he would want to spend the rest of his life with her? Was he so shallow that he would fall for a woman like her? She would not make a very charitable wife for a wealthy duke. He imagined she would give even less notice to a beggar child she saw on the street than the friar did. At least the friar had given those children some thought. From what he knew of Lady Mirabella, she would have only looked away, if she saw them at all.

The sun was starting to go down as they left with a day's supply of food and water.

The friar pointed to the last building on the road out of town. "I suppose she shall sleep at the inn there?"

Louisa stumbled and her eyes went wide.

Charles stopped, bringing his horse to a halt as well. "Pardon me?"

"Her." Brother Matthew hooked his thumb in Louisa's direction with an angry expression. "Did you think I wouldn't notice that she was a woman? Did you not know?" The friar was staring hard at Charles now.

All the blood seemed to have drained from Louisa's face as she stared not at the friar but at Charles.

"That's Jack," Charles said. "Jack, tell the man."

"Yes, my name is Jack." But neither her expression nor her voice was very convincing.

"Jack?" The friar's face split into a sarcastic smile. "Come, come. We all know you are no boy. Did you not know?" He looked pointedly at Charles.

"I let the boy travel with me. He said his name was Jack. There can be no harm in him sleeping on the ground around our fire tonight."

"See here. Confess," the friar said to her. "You are a woman. Tell the truth."

"I . . . What does it matter if I am a man or woman? I have done nothing wrong, and Sir Charles is my protector."

"Is something going on between you that would be considered fornication?" The friar's face was quite stern.

"No!" Charles and Louisa both said simultaneously.

Louisa's hands were clenched into fists. "I told him I was a boy and he believed me. There is nothing wrong between us. He is a noble knight and I am innocent. I have done nothing wrong."

"Nothing wrong, eh? Where do you belong? Where is your home? Young women do not travel. They stay where they were born, serving their family or their master until they are married."

Louisa crossed her arms over her chest and lifted her chin in a defiant stance.

"This is preposterous." Brother Matthew looked to Charles. "Sir Knight, you cannot condone such behavior from a woman. You cannot, you must not aid in her rebellion, for such it surely is. And rebellion is as the sin of witchcraft, so says the Holy Writ."

"So it does. But perhaps she has a very good reason for traveling from home. I shall not condemn her."

The friar's face was growing red. He turned to the maiden. "Look at you, wearing a man's clothing. Shameful. Go home, I say, and repent."

She looked from Brother Matthew to Charles. "I will not go home, and I wish to travel under the protection of Sir Charles, if he is still willing."

This was a quandary. How could he allow her to go with him now that the truth was out in the open?

Louisa and Brother Matthew were both looking at him, waiting for him to make a judgment. He had to make a decision. Finally, he let out the breath he was holding.

"I see nothing wrong with her traveling with me, if she

wishes to continue pretending she is a man. It may cause some awkwardness, but we can behave wisely. Even Jesus traveled with women during His ministry."

The friar shook his head, a look of disgust scrunching his face, while Louisa's expression was guarded and unreadable.

If only they'd never encountered this friar. He wasn't sure why the friar was so bent on condemning her, but he thought it was because he did not like the way Louisa had shown more Christian charity and compassion for the orphan children than he had. Not only that, but he was probably also angry at being fooled into thinking that the young woman was a man.

Whatever the reason for his anger, Charles had a bad feeling that the friar was going to cause them trouble.

Six

Louisa hated being falsely accused. Brother Matthew had judged her for wearing a man's clothing and for leaving her home, without knowing or caring why she had left. How narrow her place was in his eyes. But she need not concern herself with what he thought of her. Indeed, she did not care. He was judgmental and coldhearted. She'd seen the way he'd treated the poor beggar child. He'd condemned the little boy without knowing anything of his situation in life. And now he was condemning Louisa, even insinuating that she and Sir Charles had done something indecent.

What did Sir Charles think? She could tell he was worried about the friar's accusations. But he didn't seem surprised to learn she was a woman. Had he known all along?

Apparently she wasn't fooling anyone with her disguise.

Her stomach twisted, but she maintained her defiant posture. She couldn't let the friar think she was afraid of him. At least Sir Charles had not sent her away. Yet. She would talk to him when the friar wasn't around and find out exactly what he was thinking.

"I will allow you to sleep by our fire tonight," Brother Matthew said, shaking his finger at her face.

She found it amusing that he called it "our fire," as if he and Sir Charles were partners of some kind.

"But I only allow it because I will be here to watch over your virtue."

"Oh, thank you so much." Was it wrong to be sarcastic? Perhaps she should refrain from antagonizing the friar.

He scowled at her, watching as she walked beside Sir Charles.

She couldn't help looking to the knight who had been her protector, even if only for a short time. His expression was deflated. What was he thinking? Was he disappointed in her for deceiving him? Was he contemplating what consequences he might reap for traveling alone with her?

He'd said she could stay with him if she continued to pretend to be a man. She understood the condition. They were neither married nor related to each other. Everyone would assume they were behaving in an unseemly manner.

If only she and Sir Charles could have made it to Yorkshire without anyone realizing she was a woman.

Sir Charles was building a fire, Louisa helping him gather wood, when the friar went into the woods to relieve himself. As soon as he was gone, Louisa said, "I know you don't want to travel with a woman, and I'm sorry I deceived you, but—"

"Don't worry. I understand why you disguised yourself. It's all right. I will not treat you any different than before."

"Thank you." She felt her cheeks burning, so she turned away from him and continued gathering sticks.

What were these feelings that settled in her chest, making her feel like crying? Was she just embarrassed? Grateful? It was both those things, but more so it was the fact that this was not how she'd wanted things to go with Sir Charles, with him seeing her only as a good deed, a vulnerable person who needed his protection but who also might damage his reputation.

What did she want? Her feelings were so confusing, but she wanted him to see her as a woman who was lovely and . . . But that would never happen, and she shouldn't think past that.

Three days had passed since Brother Matthew had revealed that Louisa was a woman. No one had asked her name. Sir Charles still called her Jack, and when the friar wanted to get her attention, he said, "You there."

They had all been rather quiet. Brother Matthew spoke the most, often talking about the dangers for a woman alone, a rebellious woman's many faults and pitfalls, and various tales of woe, most of which were not in the Holy Writ at all. She knew, because she'd read the Holy Writ herself, a fact she enjoyed telling the friar.

As they were speaking about where they should eat their

evening meal and sleep for the night, they passed a sign pointing the way to a monastery.

"We may all spend the night here tonight," Brother Matthew said. "I will stay for a few days, and since I assume you both wish to be on your way, this is where we shall part."

He gave them both a stern, disapproving look. When they did not reply, he continued. "If you go on your way together, the two of you alone, you will be committing a grave sin."

"Which sin is greater—traveling with her and protecting her, or sending her off alone and unprotected?" Sir Charles asked.

Brother Matthew stopped beside his donkey. He started to speak, then closed his mouth. He huffed out a loud breath. "She is responsible for whatever happens to her. She is the one who left her home to travel the countryside unprotected."

Unruffled, Sir Charles said in a calm, even voice, "That is a cold way of thinking."

"Cold?" Brother Matthew's shoulders stiffened.

"Coldhearted, unkind, unchivalrous, un—"

"I understood your meaning." He glared. "Only remember, narrow is the way that leads to righteousness. And broad is the way that leads a soul to hell."

Louisa thought she saw Sir Charles roll his eyes.

"You do believe in the Holy Scriptures, do you not?"

"I do. I remember that in them, the only people Jesus condemned were the Pharisees and the teachers of the law. He said they were hypocrites for proclaiming themselves righteous and condemning others while they themselves had no love in their hearts for their fellow man. Mercy was important to Him, and

He told people not to judge others or they would then be judged in the same way."

Louisa wanted to cheer and tell Sir Charles how wise and noble he was, but they continued walking in silence. As they neared the monastery, a young man started toward them.

Brother Matthew suddenly rounded on them and said in a quiet but hissy voice, "Sir Charles, you will have learned in your training that obedience is of utmost importance—obedience to those who have authority over us and obedience to God. If anyone asks me about your character, I shall be forced to tell them that I cannot vouch for your integrity, I am sad to say. And as for you"—he looked with squinty eyes at Louisa—"if you do not repent and go home forthwith, I fear greatly for your soul. If you care naught for your own future, you should at least have a care for Sir Charles's."

Louisa felt the blood drain from her face, first at hearing Sir Charles so criticized because he had stood up for her, and then at the way Brother Matthew spoke to her as if she were the worst kind of sinner.

God, is he right? Am I so very bad for leaving home, even though I did it to save myself and Margaret from bad marriages? And will I bring harm to Sir Charles?

She felt sick.

"You go too far." Sir Charles's jaw twitched as he glared at the friar.

Soon their horses were being taken to the stable and they were ushered in different directions—the men with one servant and Louisa with another.

She was shown her own spartan room and given water for bathing. Then she was escorted to a hall where she ate a rather meager meal with some nuns and serving women.

It seemed no one was allowed to talk. Sitting in silence, with the other women around her so quiet, Louisa felt the weight in her chest grow heavier. As she ate her bread and frumenty made of oats, peas, and onions with a bit of pork fat, tears welled in her eyes and spilled down her cheeks. She found herself praying for Sir Charles, that no harm would come to his reputation because of her.

Later, as she lay on her narrow cot in her cold room, she realized what she had to do. She would sneak away early the next morning without Sir Charles. It was for his own good. He would probably be grateful to her for making it easy on him. This way she could continue on to Yorkshire and the treasure and he wouldn't be forced to choose whether or not to travel with her and compromise his morals as a knight.

The friar was wrong, though. God would not condemn Sir Charles; Louisa knew that in her heart. Someone so just and kind could only be blameless in God's eyes. Still, if traveling together caused people to assume bad things about Sir Charles, then she would do the right thing and leave before he woke.

She felt a tiny measure of peace after making the decision, but as she lay on her cot waiting for sleep to overtake her, tears began to creep from the corners of her eyes, running over her temples and into her hair. She would miss Sir Charles, his quiet strength, his warm eyes and smile. She had come to trust him.

"What a foolish girl I am," she whispered, wiping at the cold tears that were sending a chill over her shoulders.

This was no time to cry. This was the time for courage, as she would now be traveling alone and would need to protect herself. The most important part of protecting herself was to look like a boy. And since the friar, who did not strike her as an extraordinarily clever man, had figured it out, she needed a better disguise. But first she needed to sleep.

She closed her eyes and breathed deeply, willing herself to stop crying and find her peace again.

Charles rued the day they had met Brother Matthew. But now they would leave him behind, thankfully.

Charles was up before dawn. He knelt beside the small candle stub in his room and prayed. "Lord God, let me continue to protect the weak and do what is right in Your eyes. Help Brother Matthew understand that You desire mercy more than sacrifice, and if he judges others without mercy, he will be judged in the same way. And forgive me for resenting what Lady Mirabella did. I forgive her. Help me forgive her completely."

When he finished praying, he felt quite hopeful, as if good things were just around the next bend in the road. He went to the stable to saddle his horse. As the servant assisted him, Charles noticed Louisa's horse was not in its stall. "Where is my friend's horse?"

"The girl dressed as a boy?" the servant asked.

"Yes."

"She took the horse and left."

"Left? When?" His heart beat faster.

"Half an hour ago. Perhaps more."

Charles quickly finished saddling the horse and tying down his pack and saddlebag. He gave the servant a coin, mounted his horse, and set out to find Louisa.

After traveling until the sun was halfway up the sky, wondering if he had somehow missed her, he caught a glimpse of her up ahead guiding her horse off the road.

Charles urged his horse into a gallop until he reached the spot where she had turned off the road into a wooded area.

He went after her, catching glimpses of her through the dense trees and leaves. A tiny limb slapped him across the cheek before he could dodge it.

"Wait," he called. "You can't get away from me. I can see you." When she didn't answer, he said, "I just want to talk to you."

She stopped in a tiny clearing. He soon reached her, still feeling the sting of the welt across his cheekbone.

"Oh." She was staring at him with a strange look.

"Listen, you shouldn't care so much about what the friar said. I don't want to let you travel alone. What kind of knight would I be if I left you to be attacked on the road?" She was still looking at him oddly. "What?"

She pointed at his face. "You're bleeding."

He dabbed at his face with the back of his hand. There was only a little blood. "It's just a scratch."

"I'm sorry, but I just don't want to be the cause of something bad happening to you or to your reputation. You are not responsible for me, and it's true that I left home without permission, alone."

"I know I'm not responsible for you, but I wish to ensure you are safe on your journey."

"I cannot let you travel with me. It appears unseemly, and you must stay away from all things unseemly."

He saw the stubborn set of her mouth and jaw. She was not giving in.

"Very well. But you cannot stop me from going to Yorkshire as well."

She seemed to consider arguing with him but then said, "I suppose I can't stop you. But you must not travel with me."

"Very well." He would ride behind her. "Shall we get back on the road?"

"Did you know all along that I was a woman?" she asked in an accusatory tone.

"I did. But your disguise fools people at first glance. It fooled the men who were looking for you."

"How did you know . . ." She sighed. "That was only because I kept my head down. They thought I was a servant, so they barely paid any attention to me."

"So those were your uncle's men?"

She didn't answer right away. "I don't want to cause you any trouble."

"Your uncle is a wealthy man, then?"

"He took my father's wealth and land and income. But he is not so wealthy as he wishes to be. That's the only reason he wants me back. He doesn't care about me."

"Your sister is probably worried about you."

"She knew I left and why. She won't worry. But as I said, I am not your responsibility. No doubt you think I'm being foolish, searching for treasure, and that I should go back and marry whomever my uncle wishes me to. But there are many men who are just . . . evil. I cannot allow my sister to marry someone who is evil."

He understood how she must feel, but he also knew she had little choice. Women married, and they married the person of their guardian's choosing. It was the way life was. At least if she let her uncle marry her and her sister off, they'd each have a home, wealth, and the protection of a husband.

She passed him on her horse, making her way back onto the road, and he followed her.

When they reached the path, she turned to him. "Don't feel you have to follow me, but if you do, I want you to stay far behind me. I don't want anyone to think you are with me."

He nodded. "If that is what you wish. But will you do one thing for me? I heard your uncle's men say your name was Louisa. Will you tell me your full name?"

Her expression softened. "Of course. And I'm sorry I lied and told you my name was Jack."

"Louis Jack Smith." He couldn't help teasing her.

"Well, it's Louisa Lenton of Maydestone. My father was the Lord of the Manor of Maydestone."

"Louisa is a pretty name. At least I won't have to call you Jack anymore."

She gave him a rueful half frown and faced the road.

Her hair had a soft thickness that most men's hair lacked, and the curves of her face and the way she walked and talked were so feminine, he couldn't imagine ever thinking even for a moment that she was anything other than a young woman with a loveliness of spirit as well as of face and form.

Most knights would be glad to get rid of her. Any entanglements with women they didn't intend to marry could cause them problems later, either with the king or with the powerful fathers of women they *would* want to marry. But he couldn't leave her friendless and unprotected.

Besides, what else did he have to do? It seemed God wanted him to watch over this courageous maiden who was so determined to make her own way and control her own destiny.

He had never met another woman like her. He imagined he never would again.

Seven

Louisa wiped a tear from her cheek, rubbing furiously at the offending wetness. This was what happened when she let herself cry. She would be weepy for the rest of the day. And no good could come from that.

Why was she crying anyway?

If Sir Charles had been gruff and cold, if he had said in a grudging way that he would follow her to make sure she didn't get herself killed, if he'd been annoyed, she could hold her head high and be gruff and cold right back. But it was his kindness, his obvious compassion, that had moved her to tears.

And every time she thought of the blood on his cheek, she got choked up, knowing he'd been struck by a branch because he was trying to catch up to her.

She had to stop letting her feelings overtake her reason and put on some armor, as it were. She needed to tell herself that he was just a knight who was doing what he felt was his duty, nothing more. And once they reached Yorkshire and found the treasure, she would share it with him, if he would allow her to. Then he would be able to get married.

She imagined him wed to a wealthy baron's daughter, living in a large castle somewhere, while she and Margaret were able to live, if not in their childhood home, then somewhere where they could be independent, providing for themselves out of their own means. But for the first time, that thought did not make her happy. In fact, thinking of Sir Charles with a wife made her feel grumpy and sad, so much so that she had to push the thought away and replace it with imagining Sir Charles building a home near her and Margaret with his share of the treasure, picturing him as their neighbor who would come by their manor house every day to take a walk with them by the stream and exchange advice on everything in their lives.

There. That was better. Even if it wasn't very likely.

She traveled all that morning, stopping only at noon to eat some bread and cheese and what was left of her dried fruit and nuts. She had caught a glimpse of Sir Charles behind her when she dismounted her horse. Now he was out of sight, and she suspected he had stopped too, to rest his horse and eat. After her horse had taken a long drink in the stream, they got back on the road.

Was she leaving Sir Charles behind? She wasn't sure, but she couldn't worry about him. He could do as he pleased.

They had not gone too far when she saw a group of four men sitting on the grass. They mostly kept their heads down, but occasionally one of them would glance up. Something about their manner, the way they seemed highly aware of her but would not look directly at her, made the hair stand up on the back of her neck. She found herself holding her breath as she neared them.

The men were talking in very low voices. One of them said, looking at her from underneath low-hanging eyelids, "Good day to you."

Louisa nodded as she imagined a young man would and said, "Good day."

She picked up her pace, urging the horse into a trot even as the animal shied away to the opposite side of the road from the men.

As she rode past, a sudden movement caught the corner of her vision. When she turned her head, the men were leaping up, two of them already crossing the road and reaching toward her.

"Stop!" she yelled.

One man took hold of her horse's reins while the other grabbed her arm and yanked. At the same time, her horse reared and screamed.

Louisa hit the ground on her backside, jarring her so much that for a moment she couldn't see.

"We'll be taking your horse," one of them said. "What else do you have?"

Louisa's heart fluttered as blood surged through her limbs. She jumped to her feet, headbutting one of the men in the process. He reeled and fell back, but Louisa barely felt it.

She jerked her arm away, but the third man grabbed her shoulder.

Louisa screamed.

"It's a girl!" one of the men cried.

The man gripping her horse's reins laughed. The one

holding her slapped her across her cheek. She kicked him and screamed again, this time in anger more than fear. She fought, hitting with her fists, but they soon caught her hands and pulled them behind her back, then shoved her down on her knees.

She could no longer fight back, and panic rose inside her, making it hard to breathe. Her vision started going dark.

Where was Sir Charles? *God, help me.*

Charles reached the place where he'd seen Louisa stop. He'd assumed she was resting the horse and eating, but he'd stayed out of sight, still keeping up the illusion that they were not traveling together. But what if he'd rested a lot longer than she had and she was now way ahead of him? No matter. He'd eventually catch up to her.

He continued a little farther when a scream suddenly split the quiet afternoon.

He sent his horse galloping down the road, his blood pounding in his temples as he strained his eyes forward. Another scream, then another. But it was when the screaming stopped that he imagined something truly terrible had happened.

He pushed his horse to go as fast as he could.

As he came around a bend in the road, he saw a group of men surrounding Louisa, who was on her knees, one man holding her wrists behind her back.

Heat rose into his head like a fire. He turned his body and grasped the handle of his sword, which was strapped to his saddlebag, and drew it from its scabbard.

The men scattered, allowing Louisa to stand up.

He went straight for the one trying to mount Louisa's horse. He had just boosted himself into the saddle, tilting precariously forward as he attempted to grab the reins.

Charles knocked him out of the saddle with a hard shove. Louisa's horse reared, pawing the air with its hooves, barely missing the man's head as it came down again. Charles managed to turn his own horse around and take hold of Louisa's before it could run away.

Louisa was suddenly beside him, taking the reins from Charles. "Are you all right?"

"Yes." She nodded, but her eyes were wide, and she looked dazed.

The man on the ground scrambled up and started running down the road after the other three men, who had fled at Charles's arrival.

Charles started after them. They looked over their shoulders at him and kept running, each veering off the road in a different direction.

He couldn't catch them all, and what was he to do once he caught them? He would inform the authorities in the next village about them.

He hurried back to where Louisa was still standing beside her horse, talking softly to it.

"What happened?" he asked as he dismounted and put away his sword. Her shoulders were shaking.

His stomach twisted.

She seemed to make an effort to stop the tears, wiping her face with the back of her hand, then taking a deep breath and blowing it out. She remained facing the horse, but he didn't want to embarrass her by insisting she look at him.

"I saw those four men beside the road. I tried to ride past them, but they grabbed Millie's reins and—" She turned her head slightly and let her watery eyes meet his, but only for a moment.

He nodded, even though she wasn't looking at him. It made his chest ache to hear the fear in her voice. He leaned closer so he could better see her face.

A tear dripped from her eye to her cheek, and she wiped it away with a quick swipe of her hand.

A fist squeezed his heart. A moment later, he was wishing he had chased down those evil men. He imagined impaling them with his sword for putting their hands on Louisa, even as he knew he would never use his sword to kill an unarmed man, especially if he was running away. But it felt good to imagine, just for a moment, meting out justice on them.

Vengeance is mine. That was what the Holy Scriptures said. Vengeance belonged to God, not to man.

"They were going to steal my horse and whatever else they could find." She wiped her face and took another deep breath, and this one seemed to effectively dry up the tears.

"Evil blighters. We will make sure to spread the word at the next village and to every traveler we see to watch out for them. Are you sure they didn't hurt you?"

"I am well enough."

Her hand was touching her cheek, which he had noticed was red. They had either struck her or she'd fallen.

"You said they pulled you down on the ground. Then what happened?"

"I got up and fought them, kicking and hitting them, but they grabbed my arms and pulled my wrists behind my back. Then you came." She shuddered and wrapped her hands around her arms, hugging herself.

"Did they take anything?"

She shook her head. "I don't think so."

He wanted to comfort her. But how did one go about comforting a woman? If she were a man, he would stay quiet and let him talk about it if he wished. He'd seen his father pat his older sister, Delia, on the head or the shoulder when she was upset. And his mother would embrace her. But he wasn't sure if he should put his arms around Louisa. She wasn't his sister, after all.

And he was afraid he might enjoy it too much.

"Is there anything I can do for you?"

"No. I'm well."

"Should we stay here and rest for a bit?"

"No, but you can help me onto my horse, if you don't mind." She sniffed and grasped the pommel of her saddle.

He bent and laced his fingers together, letting her place her foot there, and boosted her up. He was still worried about her, as she was obviously shaken by what had happened.

Once she was in the saddle, he could see that her hands holding the reins were trembling. Again, his heart contracted as he desperately wanted to comfort her. She looked down at him and said in a hoarse whisper, "Thank you."

"Of course." He took a chance and covered her hand with his. She didn't pull away.

A tear fell from her eye. She sniffed and shook her head. "I'm all right."

She wasn't looking at him, so he let go of her hand and mounted his horse, and they started down the road again.

They rode at a slow pace. At least she was no longer insisting on traveling separately from him. But he wouldn't berate her. She couldn't have known those robbers would be on the road. Indeed, such attacks were relatively rare.

As the afternoon progressed, she was so quiet he began to worry that they had hurt her more than she'd said.

Finally, she glanced at him and said, "Thank you for coming to help me."

"Of course. I only wish I'd been closer when I heard you scream."

She hung her head and did not look at him.

He wished he knew how to cheer her. He hated feeling helpless. But at least he had saved her from those evil men. He'd fight them many times over if it would take away the sad, somber spirit that had settled on her.

Louisa kept her head down so Sir Charles wouldn't know she was crying.

If he had not come when he had, there was no knowing what those men would have done to her. They certainly would have stolen her horse and all her belongings, at the very least. She was glad she'd told him thank you, but her heart was too sore, too sad to say more.

Had she made a terrible mistake by leaving her home and coming on this quest for a treasure that might not even exist? The friar certainly thought so, reminding her of her uncle with his cold, accusatory tone. And now it seemed the attack by the robbers had confirmed that she was foolish indeed.

Since she was a little girl, she had dreamed of finding the Vikings' treasure. And when the future had begun to seem so bleak for herself and Margaret, she'd based all her hopes on it. How childish! Was she truly so misled by her own imaginings, thinking she could actually find a treasure that no one else had been able to acquire in the last two hundred years?

She should probably turn around and go home. But the truth was, she was afraid. Would the robbers find her again? Would Sir Charles be willing to continue traveling with her? For she realized now that she needed his help wherever she went. And how could she ask him to go to Yorkshire with her when surely there was no treasure?

If she was going to turn around, she should decide sooner rather than later. As it was, they were getting farther away from home by the minute. But she just couldn't bring herself to tell Sir Charles that she was unsure about whether to continue on after the treasure. Besides, even though she was terribly discouraged, she wasn't ready to give up.

They came to the edge of a village.

"We can buy food here," Sir Charles said. "And I will spread the word about the vicious men we encountered. You can come with me or wait for me by the well."

Her stomach sank at the thought of meeting strangers and having them stare at her, probably wondering if she was a girl and why she was dressed as she was. They might even ask her questions about the attack if she went with Sir Charles, and she certainly had no desire to recount the awful event to people she'd never met and who did not care about her.

"I'll wait for you by the well," she said.

"I shall return soon."

She took his water flask and her own and filled them up at the well. Soon two women came to fill their buckets. They greeted her briefly. Could they tell she'd been crying? She wanted to hide her face, but it would seem strange if she hung her head or turned away from them.

They went on with their gossip about a woman named Maud, giggling about how she had fallen into a rabbit snare and broken her ankle, then one said, with a look of disgust, "And now she can't do her share of the boon works."

Were most women as cruel as these, to laugh at a poor woman because she'd been clumsy and broken her ankle? Louisa had had very few friends, most of them village girls who paid her father, then her uncle, labor and a share of their crop for living on the land, and Louisa had always suspected they were kind to her only because they were afraid not to be.

Louisa was relieved when the two women left. She sat on the

edge of the wall around the well. The longer she waited for Sir Charles, the more she wished she had gone with him.

Perhaps she should go search for him. But the thought was rather demoralizing. After all, she'd been insisting he not travel with her. And now would she search for him like a child who hated to be left alone, even for a short while?

The whole day had been demoralizing. Her mind went over and over the ugly things Brother Matthew had said about her leaving her home and endangering the reputation of a noble knight in the king's service. In her mind she rebelled against his cruel shaming, talked back to him, and even accused him of being pharisaical and not Christlike at all. But after the robbers' attack, all the fire and vinegar had left her, and she could only wonder if the friar had been right.

She had to think of Margaret, of her little sister who needed her to be strong. How could she better her sister's situation if she went home and waited for her uncle to marry them both off to men even more indifferent to them than he was? Or someone as judgmental as the friar?

The treasure might not exist, but Louisa had to at least try to get it. Maybe it was real and God would bless her with it if only she believed. Maybe it was God's will for her and Margaret to be free. If God did allow her to find the treasure, she would petition the king to let her pay her uncle for what he had inherited from her father and allow her to be the Lady of the Manor of Maydestone. Her uncle and aunt would still have Reedbrake. And if her uncle would not take her money, or if the king sided with her uncle, she and Margaret could find a nice, quiet place where they could make a home for themselves.

Her spirits lifted as she saw herself and Margaret living in their own home, giving woolen blankets and food to their tenants on Christmas, paying traveling minstrels to play music for the entire demesne so they could dance, and even settling disputes among them with fairness, not according to who might give the largest bribe.

Margaret, her sweet sister. She deserved the best husband, a man who would truly love her. The very thought of her with a bully who would belittle her or otherwise treat her badly made Louisa's hands shake.

Margaret believed in Louisa. She couldn't fail her.

"I know you will take care of me." That was what Margaret had said when she was only five years old, when their mother and father had died. She'd looked up at Louisa with big, solemn but hopeful eyes.

Louisa could feel the tears returning, so she rubbed her face to distract herself from that memory.

Two more women were coming toward the well with their buckets. Louisa turned and walked toward a tree at the edge of the village square and pretended to inspect it, breaking off a leaf and twirling the stem between her fingers.

She peeked at the two women from the corner of her eye. They looked kinder than the other two. These women were perhaps in their thirties and spoke quietly together.

When Louisa was their age, would she have a friend like that?

Someone who would do mundane tasks with her, someone who was her equal? Even though she loved her little sister with all her heart, their age difference of six years made it hard to confide in her about certain things. Louisa longed for a friend who would understand everything she wished to share.

As the two women were leaving with their well water, she saw Sir Charles coming toward her. Her breath went out of her, a sigh of relief, at the sight of him.

"Did you tell them about the robbers?"

"Yes. They thanked me and said they had come through here and tried to steal food and had been run out of the village. Also, the villagers offered a barn where we might sleep tonight, but I told them we wanted to be on our way. Unless you wish to stay and have a rest?"

"No, thank you. I'm ready to go." She didn't want the entire village knowing that Sir Charles was traveling with a woman. They would surely think bad things about them both.

"Is something wrong?" he asked as they were walking their horses out of the village and back on the road to Yorkshire.

"No. Why do you ask?"

"You look sad."

"I am very well." She quickened her pace to show him she was all right.

What kind of man noticed when she looked sad—and asked her about it? Truly, Sir Charles was different from any man she'd known before.

EIGHT

CHARLES WAS GLAD TO BE LEAVING THE VILLAGE. THE villagers had been pleasant enough, but they asked too many questions.

Traveling was a tedious process. It was faster and easier with horses, but they had to stop often for the animals to rest and drink water, not to mention making sure they had enough to eat. And since they weren't in an area with any large towns, they often went long stretches without seeing another person.

As the day wore on, Louisa seemed to relax and gradually began to talk more. He marveled at the fact that she was interesting to talk to. He never grew tired of her or wished he was alone.

"Tell me about your childhood," she said as they were going down the road.

"I played with my brothers and sister. We ran all over the woods, fishing and setting snares, and then I turned seven years old and was sent to train as a knight. I thought it would be a great adventure, but it was really just work. I missed my mother and father and my sister and brothers." He missed his childhood. But he was surprised he was telling her this. "It was what my brothers had done before me, so I knew I couldn't complain."

She was gazing at him with the sweetest expression on her face. At that moment, the sun peeked out of the clouds and sparkled in her eyes.

"That sounds sad. I hope you weren't mistreated."

"No, not mistreated. I just wasn't allowed to run about and do as I pleased anymore. But I learned many things besides sword fighting and horsemanship. And I gained lifelong friendships with some good men I never would have been able to meet if I'd stayed at home."

Louisa seemed to be mulling this over. Then she let out a deep sigh. "I do think it would be best if children could just be children, if nothing bad ever happened to them. If they didn't get sent away from their mothers, if their mothers and fathers never died and they could play and be happy."

"Don't you think they would become spoiled and obnoxious?"

"Not if they were required to treat others with respect." She looked sharply at him from atop her horse and said, "You are smiling. You think I'm daft."

"No, just perhaps a little too softhearted. A boy needs a firm hand, but I suppose that's what fathers are for." At the same time, he liked her all the more for her tender heart. She would make a good mother.

She sighed again. "It is true I have little experience with boys."

"What about your childhood?"

"It was similar to yours, I think, running about and doing as I pleased. I wasn't sent away when I was seven, but my mother and father began to teach me reading and writing and arithmetic at that age. When I was nine, they found a tutor who could teach me languages and science. He was very adamant that we use the Holy Writ in most of our lessons. I'd read the entire Scriptures all the way through at least three times by the time I was thirteen.

"My parents both died when I was eleven and Margaret was five, and things changed a great deal after that. My uncle eventually sent my tutor away, but I continued to study on my own. Mostly I just read whatever books I could get. And I taught my sister Latin and French and English, but she was not very inclined toward studying. I gave up trying to teach her languages about a year ago. She told me she knew enough." Louisa laughed, a happy sound. She always looked happy when she spoke of her sister.

"Did something happen that made you decide to finally go in search of the treasure? Weren't you afraid to travel by yourself?"

"I was afraid, but I was more afraid my uncle would marry my sister off to some disgusting, perverted old man." She proceeded to tell him about the last suitor her uncle had invited to the manor and about how he even put Margaret before him as a potential wife.

Charles's face heated at the thought of her uncle marrying off a twelve-year-old girl, although he knew it happened all the time. He also didn't like the thought of Louisa being forced to marry some old man. Louisa was too special to be given to just anyone. But it wasn't that as much as . . . He probably shouldn't acknowledge the real reason he hated thinking of her marrying.

"But another reason I decided to leave home and go search for the treasure . . . It happened about a year ago, and it made me realize I had to come up with a plan to get Margaret and me away from my uncle and aunt. It caused me to decide I didn't want to marry at all."

She told him the story of one of her uncle's suitors trying to steal her virtue, coming into her bedroom that she shared with Margaret while they were asleep.

"I fought him off and knocked him out with my iron candle-stick holder."

Charles felt slightly sick. "What is his name? I will make him pay for that."

"To be honest, I don't remember. I think I blocked it from my memory, it frightened me so much. I'm surprised I'm even telling you about it. I never speak of it. But when those men tried to rob me, it brought it back into my mind." She frowned and shook her head slightly.

He hated that she suffered so. He wished he could have saved her from those experiences. Thankfully, he could protect her now, and he tried to think of what he could say to change her mood and cheer her. Maybe an amusing story? If she were one of his fellow knights, he'd probably start singing a funny song, but he couldn't think of anything that seemed appropriate. Maybe when they stopped for the night, he would set a trap for a hare or a pheasant. A good meal always cheered them both.

They came to a long stretch of road with no hills or bends.

Far ahead they could see someone riding on a horse. As they gradually caught up with the traveler, he could see it was a woman on a chestnut mare.

"Good day," Charles said.

"Good day to you," the woman said cheerily.

"Are you traveling far?" Charles asked, worried about her since she was a woman traveling alone.

"To Yorkshire, another few days' ride. And you?"

"We are headed to Yorkshire as well. Would you like to ride along with us?" Another woman might make Louisa feel more at ease.

"That is very kind of you." She smiled so big he could see that she had almost a full set of teeth. "I am Richenda Kemp of York."

"Sir Charles Raynsford of Dericott, at your service."

"You are a knight, then. Very good. And is this your squire?"

"This is my fellow traveler . . ." He paused, not sure if he should introduce her as Louisa or Jack.

"I am Louisa," she said. Her eyes were staring straight at the woman, as if waiting for her reaction.

"I am so pleased to make the acquaintance of two fellow travelers. You both may call me Richie. It will be quite pleasant to have the company of a noble knight and a fellow woman traveler. And you said you were headed to Yorkshire as well? Where in Yorkshire? It is a big county."

"The northern part. Swaledale, actually," Charles said to the friendly woman.

"Very good, very good. This is a lonely stretch of road, is it not? I have lost my servant, and I don't relish traveling alone.

I am so glad we happened upon each other. My husband died ten years ago, and when my daughter became sick, I decided to make the pilgrimage to Canterbury to the shrine of St. Thomas à Becket, to procure some St. Thomas's Water for her. My servant went with me as my protector, but I have been forced to travel alone ever since I left London."

"I'm sorry you lost your servant. May I ask what happened to him?"

"He was rather old, and the long journey tired him out, poor fellow. I left him in London, saying he could go no farther. I do wonder that the visit to St. Thomas à Becket's shrine and his saintly relics did not revive him. Even touching the vial of the saint's blood mixed with water did not restore his strength. I put a drop of it on his forehead in the sign of the cross. But as I said, he is rather old, fifty-five years."

"We are pleased to have you travel with us," Charles said. "There is safety in numbers." In fact, this might be just what they needed to keep Louisa from worrying about his reputation.

"I gratefully accept your offer." She grinned first at him, then at Louisa.

Now they would have Richie's presence to ensure Louisa's virtue was not questioned.

He only hoped this woman wouldn't browbeat Louisa the way Brother Matthew had.

Louisa liked Richenda Kemp immediately.

"Thank you for allowing me to travel with you and Louisa,"

Richie said a few miles down the road. "My daughter is also a beauty, and brave like you." She smiled at Louisa.

I am brave, Louisa thought, remembering how she had kicked the robbers and fought them.

Besides speaking to Louisa as if she was a person and not someone to look down on, Richie was very enthusiastic about nearly everything, and she talked a lot. It made the time go by faster.

Late in the day, when the sun was low, they stopped for their evening meal. While Sir Charles tarried in the woods, Richie turned to Louisa.

"I can't help but notice that you're wearing men's clothing."

"Yes, I left home without my uncle's permission and didn't want him finding me. I also was traveling alone and didn't want any unwelcome attention."

"I thought it was something like that." Richie nodded.

"I came upon Sir Charles not long after I left. I told him my name was Jack and he let me travel with him. He knew I was a woman, but he didn't say anything."

"He seems very kind and noble, more so than most knights I've encountered." Richie gave her a knowing look from underneath pale-brown brows. "How was it revealed—how did he acknowledge—that you were a woman?"

"We came upon a friar on the road. His name was Brother Matthew, and he told me I was endangering Sir Charles's reputation and that I should go home. He said it was obvious I was a woman."

"Well, Brother Matthew sounds perfectly . . . awful."

"Perhaps he wasn't very kind, but I decided he was right and so I tried traveling separately from Sir Charles, but I was attacked by robbers."

"Oh my! How dreadful! Were you hurt?"

"No. Sir Charles heard me scream and he came before the men could steal my horse or hurt me."

"How wonderful that you have a guardian angel like Sir Charles."

"Yes, and I'm also very thankful that you are traveling with us. Now no one can accuse me or Sir Charles of anything."

"It works out well for all of us, I daresay. Sir Charles would be all alone without us." She gave Louisa a wink. "How much better to have the company of two intelligent beings such as us?"

Richie's smile was quite contagious. Louisa couldn't help but return it.

"Would you like some more comfortable clothing?"

The morning was dawning warmer than the day before. Richie lifted her head from searching through her saddlebags and wiggled her brows at Louisa.

"Comfortable?"

"A dress. Something more womanly. You can continue wearing the hose, unless it gets too warm."

"I don't want to take your clothes," Louisa said. "You will need them."

"I am happy to share with you, though my dresses will

certainly be too big for you. But when next we find a market town on market day, we will purchase you something. A beautiful woman like you should be wearing pretty clothes. And I have a few ideas to dress up your hair. It is short, but a pretty coif and veil will hide that and make you look quite feminine."

Perhaps the woman's attention to her appearance should have made her uncomfortable, but it actually cheered her. The longer she dressed as a boy, the less she liked it. Which probably had more to do with how she wanted Sir Charles to see her than anything else.

As fate would have it, two days later they happened upon a market town on market day.

The atmosphere was festive, with music from a traveling minstrel, who was singing and playing on his lute in the town square near the well. Sellers had set up booths in rows, hawking their wares to anyone who walked by.

Richie said to Sir Charles, "Louisa and I have a quest. You may meet us at the well in two hours."

"Two hours? Very well." He raised his brows but asked no questions.

Richie looped her arm through Louisa's and grinned. "We shall find you something that will make you stand out anywhere, even in the Great Hall of a duke or prince."

Louisa laughed. Richie had a way of making everything seem festive and lively.

"Do you not believe me? I shall make a believer of you." Richie waggled her brows at her, which only made Louisa want to laugh again.

They found a fabric merchant who also was selling premade kirtles and bliauds. Sitting behind him was a seamstress who was bent over her work, sending a needle and thread in and out of the fabric in her lap with great speed.

"If we find a dress we like, can the seamstress alter it for us?" Richie asked the merchant.

"Yes, of course," the merchant said. He proceeded to show them his most expensive dresses, made of silk imported from the East.

Louisa's stomach did a flip at the price he quoted. It was more than twice the cost of everything Louisa possessed. But Richie did not bat an eye. She picked a pale-green one with bright flowers and leaves embroidered around the neckline and the ends of the wide sleeves. She held it up to Louisa, stretching the dress over Louisa's shoulders.

"This one looks very becoming. What do you think?"

"I think it's too expensive," Louisa whispered.

"Nonsense. My husband left me a wealthy woman. I will buy it for you."

How fortunate for Richie that the robbers had not attacked *her* instead of Louisa.

She looked through the slightly less expensive dresses made of fine linen and chose a deep-blue bliaud and a belt with more brightly colored embroidery.

"This one will match your eyes perfectly." Richie held it up to her chin and sucked in a loud breath. "Oh yes, this one is just the thing."

Soon the seamstress was pulling the first dress over Louisa's head and pinching it tight at her waist.

"You will also need an underdress," Richie said.

The merchant was showing her his selection of underdresses as the seamstress finished estimating where she would need to make her stitches and snatched the second dress over Louisa's head.

"Give me an hour," the seamstress said. "They will be ready."

Richie purchased the white, fine linen underdress and said, "Let us go get some food now."

She found a woman selling hot stuffed buns filled with some kind of meat, boiled cabbage, and leeks, and they put them in their packs and ate one while they walked through the market vendors. They also bought bread and cheese and dried fruit and nuts. They filled their packs and finally made their way back to the booth where they'd found the dresses.

The seamstress insisted on Louisa trying them on without her bulky outer tunic and with the fine linen underdress. She took her behind two screens and pulled each dress over her head. Everything fit perfectly.

The second one she put on was the deep-blue bliaud. When Richie saw her, she exclaimed dramatically, "Dear saints above! You are beautiful!"

Louisa felt herself smiling, even though she knew Richie was exaggerating.

"Oh, my dear." She actually seemed to have tears in her eyes as she placed her hands on either side of Louisa's face and looked her in the eyes. "Such beautiful eyes and skin and teeth. You are a vision of loveliness."

Louisa let out a nervous laugh. She couldn't believe Richie was telling the truth, especially since she had not been taking care of her skin by letting the sun shine on her every day. Her face was probably as brown as a chipmunk by now. Richie was too kind.

"I should take it off." Louisa turned to go back into the privacy of the screens, but Richie stopped her.

"Leave it on. You should wear it."

"But it will get soiled on the road."

"What good are new clothes if you're not going to wear them? Never save anything for tomorrow that you can enjoy today, I always say. Come. Humor an old woman and leave it on."

"Very well."

Louisa felt her heart rise into her throat. What would Sir Charles say when he saw her?

"One more thing before we go." Richie steered her toward a booth that sold coifs and ribbons and veils.

They browsed through the hair accessories, and Richie chose several items and purchased them. Again, Louisa's stomach churned at the money her new friend was spending on her. She only hoped she really was as wealthy as she said.

"Is it time to meet Sir Charles now?" Louisa didn't want to keep him waiting.

Richie grinned. "Not just yet. I want to prepare your hair." She grabbed Louisa's arm and pulled her behind the privacy screens and sat her on a stool. Then she started pulling and tugging on Louisa's short hair, pinning and muttering to herself.

Finally, she came around to stand in front of Louisa, tucking and arranging for another few moments before saying, "There."

She hugged herself and made a tiny squeal under her breath as she stared at Louisa, obviously quite pleased. "I am only sorry I don't have a looking glass for you to see yourself, but you may depend upon it—you are the most beautiful woman here."

Louisa gingerly touched the veil that was covering most of her hair, all but a bit in front. She gazed down at her lovely new dress and felt . . . quite different than she had since she'd left home in her oversized men's clothing.

But would her uncle's men recognize her if they came across her again? Possibly, but she hoped she was far enough away that they would not come looking for her here.

"Come." Richie once again tucked her arm through Louisa's and led her through the crowded marketplace with their packs and new purchases under one arm.

She couldn't help but notice that people were looking at her much differently than they had when she'd walked into the market. Men stared appreciatively, and even women took a second look at her, obviously admiring—or envying—her dress. She couldn't decide whether the new attention made her feel embarrassed and uncomfortable or . . . good.

She caught sight of Sir Charles standing at the well. Her cheeks began to burn. What would he think when he saw her? Would he laugh at her for trying to look like someone she was not? Would he be surprised? Or would he even care? Maybe he would behave as if she looked the same and nothing had changed.

Perhaps that would be best, for she suddenly felt afraid that his reaction would hurt her.

He was lounging against the stone wall of the well, looking content but alert, chewing on a long piece of straw.

She walked slowly, holding up the hem of her dress with one hand and holding on to her things with the other. She was only twenty feet away from him when he suddenly saw her coming toward him.

He straightened, pushing himself off the wall, his eyes widening ever so slightly, and the straw fell out of his mouth.

"Richie bought me two new dresses," Louisa said, trying to act as if nothing important had happened, as if she wasn't feeling very self-conscious. "She insisted I wear this, even though I told her it would get dirty on the road."

She glanced at Richie, who was watching Sir Charles like a cat watches a mouse, an anticipatory glint in her eye.

"Do you approve?" Richie asked.

Sir Charles opened his mouth, closed it, then stammered, "Uh . . . of course. That is, whatever Louisa wishes to wear is fine. And now that you're traveling with us . . . It is well. Did you get everything else you need—food?"

Was he pleased to see her dressed this way? She couldn't tell. But the way he was stammering told her that he was at least surprised.

"The dress is very pretty, is it not?" Richie asked.

Louisa's stomach sank. Would she embarrass them both by forcing him to tell what he thought?

"It is a pretty dress. And Louisa looks very pretty in it." He immediately turned away from them and headed to the tree nearby where their horses were tied.

Richie gave Louisa a satisfied smile and followed slowly after Sir Charles.

Louisa tried to walk regally, the way her aunt had taught her to, holding her head high and looking straight ahead, as a lady should.

She had grown so accustomed to the men's hose she'd been wearing that it seemed strange to ride her horse in a dress. But she also knew the hose would be too warm under her skirts. Besides, she felt happy to be wearing a dress again, to cease the pretense that she was a man, wondering all the time if anyone was even fooled by it.

She wanted Sir Charles to think she was pretty, but now that he did—possibly—he didn't talk to her as much. He even seemed afraid to look at her, though she couldn't imagine why. She sighed, wondering if things would be awkward between them now.

NINE

CHARLES NEARLY SWALLOWED HIS TONGUE WHEN HE SAW Louisa dressed as a wealthy lady. Was this some sort of game Richie was playing? She must realize how pretty Louisa looked and wanted Charles to notice. But why?

What she didn't realize was that he had already noticed how pretty Louisa was. It was simply more comfortable to talk to her and travel with her when she was not looking so obviously feminine. To have a beautiful young woman constantly by his side made him slightly uncomfortable.

He'd grown fond of Louisa, but he knew from his experience with Lady Mirabella that falling in love with an unattainable woman meant only pain for him. That pain was not something he wished to repeat so soon. Louisa was obviously the daughter of someone of some wealth and means, and from what Louisa had told him, her guardian expected to be paid handsomely for the privilege of marrying her.

It was hopeless, so he did his best to treat her as he had before.

Two days later, they came to a small village and went to the well, as they always did, to fill their flasks and water the horses. They were just starting to draw water when he heard someone yelling not far away.

A woman and a very small child, probably about three years old, were cowering before a man who was gesturing violently, shouting at them to leave his village.

The woman gathered the child in her arms and was slowly walking away, but the man followed and continued yelling at them.

"What is the matter here?" Charles walked up and stood between them.

No one spoke right away. The man's face was red, and he was still glaring at the woman. Then he turned his scowl on Charles.

"I will not have this cursed woman and her cursed son living in this village!" He pointed at the woman and her little son, who was hiding his face behind his mother, pressing close to her side.

"Cursed? What do you mean?" He felt his ire growing.

"Look at him! I will not have the crops of everyone in this village blighted because of their curse." He grabbed the child's arm and pulled him out from behind his mother, and Charles could see that his other arm was missing.

"He was born with only one arm. Then her husband and five other people in her village died of a fever. Does that not sound like she and the boy are cursed? I will not have it! I will not have her cursing my village." He turned to the woman, who held her son close, and waved his arms at her. "Go! Get out of here! We don't want you here!"

A small group of people had gathered not far away. None of them spoke, but all of them stared back with varying degrees of agreement with the man showing on their faces.

Charles could tell him that he hardly thought that this woman or her son could have caused that misfortune, or that they would cause misfortune here either, but his words would only anger the man further.

However, he did have something to say. "I am Sir Charles, a knight in the service of King Richard. Regardless of what happened in her village, it is wrong to mistreat them. Show some Christian charity."

"Christian charity? What about my family? What about my village? Should they suffer while we show charity to the cursed? Look at him! You saw the boy."

The woman was visibly shaking, and the boy had tears rolling down his cheeks. He was far too young to experience such cruelty.

Charles looked at the woman. "Do you have family or property anywhere?"

She shook her head. "Our lord took back my land when my husband died. My sister lives here, but she doesn't want us."

"Take her with you," the man shouted, "if you are so willing to show Christian charity to the cursed!"

"Get back. I've had enough of you." Charles wished he had his sword strapped to his back, but he wouldn't stand for this bully mouthing off. He pointed past the man. "Go. Out of my sight."

The man immediately backed away toward the small crowd of people. When he was far enough away to suit Charles, the knight turned to the woman and her child, who were crouched on the ground, as if bracing themselves for blows.

"You may travel with my companions and me. Come." Charles motioned with his hand and the woman stood and picked up her son, holding him close to her.

As they walked back toward the well, where Louisa and Richie were watching, he turned his head and asked the woman, "Do you have any other family?"

"No, sir."

What was he to do with this woman and her child? He had no idea, but he knew he had to help them. People were so fearful of the devil that they often forgot that God was more powerful. Had the Lord not admonished His people many times, "Be not afraid"?

He studied the looks on Richie's and Louisa's faces. Richie seemed a bit uncertain, but Louisa stepped forward with an empathetic expression.

"You will be safe with us," she said, smiling at the woman, then at the little boy. "I am Louisa, and this is Richie. And what are your names?"

"Sybil and Elias." Sybil kept her head down, her voice quiet. They both looked as if they'd been sleeping on the bare ground for many nights.

They were still watering the horses, so Charles asked the woman, "Where are your belongings? Do you need to go get them from your sister's house?"

"They are hidden. I shall fetch them." She hurried away, the little boy bouncing on her hip.

Charles decided to follow at a distance to make sure no one else harassed her.

She didn't go far outside of the village before she moved off the road and went to a large oak tree with exposed roots. She reached into a hollow under the roots and drew out a small pack, too small to contain more than a few pieces of clothing for each of them.

She grasped the bundle to her chest with one hand while holding the child close in the other and hurried back toward him.

"Thank you," she said.

"Of course. I am pleased to be of service to you." He studied her for a moment and said, "You know you are not cursed, do you not?"

She seemed to think for a moment, then said meekly, "I don't feel in my heart that I am cursed, and I know my precious child is not cursed. We are just a bit unfortunate, perhaps, like Job. Though I know I am not perfect, I think I am as good a Christian as most."

She hung her head again.

The child's eyes were big and round as he stared up at Charles. He looked like any normal child, only sadder and with one arm missing. But Charles knew the fear of most people—the fear that their crops would fail and that they and their children would go hungry. Fear fueled their thoughts and controlled their beliefs. Anyone who was different was blamed for any misfortune that befell the community—a disease that wiped out the animals, a plague that killed large numbers of people, a drought or pestilence or blight that destroyed their food crops.

And a child born with only one arm would be thought to be a sign of the devil's curse.

Of course it wasn't the child's fault. Charles had had the privilege of reading the Holy Scriptures in their entirety, and never was a child blamed for misfortunes that befell anyone, nor did God tell anyone to be afraid of the devil. But to provide for widows and orphans was the definition of pure religion, according to the apostle James.

Charles was gathering quite a group of widows and orphans, it seemed.

Louisa was glad to have a little band of people, including two women, to converse with. Even though Sybil did not talk very much, she seemed eager to please. She often smiled or offered help, but she was also timid and easily startled, which was understandable, as she had obviously been mistreated quite a bit.

Louisa entertained little Elias and played games with him, repeated rhymes that she'd learned as a child, and sang songs to him, which mostly erased the sad, frozen look he wore when they'd first encountered him. It thrilled her heart when she was able to make him smile. She still had not been able to coax a laugh out of him, but she would not give up.

One morning when Sybil had gone into the woods to relieve herself, Louisa was holding Elias and trying to amuse him as

Richie looked on with a wan smile from where she was brushing her horse. Sir Charles walked up, his hair wet from a quick wash in the river next to where they had slept the night before.

Her heart lurched in her chest at the way he looked—his dark hair slightly curly as water dripped from a strand at his temple. His eyes seemed even bluer than normal, reflecting the sun that glinted through the leaves. He was staring right at her and smiling.

If she could freeze this moment and relive it again and again, she would.

She came to the end of the rhyme she had been reciting to Elias, and he gave a slight bounce on her lap and said, "Again."

"You have made a friend," he said, still smiling.

"Again," Elias repeated while Sir Charles started checking his horse's hooves a few feet away.

"Do you like this one?" Louisa asked Elias as she began a rhyme she hadn't thought about in years. She was nearly finished when she realized she had forgotten how it ended. She faltered, Elias staring at her.

Suddenly Sir Charles filled in the missing words.

Sir Charles said, "My old nurse used to tell me that one every morning," then sat down in front of them. "Do you know this one?" He started to sing a silly song about a bird and a fox, using his fingers like they were a ladder for the fox to climb to get the bird.

As he was leaning close, Louisa's heart beat erratically, as if the bird had found its way into her chest.

Sir Charles showed Elias how to use his hand with Sir Charles's hand to make the ladder. Elias gasped as he figured out how to touch the tips of his fingers to Sir Charles's and make the fox climb the ladder, as it were, while Sir Charles sang the song again. When the fox caught the bird, the boy squealed, then giggled.

Louisa smiled and her eyes met Sir Charles's. She wanted to tell him he was good with children, that she'd been longing to hear the boy laugh. Instead, she sighed, her breath rushing out of her at how handsome he was—handsome and kind and . . . wonderful.

Just then a man walked into the small clearing. He was leading a donkey loaded down with bundles.

"Pardon me," he said. "I heard a child squeal and thought I would ensure he was not hurt. I see that he is well."

"Oh yes, we were just playing a little game," Sir Charles said.

The man looked to be around thirty years old, with a pleasant face.

"Your son is very like you both—hair like his mother and eyes like his father."

"He is not our son." Sir Charles looked amused.

"No?" the man asked.

"No," Louisa said. "That is, we are not married." She inclined her head toward Sir Charles. She suddenly gasped at how her words sounded. "What I mean is, the child is not ours, is not mine either." Why was she getting so flustered? Her cheeks were starting to burn, but she wasn't sure if it was because her explanation sounded, for a moment, as if she had had a child out of wedlock, or because she was imagining how it would feel to say that Sir Charles was her husband.

"Butterfly!" Elias pointed, then jumped up and ran after a yellow butterfly. At that moment, Louisa saw that Sybil was coming toward them, and his mother followed him as he chased the butterfly.

"I am Morten," the man said.

"Sir Charles of Dericott, and this is Louisa."

Richie came into the clearing and Sir Charles introduced the man to her. "You may call me Richie. Where are you bound?" she asked.

"Any number of places. I travel to market towns selling shoes made by my father and brothers in Chesterfield."

When Sybil walked back to the group with Elias on her hip, Morten turned to look at her. She mumbled meekly, "I am Sybil."

"And her adorable little boy is Elias," Louisa said. Even though Sybil obviously didn't want to attract attention to him, Louisa wanted to make sure the stranger knew that they all accepted Elias and were protective of him.

"What a handsome little man," Morten said with his polite smile.

After a few minutes of conversation, they were all ready to get back on the road.

"Would it be all right if I traveled with your group?" Morten asked.

"I don't mind," Sir Charles said. He looked around at the rest of their group. "Does anyone mind?"

"The more the merrier!" Richie said.

"It is all right with me," Louisa said.

"Sybil?" Sir Charles asked.

"Yes." Sybil's voice was barely audible as she nodded and smiled her painfully agreeable smile.

They traveled along while engaging in pleasant conversation. Richie talked the most, but when they stopped to rest the horses, Louisa took note of what seemed to be the first time Morten saw that the little boy had an infirmity. His expression changed from pleased curiosity to surprise but just as quickly morphed into compassion and understanding.

While they sat and had a small repast of bread and cheese, Louisa noticed that Morten moved closer to Sybil and Elias and shared something that looked like a flat piece of bread with the boy.

"It is sweet," Morten said. "Taste it."

Elias took a bite, then another and another, obviously liking what he tasted.

"I bought those in a village to the west, the baker's special sweet bread. He called it honey bread. Take one," he said, offering one of the small flat cakes to Sybil.

She mumbled something Louisa couldn't make out.

"Please take it. I have a lot more," he said.

She finally accepted the cake and took a bite, nodding and thanking him, then gave the rest of it to Elias.

That day and the next progressed just as pleasantly, even though they were plagued with a light rain most of the time. At least it was warm and they did not have to worry about freezing. Richie and Louisa had enough extra clothing, and Sir Charles and Morten enough extra blankets, to share with Sybil and Elias.

Morten told them, "I'm heading to the largest market town for many miles, Ashbourne, and will stay there through the Midsummer Festival. Is Ashbourne on your way?"

Sir Charles nodded. "If I'm not mistaken, we should arrive there either today or tomorrow."

The land was becoming less flat as the road passed through valleys with hills on either side.

In the late afternoon, Elias and his mother were riding on Sir Charles's horse while he walked. The child became so fussy, crying and whining, that Louisa offered to take him onto her horse. She sat him on the saddle in front of her, holding on to him, and he soon fell asleep with his head resting against her stomach.

A warm feeling swept over her as she held the sleeping child. She was also glad to give Sybil a break from caring for him, since she always looked so tired.

An hour or so later, they were keeping an eye out for a good place to bed down for the night when they caught sight of a large manor house not far off the road.

"I believe that is Ashbourne Hall," Sir Charles said.

"That means we are very close to the town of Ashbourne," Morten said, a note of excitement in his voice. "And they are sure to offer us a place to sleep tonight."

Louisa looked at Sir Charles. He did not disagree, and they took the lane that would lead them to the great manor house.

Ashbourne Hall was no castle—it was rather plain, as most manor houses were—but it was grand, with three levels, which was one more level than her father's manor house in her home village of Maydestone. They would surely have room for a few travelers and would probably share some warm frumenty with them.

As they started up the lane, Elias awoke from his nap wanting his mother.

"I'll carry you on my shoulders. Would you like that?" Morten asked in a cheerful voice.

The boy stared at him as if uncertain.

"You'll be taller than me, taller than your mother."

The boy held out his arm, so Louisa stopped her horse and helped settle the boy on Morten's shoulders. Sybil looked on anxiously, but Morten held the boy's legs firmly while Elias held on to Morten's hair like he was holding a fistful of a horse's mane.

Morten started singing a riding song and mimicking the galloping of a horse, gently jostling the boy and making him laugh. Sybil looked on with a trembling smile just before a tear dripped from her eye onto her cheek. She flicked it away with her finger, still smiling.

At the manor, the grooms took their animals, and they were immediately given some bread and shown into a large room that was divided by a partial wall, one side for women and the other for men, with several narrow beds on each side.

"You may sleep here," the old woman servant said. "And you may eat with the servants in the kitchen. We will ring the bell when it's ready."

When Louisa, Richie, Sybil, and Elias were alone on their side of the room, Louisa stretched out on one of the beds. How good it would feel to sleep on a bed again. Except for the night at the monastery, she had only slept on the ground since she left home. How long would it take for her to get accustomed to sleeping in the bed with Margaret and Hanilda when she was home again?

Then she remembered that once she retrieved the treasure, she and Margaret would be rich enough to have their own place. Her uncle probably would not agree to sell her Maydestone Manor, but she would find a new home where they could live without answering to anyone.

For tonight she would enjoy sleeping on something softer than the ground and dream of her new home where she and Margaret could themselves offer food and a bed to weary travelers.

TEN

THE NEXT MORNING LOUISA WAS GATHERING UP HER things when Sir Charles appeared and announced, "The lord has invited us to stay for the Midsummer Festival, which is in two days."

Louisa expected Richie to want to get on the road, since she was on her way back to her daughter. Instead, she seemed happy to delay their journey another couple of days. Perhaps she figured a few more days wouldn't make a difference.

"Midsummer in Ashbourne sounds very festive." Richie's eyes were wide as she clasped her hands. "I love a good Midsummer Festival."

"I am staying to ply my wares," Morten said. "I'd be very glad of the company."

"I would like to stay for the festival." Louisa had only ever experienced Midsummer in her tiny village where they had to make their own entertainment without professional singers and musicians. But it was one of Louisa's favorite festivals, with its enjoyable traditions such as dancing, singing, and lighting bonfires. And if Ashbourne was as large and prosperous as she had heard, this Midsummer Festival should be better than any festival she'd experienced before.

Everyone seemed a bit awed that the lord had asked to speak with Sir Charles privately and then invited them to stay. Richie especially seemed pleased and asked him several questions about the Lord of the Manor of Ashbourne. Then she said, "Let us go to the town of Ashbourne and see it for ourselves. Shall we?"

Everyone was agreeable, so they soon set out.

Ashbourne was a large market town, and Louisa gasped when she saw the church and its spire. Could the cathedrals of London and the other great cities be any more impressive than this one?

"May we visit the church?" she asked, realizing she was already moving toward it.

"Of course." Sir Charles followed her.

"Let us all go and light a candle," Richie said. "I never lose an opportunity to say a prayer and put a penny in the poor box at every church I see. Who knows where one might meet the very Spirit of God and gain His favor for a miracle?"

Louisa had never thought of it that way before. But on this journey, she had found that she loved visiting churches. Though she did like to say a prayer and light a candle, her main desire was to admire its beauty and feel the awe of praying in the same place where many others before her had made their petitions to God.

The beauty of the churches she'd seen, even the small village churches, had indeed inspired her and given her memories that she would always hold dear, but this one—St. Oswald's Church, as it was called—promised to be the most beautiful of all. The spire took her breath away. The stained glass windows were beautiful beyond compare, and the nave was enormous, with the highest ceiling she had seen yet.

Louisa walked to the chancel, genuflected at the crucifix, and knelt to pray. As she prayed, a thought nagged at the back of her mind even as she nudged it away and concentrated on her prayer. Finally, the thought intruded on her. If there really was a giant who guarded the Viking treasure at the top of a mountain, and if she was clever enough to take it from him, that would be stealing. And stealing was clearly a sin.

"God," Louisa whispered, low enough that no one would hear, "I don't want to be guilty of stealing. When is taking not stealing? Is it not stealing if the giant is evil and cruel?"

Louisa often spoke to God in such a manner, asking Him questions and speaking to Him as if He were a human. There had been only one or two occasions when she felt God spoke back to her—more of a thought appearing in her mind than an audible voice. She wasn't surprised when she did not get an answer, but she did feel unsettled in her spirit, almost a feeling of rebuke.

Her father had never mentioned a giant. She very much doubted that the giant even existed. But if it was wrong to take the treasure, then her whole quest was wrong. Even if she succeeded, she was failing.

She prayed silently, *God, what should I do? Should I go home and accept my fate?*

She waited, a heavy feeling in her chest. If God told her to go home, that would hurt so much. She'd always believed God would save both her and her sister from her uncle's marriage schemes, always believed God cared for her and would give her a good life while enabling her to care for Margaret. But perhaps that had been only her own strong desire. After all, God never promised to give anyone an easy life. Even Jesus' own mother's life had not been without trouble. Mary must have suffered greatly from other people shaming her, gossiping that she'd had her first child outside of marriage, and later watching as her own dear Son was cruelly mistreated and hung on a cross to die a horrible death.

As these thoughts went through her mind, she realized God had not answered her. So she tried again. *God, please give me a sign. If You want me to go back home* . . . She glanced up and caught sight of one particular candle that was burning apart from the others, the very candle she had lit.

If You want me to go home, then snuff out that candle.

She stared at the candle. It continued to flicker and burn as it had before. She closed her eyes and focused her mind on Jesus, the picture of Him hanging on the cross that she'd seen so many times on the crucifix in her village church. Then she opened her eyes to look at the candle. It was still burning.

Perhaps there was no Viking treasure. But if her journey was futile, all the more reason for God to send her home. Unless there was something else she was to find on this journey, a lesson God had for her or some kind of blessing that she would only find away from home.

She went back to praying, asking God this time for wisdom and understanding.

Louisa had once explained to her priest her way of asking God for a sign, but the priest had not looked pleased. He'd frowned and said, "I do not encourage asking the Lord God for signs."

"Why not? Gideon asked for a sign."

"You are not Gideon," was his only answer. That was not good enough for Louisa.

The difference between her and Gideon, it seemed to Louisa, was that God had asked Gideon to do something and then Gideon wanted confirmation, so he asked for a sign from God. Was Louisa not more justified in asking for a sign, since she didn't have the benefit of hearing from God first? Should she not ask for a sign when she was unsure if something was only her desire and might violate God's wishes for her?

She also understood that asking for a sign was not something to be done lightly or in any and every situation. She had to truly believe and not doubt, and to go against what God was telling her would surely be a grave sin. She could understand how Job must have felt when he said he wanted to speak to God face-to-face and get answers to all his questions.

She continued to pray, but soon Louisa's mind was wandering. Since she didn't want to inconvenience her fellow travelers—or be left behind—she concluded her prayer, then took one more turn around the magnificent church.

In the corner of the nave near the front door, she noticed some sort of carving in the wall. When she went toward it, she saw that it was a crude drawing of a hill and a cross beside it. The hill immediately reminded her of the mountain where the Viking treasure was supposed to be hidden.

Was God trying to give her a sign? Did this mean she was supposed to continue on to search for the treasure? Or was that only what she wanted to think?

She noticed other carvings on the wall beside it. Some were names and dates carved into the wood beams. One was a boat with a cross over it and underneath were the words *God save.*

Another was a date and the words *God heal my son.* Another wrote, *God is good.*

Obviously there were people in this market town who knew how to read and write, people who were desperate enough for God's blessing and mercy that they would carve their message on the walls of the church itself.

Louisa closed her eyes and said a quick prayer for all those who needed saving and healing, then for every person in her group—Sir Charles, Richie, Sybil and Elias, and Morten. "Keep us safe in our travels and lead us in the ways of righteousness," she whispered.

When she left the church, she saw the others standing outside.

"We are going with Morten to set up his stall in the market square," Richie said.

"Are you well?" Sir Charles asked quietly after helping her onto her horse.

"Very well, I thank you." She had cried only a few tears, something that always happened while she was praying. Could he tell?

He gazed into her eyes for a few moments before turning away.

Even though Sir Charles was a man, she felt closer and more trusting of him than of any of the other travelers. But she had been with him much longer than she had known the others and had seen his integrity many times. She just had to not think about how handsome he was.

They made their way to the center of the town. Already there seemed to be a festive air about as a few merchants had set up their tents and were working on readying their stalls on the cobblestones of the marketplace.

Richie started a conversation with one of the merchants, who was selling spices and silks from the Orient. What must it be like to be so friendly and able to talk so freely with strangers?

Sybil was glancing around and holding Elias close to her, as if afraid someone would harass them. But instead of clinging to her as he used to do, Elias was fussing and stretching out his arm, trying to pull away from her.

"I'll walk with him if you like," Louisa said.

Sybil shook her head and pulled him closer, speaking quietly into his ear.

"Look what I found." Morten came toward them and showed Elias what was in his hand—two wooden toys. "It's a knight and his horse."

Elias took the toys and instantly calmed, staring at the wooden figures and turning them. He started talking in his little child voice, the most words Louisa had ever heard him say, but she could only make out a few—"Knight," "horse," and "fight."

She noticed Morten looking at Sybil, and then she was gazing back at him. Certainly Morten had never looked at Louisa that way, and she couldn't imagine him looking at Richie or Sir Charles that way either. Could there be something between them? He had better not think of behaving dishonorably toward Sybil. Sir Charles would not stand for that, and neither would she.

She had already been thinking ahead to the Midsummer Festival, wondering if Sir Charles would dance with her, for there was sure to be music and dancing. He had been different since she started wearing the fine dresses Richie had bought for her. She wanted so much for him to think she was pretty, but for many reasons, she was too afraid to be flirtatious with him.

Her thoughts in regard to Sir Charles were such a tangle. She didn't want to feel about him the way she did, but there was no getting out of it.

Sybil was probably not much older than Louisa, even though she had been married and had a three-year-old child. Did she think about Morten the way Louisa thought about Sir Charles?

This could be a very interesting Midsummer Festival.

Louisa sat around the bonfire outside of town, its flames so high and hot that she had to sit quite a long way from it. Sir Charles and Morten were standing and talking, watching over Louisa, Sybil, and Elias. A large crowd had formed, drinking and singing by the garish but warm light of the enormous fire.

Richie came hurrying up to them, holding her skirts in one

hand and a blazing torch in the other. "I have found some young maidens who know where to gather the correct herbs," Richie said to Louisa and Sybil. Her face was bright and smiling. "Come, you must go with them. Hurry or they will leave you."

"Herbs? What are you talking of?" Louisa asked. Sybil looked as confused as she was. But then Louisa remembered the Midsummer Eve ritual.

"The herbs that you must pick tonight. You must put them under your pillow and when you sleep tonight, on Midsummer Eve, you will dream of the man you will marry."

Sybil shook her head. "I need to stay with Elias."

"Very well. I understand." Richie grabbed Louisa's hand and pulled. "But you must come! You will dream of your future husband tonight."

Louisa did not want to admit it, but for the first time in her life, she liked the idea that she could dream of the man she would marry. So she let Richie drag her along to the outskirts of the town, where a group of young women were waiting. They were all dressed in white, with flowers arranged in a circle on top of their heads, their hair flowing freely over their shoulders and down their backs. They were smiling and giggling, talking among themselves.

"We are ready!" Richie cried.

One of the young women, a petite girl, approached Louisa and took her by the hand, and then they all started into the forest.

Louisa realized Richie was not with them.

"Aren't you coming with us?" Louisa asked her over her shoulder.

"Goodness, no! I don't intend to marry again. Go on." She motioned her on.

Louisa went with the rest of the girls into the woods. Several of the maidens were carrying torches like Richie's and the fire from each one bobbed up and down, throwing dense shadows all around them on the trees, bushes, and the leafy fern-covered ground.

"My name is Aurora," the girl who was holding Louisa's hand said.

"I'm Louisa. How old are you, if you don't mind my asking?"

"Sixteen, and I know exactly who I want to dream about tonight. Do you?"

What should Louisa say to that? "I want to know who I will marry, but I don't know who it will be."

"Who do you want it to be?"

"Someone kind and good-hearted."

"And handsome. I'm sure you wish to marry someone handsome."

"Yes, I hope he would be handsome. Who is it you want to marry?"

"John Lakewood. I've been in love with him since I was a little girl, but he hardly knows I exist. But tonight I hope I dream of him, and tomorrow I will dance with him. I hope." She smiled, scrunching her face with excitement.

Louisa couldn't help smiling back. Aurora reminded her of a young Richie.

Louisa and Aurora followed the girls, but soon Aurora led her away from the others until Louisa could no longer see any of their torches.

"Shouldn't we stay close to the others?" Louisa asked.

"Don't worry. I have my torch. And I know exactly where to go to find the herbs we need. St. John's wort is just over here in this clearing."

Aurora hurried forward, holding up her skirt and high-stepping among the thick undergrowth of ferns and bushes and small trees. Finally, she found the clearing and bent to pick the small, yellow flowering plants.

"You must pick some too. I will pick enough to share with the others, in case they don't find any."

Aurora picked an enormous handful and stuffed them into the bag that hung from her arm. Louisa did not have a pocket, so she held her plants in her hand.

"We also need some thyme and mint." Aurora led them farther into the forest.

"Are you sure we won't get lost?" Louisa said.

Aurora blew out a breath as if to scoff at the idea. "I've been roaming these woods all my life."

It was quite dark, and Louisa hoped her new friend's confidence was justified. They ventured farther into the forest, which became even denser with trees, bushes, ferns, and vines. Then Aurora's torch began to flicker.

Aurora still looked confident, as her expression was highlighted by the light of the torch.

"Should we turn back?" Louisa asked. The flickering was getting worse.

"No, it's not far now. There's a patch of mint next to the thyme. Come."

She proceeded past a large oak, then sank down and started grabbing the plants growing by their ankles with her one free hand. Louisa did the same, hoping to hurry her along.

"Here, put them in my bag so you don't drop anything. I'll share with you when we get back to town."

Louisa did as she bid, her heart leaping into her throat as she watched the torch's light grow dimmer.

"We should hurry," Louisa said.

Aurora stuffed a handful into her bag as she stood. "This is enough." She turned around to go back the way they had come, but before they could take more than two steps, the torch went out.

They were plunged into darkness, unable to see even the moon or stars in the dense, overgrown woods.

ELEVEN

CHARLES HAD SAT AROUND THE BONFIRE LONG ENOUGH.
He stood to go find Richie and Louisa when he saw Richie
hurrying toward him.

"The other maidens have returned from gathering herbs in
the forest, but Louisa isn't with them."

Charles's whole body tensed, but then he recalled his training, how to steel himself from emotion when there was danger
afoot.

"Take me to the other maidens."

Richie led him to a group of young women standing around
talking to an older man and woman. Richie began asking questions. Moments later she turned to Charles.

"They think Louisa went with the maiden Aurora. She also
has not returned."

"How long have they been gone?"

"At least an hour," one of the girls said. "That is Aurora's mother and father." She pointed to the older couple. The woman was crying.

"Where exactly do you think she went?" Charles asked them.

"We don't know. She likes to wander the woods." The crying woman shook her head.

"Who can show me where they were last seen?" Charles barked at the young maidens.

"We can show you," one of them said.

Someone handed Charles a torch and he followed two maidens toward the forest.

God, let me be able to find them, he prayed. He knew how easy it was to become lost in the forest, especially at night. It was all too likely that Aurora had missed her landmarks and was now lost. And after getting lost, many things might happen to them—falling and breaking a leg, getting caught in a snare, not to mention the wild animals in these woods that were capable of attacking two young women.

They hadn't gone far when one of the maidens said, "Here is where I last saw them."

"What direction were they going?"

"I'm not sure. Maybe that way?" She pointed into the dark.

"Thank you. You had better go back. Do you know the way?"

"Yes." The two maidens stared at him, casting shy smiles his way. "I hope you find them," one said.

"You are very brave," the other said, and they both giggled as they hurried back the way they had come.

Charles continued through the thick forest. He took out his

knife and marked the trees as he went, carving an arrow to show which way he was going so he would know how to get back.

Truly, Louisa and the other maiden could be anywhere. They could have been walking for an hour in the wrong direction, or they could have been walking around in circles and therefore not far away.

He began calling out, "Louisa! Can you hear me?" He kept calling out every half minute or so, not knowing if he was going toward them or away from them. But he kept carving arrows in the trees every few steps, deliberately breaking branches and clearing out big swaths so he would recognize where he had walked, all the while praying, "Lord God, guide me and help me find them."

Louisa's heart beat hard, her eyes straining to see anything in the dark forest, Aurora clutching her hand in a tight grip.

"I'm so sorry I got us lost," Aurora said, her voice catching on a sob.

"It's all right. It wasn't your fault. We will be all right." Louisa was trying to assure herself as much as Aurora.

"I don't know which way to go," the girl wailed.

"I think it best if we just stay here. Someone will come looking for us."

Just then they heard a wolf's long, mournful howl.

Aurora screamed. "The wolves will eat us."

As if to confirm her words, another wolf, then another, joined in the howling. Aurora was crying in earnest now.

"Listen to me. Those wolves are a long way off. We will be all right. They won't come this close to the town." Louisa wasn't nearly as sure of what she was saying as she sounded. But she needed to stay calm for Aurora, and strangely enough, the girl's uncontrolled fear forced Louisa to stay strong. "Come, let us sit here and sing some songs to keep ourselves calm as we wait. I'm sure someone will come and find us."

Louisa sank to the ground and Aurora joined her. She started singing a familiar chant she'd heard many times in church. It sounded a bit mournful, so after the first verse she changed to a lively song her mother used to sing to her and Margaret. Aurora finally joined in.

When they had sung all the verses they knew, Aurora said, "This is good. They will hear us singing when they come looking for us."

"That's right." Louisa patted the girl's arm. "No need to worry." But she also knew how difficult it would be for any-one to find them in the wide, vast forest. "Let us say a quick prayer."

Louisa spoke a prayer aloud, asking God for help, to lead someone to find them and help them get back to town. Silently she hoped it was Sir Charles who would find them, but indeed, anyone would be a welcome sight.

She didn't like the sounds around them—a rustle here and the hoot of an owl there. So they started singing a well-known ballad.

They both sang loudly. But after a few verses, they heard

the wolves again, and this time they sounded closer—much closer.

Charles could tell the wolves were nearby, but instead of hating them for their howling, he thanked God for it. As long as they were howling, he knew they were not attacking, for a howl was not the sound they made when they were drawing close to their prey. And the howling gave him a direction to go in, for he was becoming convinced that they were stalking some large prey, and what bigger or more helpless prey than two young maidens lost in the forest?

He quickened his step, taking less time to mark his path now.

"Louisa!" he kept calling.

What if he was going farther away from them? Perhaps they had already found their way back. But he kept going, believing that following the sound of the wolves' howling would lead him to Louisa. He had his sword, and he would search all night and face a whole pack of wolves if he had to.

The howling of the wolves made the hair on Louisa's arms stand up, and she turned toward Aurora.

"I think I know how we can find our way back," Louisa said.

"How?"

"We will go away from the sound of the wolves' howling. Wherever they are is the opposite of where the town is." She wasn't certain of this, but it sounded reasonable.

Aurora clutched her hand as they started walking. They hadn't gone far when Aurora smacked her face into a tree.

"Are you hurt?"

"No. Let's keep going."

They held on to each other, walking slowly as they stumbled and picked their way along. But their progress was so slow that Louisa couldn't imagine they were getting any farther away from the wolves.

Aurora grabbed Louisa with both hands. "What is that?"

They stopped and listened. "I don't hear anything."

"It sounded like a hiss."

Could it be a poisonous adder? They were active this time of year if it was warm, and it had been very warm the past few days.

"There it is again!"

Louisa heard it too. It seemed to be just to their right.

Aurora let out a stifled shriek and started to run, pulling Louisa along with her.

Louisa's foot hit something and she stumbled. She tried to catch herself with her other foot, but it sank into a hole. She fell, barely getting her hand in front of her to keep from hitting her face.

Aurora screamed. "It's got you!"

"I'm all right. I just fell." Louisa scrambled to her feet, knowing if the hissing sound was being made by an adder, it was capable of closing the gap between them very quickly.

When she stood, a sharp pain went through her ankle, and she almost fell again. She limped a few steps before saying, "We have to go slowly."

"But the wolves and the hissing . . ." Aurora was crying again.

"You have to be brave, Aurora. The wolves are still a long way away, and whatever is hissing is probably as afraid of us as we are of it."

Once again, she was saying something she wasn't sure was true, but she forced herself to believe it.

"Be brave. Be brave," Aurora chanted several times, holding on to Louisa with both hands.

Louisa limped as fast as she could, but terrified of falling again, she wasn't moving very quickly. She let her thoughts go to other things, including the Midsummer Festival tomorrow. Her ankle hurt, but she didn't think it was broken. Surely it would be better by morning. She wanted to be able to dance at the festival.

What an ill-fated night this had become. And if she continued walking on her sore ankle, would it get worse? It might swell and be too painful to walk on. Then she could become a hindrance to her traveling companions.

If she kept thinking like that, she'd be crying along with Aurora. She had to stop borrowing trouble and focus on surviving this night.

The wolves howled again, and this time they sounded like they were just over her right shoulder, maybe a hundred feet away.

Aurora screamed.

God, are we going to die?

Just then she thought she heard a voice calling her name.

"Is someone there?" she cried.

"Louisa!" Sir Charles's voice was dim, but it was he!

"I'm here!" Her heart soared and tears of relief stung her eyes.

Aurora squealed, then giggled hysterically.

"Keep yelling," Sir Charles's voice said. "I'm coming."

She could hear the wolves growling, a low, quiet sound, sending a prickling sensation down the back of her neck.

"Please hurry!" she cried.

"Keep talking," he answered.

"I can't move fast. I hurt my ankle."

She suddenly caught sight of the light of his torch flickering and bobbing through the branches and leaves between them.

A wolf growled behind them, closer than before. Her heart was beating and roaring in her ears. Aurora screamed again.

In front of her was the *whoosh*ing and breaking of branches as Sir Charles crashed through the underbrush. Ducking under a branch, his face was fierce and beautiful in the light of the torch in his left hand, his raised sword in his right hand.

"Stay here," he ordered and walked past them.

Louisa turned around and saw the glowing eyes of four or five wolves in the bushes behind them.

Aurora screamed and screamed as Sir Charles brandished his sword, waving his torch at the snarling animals.

One of them jumped at him. Sir Charles slashed its throat in midair. It fell on the ground and didn't move.

The other wolves took a step back. Sir Charles jumped at them, lunging with his sword and yelling.

They were slow to back away, taking a step only when he moved in their direction.

He kept going, chasing them, yelling and raising his arms over his head until he was almost out of sight.

Aurora screamed. A wolf was standing right in front of her, baring its teeth. Louisa pulled Aurora, moving so that she was between the wolf and Aurora.

Sir Charles ran up behind the wolf, which rounded on him. He stabbed the animal in the neck. Louisa turned her head as she heard the wolf's death gurgle.

Sir Charles moved his body between the wolves and Louisa and Aurora. He stood with his sword at the ready, so close to Louisa that she felt the brush of his clothing against her arm. He held out his torch in the direction the wolves had retreated. Louisa strained her eyes but could no longer see the red, glowing eyes.

Aurora gripped Louisa's arm so tightly it ached.

Finally, Sir Charles turned to Louisa. "I think they're gone. Are you all right?"

"We are well." Louisa's voice shook, so she cleared her throat. "Are you hurt?"

"No." He stepped toward them, sheathing his sword.

"Thanks be to God for sending you to find us," Aurora said. "We were nearly killed . . . by wolves." Her hands were shaking as she pressed them to her cheeks.

"Come. Let's get back to town." Sir Charles walked between them, with Louisa holding on to his arm and Aurora holding on to his other arm.

They'd walked only a few feet when Sir Charles stopped and turned to Louisa. "You're limping."

"She fell and hurt her ankle," Aurora said.

"I'll carry you." Sir Charles leaned toward her.

"No, please, you cannot." Her heart beat double time at the thought of him lifting her into his arms.

"I assure you I can." He handed his torch to Aurora.

Louisa's cheeks were burning. How could she bear to be so close to him? "I just mean that it must be a long way back. You cannot carry me the whole way." She didn't want to insult him, but even his undoubtedly impressive strength would be hard-pressed. She'd carried her younger sister, and though she seemed light at first, it didn't take long for her weight to become too heavy for her.

Ignoring her protests, he slipped his arm under her knees and his other around her back and lifted her.

She couldn't remember anyone ever carrying her. Her head was spinning at being so close to him, her face only a handbreadth from his. His arms were unyielding, his hand clamped around her ribs. He was already walking at a brisk pace through the bushes as he said, "I assure you, I can carry you the whole way."

She closed her eyes, her breath coming fast and shallow. Did he care for her so much? She was overwhelmed with warmth one moment and fear of losing his care the next. She had been such a bother ever since he'd met her. Would he decide she was too much trouble and start to resent her? Her chest ached just thinking about it.

"I can walk," she said.

"I don't want you to make your ankle worse."

Was he afraid she would become even more of a nuisance? Louisa was quiet, her whole body tense. Finally, she could no longer keep silent.

136

"I don't want you to hurt yourself."

"Louisa, stop protesting," Aurora said. "It is faster this way."

The burning in Louisa's face increased. She was glad it was too dark for them to see it.

"I will put you down if you wish it," he said quietly. "But I'd rather carry you."

He wasn't slowing down or stumbling or even breathing particularly hard.

"Very well."

Since he was staring ahead and at the ground, carefully watching where he stepped, she let herself examine his face. He was a handsome man. And after traveling with him for so long, she knew his habit was to regularly trim his beard and moustache and shave the hair on his cheeks and neck instead of letting it grow wild, as did her uncle and most of the menservants and guards she'd known. He also bathed regularly and washed his clothing often.

Those things were appealing, but even more important was that he was a man of character and genuine compassion and kindness. And if he stopped being kind to her or thinking well of her, she wasn't sure she could bear it.

She shouldn't think about him as a possible husband, but he was proving to be her ideal in a man. Could she help thinking so?

"Do you think the wolves are gone?" Aurora asked.

"I believe so."

He was starting to sound a little winded.

"Why don't we stop and let you rest a bit," Louisa suggested, "since the wolves are gone."

"I don't need to rest, but I am looking for a break in the trees," he said. "Let me know when you're able to see the moon or any stars."

It had been a while since they'd seen anything like a clearing, but Louisa kept her eyes up. After a few more minutes she cried out, "There! I see the moon."

Sir Charles stopped and set Louisa on the ground while saying, "Hold on to me. Don't put any weight on your injured ankle."

Louisa did as she was told, holding on to his arm as he peered up into the sky. Finally, he said, "I think we're going in the right direction, but I haven't seen any of the marks I made on the trees." He looked at Aurora. "Do you see anything familiar?"

"I think we're going toward town, but it's very hard to tell."

He studied the sky some more while Louisa tested her ankle, putting a little bit of weight on it, then a bit more.

"My ankle barely hurts. I think it will be all right to walk on it."

"You could easily injure it further walking in the dark." He was already lifting her in his arms. "I know how stubborn you are about doing things yourself, but it is all right to let someone help you every once in a while."

His calling her stubborn stung. But he must be sensing that she felt guilty about him having to carry her. Could it be that he just wanted her to be grateful?

"Thank you for helping me." She watched as his expression softened.

"You're welcome," he said quietly.

She was having to strain her neck to hold her head up and

away from him. She decided to stop straining and let her head rest against his shoulder.

She had to admit that when she wasn't worrying about being a burden, it was pleasant to be carried in his arms. She allowed herself to think about how he had slayed two wolves to save her and Aurora. How powerful and strong he had looked as he gripped his sword and swung it at the deadly animals that were intent on killing them. How her heart trusted in his strength and power, in his protection. She felt a little dizzy as she dwelt on it.

Her swoony thoughts were interrupted by Aurora saying, "We are so grateful to you for finding us, Sir Charles."

She wanted to believe that he came looking for her because he cared about her. But wasn't Sir Charles always chivalrous and giving of himself for others?

She fell a pang of jealousy for the woman who would some-day win this profoundly generous knight's heart.

Twelve

Charles didn't mean to sound irritable when he told Louisa not to be so stubborn about letting him help her, but at least his words silenced her protests. She even relaxed in his arms and let herself rest against his chest.

He couldn't keep his thoughts from how close Louisa had come to being attacked by those wolves. If he had come one minute later, she would probably be dead.

He had wanted to grab her and hug her. Wonderful, brave, selfless, extraordinary girl! The world would have been a much worse place without her.

Thank You, God. Thank You, thank You.

She was not heavy, but even a small person gets heavy after carrying them so far, and his arms were aching to the point of burning when he stopped for a second break, placing her carefully on the ground. But what kind of man would he be if he let her walk back to town on an injured ankle? He wanted to take care of her. After all, they'd been traveling together long enough to become friends, and he would do anything for a friend. But if he was honest, he had feelings for her that had little to do with friendship. He had begun to wonder if it were possible for her to be more than that to him.

And she felt so good in his arms.

Besides that, her limping would slow them down, and he wanted to get them all out of these dark, eerie woods as quickly as possible.

"I see a torch!" Aurora cried.

He saw it too, a tiny flicker of light far ahead, and then it was gone. A shiver went over his shoulders as his mind went to fairies and witches and spectral lights that were whispered about. Although he suspected those were told only to frighten children into staying out of the woods at nighttime.

"Aurora!" someone called.

"Father! I'm here!" the girl answered.

More torches and people started to become visible in the dark.

"We found them!" someone shouted.

They were not yet out of the woods when Aurora's mother and father came hurrying toward them and embraced their daughter.

"Are you hurt?" her mother asked.

"No, I'm well. My torch went out and we couldn't find our way back, but Sir Charles found us. He killed two wolves that were trying to eat us. But look! I didn't lose my herbs!" Aurora held up the bag that was still hanging from her arm.

"Wolves," her mother said with a gasp. "Oh, dear saints

above." She made the sign of the cross over her chest and let out a small sob.

"We are perfectly safe now, thanks to Sir Charles." Aurora was smiling up at him.

"Sir, we cannot thank you enough," her mother said, clasping her hands together as she gazed at him with tearful eyes.

"You are most welcome. Shall we make our way out of these woods now?"

"Yes, of course," the father said, pulling on his wife's arm. He nodded at Charles. "I thank you, sir, for your kindness and bravery."

After a short rest, Charles lifted Louisa again. "It was my privilege and honor to help." He said another silent prayer of his own, thanking God for leading him to Louisa.

Louisa's hands were around Sir Charles's neck as they emerged from the dark forest amid cheers from the crowd that had gathered.

Richie ran up to them, exclaiming, "Oh, thank God you are safe! I knew Sir Charles would find you."

"Can you fetch her horse?" Sir Charles asked Morten, setting Louisa down carefully.

To Richie's questioning look, Louisa said, "I stepped in a hole and twisted my ankle. I think it is all right, but—"

"Oh, my dear! How fortunate you had Sir Charles to carry you." Richie's eyes were wide, an irrepressible smile on her lips.

"Here is her horse," Morten said, appearing behind Richie.

"Where are Sybil and Elias?" Louisa asked.

"I took them back to Ashbourne Hall an hour or so ago." Morten glanced away as he spoke.

"We should get back there too." Sir Charles lifted Louisa onto her horse, careful not to bump her foot, placing her sideways in the saddle so that she could swing her foot around to the other side.

"Wait!" Aurora came running up to her. "You must take some herbs."

Thankfully, Sir Charles had stepped back and was talking with Morten and Richie.

"Put these under your pillow tonight," Aurora whispered excitedly. She searched through the bag and drew out the three different kinds of herbs and handed them to Louisa. Her smile stretched all the way across her face. "And I have a feeling I know who you will dream about tonight."

For someone who had cried a great deal in the last hour or two, it was impossible to detect any of that kind of emotion in her now. Aurora's eyes were alight and her smile wide.

Louisa couldn't help laughing at Aurora's excitement while shaking her head at her assumption. "Thank you."

After all they'd been through together, Louisa felt genuine affection for the girl as she watched her walk away with her mother and father and the rest of the crowd. She was sad that she probably never would see her again. It had felt good to make a friend, even as fleeting as their friendship had been.

After gathering Richie and Morten and mounting their animals, they rode back to Ashbourne Hall.

Louisa felt quite weary. Sir Charles was beside her as soon as her horse stopped. He waited for her to swing her leg around, then placed his hands on either side of her waist and lifted her off the horse. When her feet touched the ground, trying to put all her weight on one foot, she had to grab his arms to keep from falling.

"Steady." Sir Charles held her elbows.

He gazed into her eyes. Louisa's heart skipped a beat, then pounded hard against her chest. Tears stung her eyes, though she wasn't sure why.

Suddenly he was lifting her in his arms. She had to bury her face in his shirt to take a moment to get control of herself.

"Sir Charles," Richie said, "are you not glad we have our Louisa back safe and sound? She might have been lost all night in that frightening forest."

"I'm exceedingly glad God helped me find her."

Louisa should tell him how grateful she was to him, but instead, she swallowed the lump in her throat and blinked back the tears. And when Sir Charles gazed down at her, she couldn't look away.

"It is the second time he has come to your rescue, is it not, Louisa?"

"It is at least the second time." If she didn't count the fact that he'd let her travel with him all these days and watched over her.

They went inside the smaller section of Ashbourne Hall only to find that the beds they'd slept in the night before were now occupied with people in town for the Midsummer Festival. But a servant quickly told them, "Lord Ashbourne has moved you all to more comfortable rooms." No doubt because of Sir Charles's position as a knight and because of his noble family.

The servant led them to a room with two beds that Louisa would be sharing with Richie, Sybil, and Elias. Sybil and Elias were already there, asleep in one of the beds. Sir Charles set Louisa down on the other bed.

"Thank you," she said.

He briefly met her gaze, then bowed and left the room with the servant.

As soon as he was gone, Richie sucked in a loud breath. "What a romantic story this would make," she said in a loud whisper. "The troubadours could make a song about you—the handsome knight and the lovely runaway maiden."

It was Louisa's turn to gasp. "Richie, no. That's nonsense."

"I think not. The way he was looking at you, and the way he insisted on carrying you. He is in love with you!"

"No, Richie. You are mistaken." Her heart raced at the thought, even though she knew it was not true. "Sir Charles is not in love with me. He is simply a noble knight who does his duty, which is to help those in need. He is not . . . No." She shook her head adamantly. "And I beg you not to embarrass him."

"I won't embarrass him. I will say no more." She used her thumb and index finger to pinch her lips closed.

They were all tired, but Richie and Sybil, who had woken up when they came in, wanted to hear her account of the night's events.

In the middle of Louisa's telling of it, Richie whispered excitedly, "Where are those herbs?"

Louisa found them in her bag, and Richie took them from her hand and shoved them under her pillow.

"Now you will dream of the man you will marry." Richie's smile was reminiscent of Aurora's.

Louisa felt a mild sting of envy at how Richie and Aurora could be so hopeful and sure of things, so enthusiastic despite the odds. Louisa had hardly ever felt that amount of assured hope about anything. Fear of disappointment was always lurking in her mind. It was truly surprising that she had put so much faith in finding the Viking treasure. Usually, if she got her hopes up too high, she feared something terrible might happen. But perhaps she thought like that because her parents had died so young, even as Louisa prayed and believed that God would heal them.

Bad things happened to everyone, eventually, as they lived in a fallen and evil world. But it seemed as though Richie had never lost her childlike surety that good things were coming. It must simply be her God-given personality.

People could be so different.

She fell asleep wondering if her ankle would be well enough that she could dance with Sir Charles at the festival—and if he would even want to.

Charles walked through the rows of stalls at one side of the market square, perusing all the wares from nearby and from as far away as the Far East. He spent a few minutes examining Morten's shoes and bought a few pairs to give as gifts to his nieces and nephews, though he'd probably end up giving them to some poor shoeless waifs this winter who had no shoes and were in danger of frostbite.

He paused beside a booth selling ribbons and scarves. As he gazed at all the different colors, he found himself considering which ones Louisa might like most. The blue would match her eyes, but the pink would match the embroidery in her dress.

This was not what he should be dwelling on. He'd already thought too much about Louisa, especially since he carried her out of the woods the night before.

He quickly moved away from the stall with the ribbons and scarves and forced his mind to empty. He did not let himself think but wandered between the rows of merchants and their goods until he came to a stall with leather boots and saddles. He searched until he found a leather saddlebag of good quality and bought it. And he immediately wondered if Louisa was in need of shoes or a saddlebag.

He knew she was not his responsibility, but that was not the issue. He genuinely wanted to take care of her, to make sure she had everything she needed. He didn't feel that way about Richie. He did have a little more of that feeling regarding Sybil and Elias, but it was not the same as he felt about Louisa.

Perhaps it was only because she'd been traveling with him longer and because she'd needed him to rescue her two times now. It had nothing to do with the fact that she was interesting to converse with, or that she was very compassionate and trustworthy, or that she looked quite pretty since she started wearing her hair back, showing the gentle contours of her face, and the way the new blue dress made her eyes even bluer.

The music was growing louder, as were the people's voices. He also heard the sounds of many feet stepping to the rhythm of the music and decided to go and watch.

When he reached the side of the square where the music was coming from, there was Louisa in her prettiest dress, watching the others dance, while a man he'd never seen before stood beside her.

He stared hard at the man, who was turned toward Louisa and appeared to be talking to her.

"Is something wrong?" Richie was walking toward him.

"No."

"You were just scowling."

Richie was much too inquisitive, with her sly little smiles.

"Is Louisa's ankle still paining her?"

"It is. That's why she's not dancing. It's a good thing you carried her and didn't let her walk on it last night." She waggled her eyebrows at him.

"Why aren't you dancing?" he asked her.

"I'm too old for dancing—bad knee. Louisa is just the right age for it. Such a pity she can't dance on her bad ankle."

He hated himself for asking, but he couldn't help it. "Who is that man standing beside her? Do you know him?"

"No. He asked her to dance, and she said no. He seems harmless." She shrugged.

Seeming harmless and being harmless were two different things.

Clapping her hands in time to the music, Richie said, "Why

don't you introduce yourself to the man and chase him away? After all, Louisa doesn't look as if she wishes to talk to him."

Richie was right. Charles left Richie's side and went to Louisa. He stared the man down and nodded a greeting, then asked Louisa, "How is your ankle feeling today?"

"I am trying not to put much weight on it, but it is a little better—not well enough to dance, unfortunately." She smiled up at him.

The man standing beside her seemed to take the hint and moved away.

"I'm sorry you can't dance on your ankle."

She shrugged her shoulders. "The music is very pleasant, though."

Her eyes, her face, and her smile were also very pleasant.

He stayed by her side as they talked and listened to the music and watched the dancers.

His mind wandered to how Richie was ever quick to push him to notice Louisa. It was as if she wanted him to fall in love with her. But he'd had a bad enough experience with Lady Mirabella to last him a number of years. Besides, he and Louisa still had a long way to go and could end up traveling the last few days of their journey alone together. He didn't want to make things awkward.

To Richie, anything that amused her was fair game, and he had no intention of making himself Richie's entertainment. But he also wasn't willing to stop talking to Louisa just to avoid being teased by Richie.

Thirteen

"I hope you're not in pain."

"Not when I don't put weight on it."

Louisa's heart fluttered at the serious expression in Sir Charles's eyes. He looked just as he had in her dream the night before.

Unbidden, the dream flooded her like a recent memory. Her heart, even now, skipped a beat when she remembered Sir Charles declaring, "I love you," as he gazed deeply into her eyes.

Her face grew warm. Could he see her blushing?

It was only a dream, but her breath hitched in her throat as if it were real. She could feel the same rush of emotion she had in her dream as she stared at him.

In the dream they were standing in a church, facing each other, and he told her he loved her. Then he touched her cheek, cupping her face with the palm of his hand, and leaned down to kiss her.

She was awakened by Elias crying out in his sleep. Sybil rubbed his back and said, "Go to sleep. All is well," and once the boy had calmed down, Louisa closed her eyes and tried to go back to the dream. But instead she just lay there reliving it, wishing it had been real.

For a long time she could still feel his hand touching her face.

Louisa did her best to bring her thoughts back to the present. She tried to smile and say in a lighthearted way, "I had hoped the ankle would have healed overnight, but in truth, when I walk on it, it still hurts as much as it did last night."

"That is a pity, since I would have liked to dance with you today."

Her heart jumped into her throat, and she had to swallow before she could answer. "I would have liked that very much."

Sir Charles kept his eyes on her, looking as if he wanted to say something else. But then he turned his head and watched the dancers.

She loved that he was so fierce and unafraid when there was danger about. But he had also held her so tenderly last night. And while it was strange at first to be carried by him, she knew she could get used to being so close to him . . . and she would enjoy it.

That Lady Mirabella was foolish indeed. To be loved by Sir Charles would mean a lifetime of protection and kindness, love and devotion. Whoever married him was truly a fortunate woman.

But she shouldn't be thinking about any of this. It would only make her unhappy. Instead, she would enjoy this time talking with him as a friend.

"You seem happier," he said, returning his gaze to her.

"Happier?" she asked.

"Since you stopped being Jack."

She couldn't help smiling. "You mean since I started wearing dresses again?"

"Yes."

She thought about it a moment, and when the song ended, she told him, "I didn't enjoy pretending to be someone I wasn't. I was always afraid someone would realize I was being deceptive."

He seemed to be about to say something, but he nodded instead and went back to watching the dancers, a thoughtful crease in his brow.

Louisa believed in miracles, of course, but surely God did not let people manipulate Him into telling her who she would marry by placing herbs under their pillows on a certain night of the year. However, just as she'd argued with her priest, perhaps Gideon using the fleece was simply an example of a child of God asking Him to confirm what they believed God had told them. Could placing herbs under a pillow and asking God to show her who she would marry be another example of the same concept?

Just before she fell asleep, she'd asked God to let her dream of the man she should marry. Was God telling her that she should marry Sir Charles?

Earlier that morning, she'd prayed, *God, if Sir Charles is the man I should marry, then please make a way.* But it was difficult to imagine how that could feasibly happen. And now she was more worried than ever that she would be terribly brokenhearted when the two of them parted ways, as they inevitably must.

Wasn't she being faithless to think that? After all, God could do anything. If God wanted her to marry Sir Charles, then He would make a way.

The only problem was, she wasn't sure God *did* want her to marry Sir Charles.

It was all rather confusing, the way her thoughts went around and around. But she could neither control the future nor predict it, so she did her best to put it out of her mind and simply enjoy the festival, her first one in a large market town.

She felt pretty as she noticed a few men looking at her. And she'd also noticed a few young women looking longingly at Sir Charles. Did he know how handsome he was? He was a confident person, but his confidence seemed to come more from a sense of competence in his skills and physical strength. She'd never noticed him behaving in a conceited way. Besides, it hadn't been long since he was rejected by that duke's daughter.

When he'd told her about how he'd hoped to marry Lady Mirabella, she'd seen a hint of insecurity in him when it came to women and love. He'd obviously had little experience with either. Lady Mirabella had thought that he and the other knights she'd manipulated would be content to love her and pine after her from afar while she married someone else. Even Louisa knew that such a thing would be completely unacceptable to a self-respecting man like Sir Charles.

She also was realistic enough to know that Sir Charles was not in love with her, nor would he allow himself to love her, especially after the disaster with Lady Mirabella, unless he thought their marriage would be possible and that it would be a wise choice for himself financially. She knew how the world worked, for her aunt and uncle had both spoken at length with her on the subject. In fact, it was the only thing they ever instructed her on.

"Should you be standing so long on your ankle?" he asked, snapping her out of her thoughts.

"I'm not really putting any weight on it."

"We should find you a place to sit."

"Truly, I'd rather go and see what Richie and Sybil are doing."

"Very well." He held out his arm to her. They soon saw Richie and made their way through the crowd of people to where she was standing.

"You two are both looking quite handsome today," she said. "I could watch the dancing and listen to this music all day. But should we look for Sybil and Elias?"

"Where did you last see them?" Sir Charles asked.

"They were sitting against that church over there." Richie pointed to the church on the farthest end of the town square from the marketplace.

"Perhaps they went inside," Louisa said.

"I will go and see." Richie hurried ahead of them and entered the church.

Louisa tried not to limp, but her ankle was too sore to put her full weight on it.

"I hope you didn't reinjure your ankle. I can carry you." Sir Charles was gazing down at her with his brows drawn together.

"No, I'm well enough to walk. I'm being careful."

He said nothing, but he still looked concerned.

"It's a bit sore, but nothing serious." She shrugged and smiled, hoping he wouldn't be overly concerned.

She felt her cheeks grow warm again at his attention. "You should be dancing, not fussing over me," she said, then wished she had worded it differently, as he might be offended at her characterizing him as "fussing over" her. Besides, the thought of him dancing with another woman sent a pang through her stomach.

Sir Charles shook his head as if to dismiss her protest. "Let's get you somewhere you can sit." He held out his arm.

Just then Richie emerged from the front door of the church and shook her head. "They're not there."

"We should keep looking for them," Louisa said.

"I'm sure they're well," Richie said, "but I'll feel better when we find them. Let us ask Morten if he's seen them."

"That's a good idea," Sir Charles said. "But first we need to find a place for Louisa to sit."

Louisa leaned on Sir Charles's arm as they walked toward the fountain, where several people were sitting on the built-in bench around it. But it was in the sun, which was becoming a bit oppressive as the day wore on.

Sir Charles led her past the fountain to a brightly colored pavilion along the edge of the merchants' stalls.

"This is the Cockayne family's pavilion," Sir Charles explained. "They assured me that it was open to us."

She remembered that Cockayne was the surname of the Lord of the Manor of Ashbourne Hall. They went inside and found some wooden chairs with cushions.

Sir Charles helped her down into a chair, pulled up a stool where she could prop up her foot, and tied back the opening in the tent. She had a clear view of several stalls and about half of the square.

"Thank you."

"We'll find Morten," Sir Charles said, "and if Sybil and Elias are not with him, we will let you know."

Louisa nodded and watched them leave. She sighed. She hardly minded the pain, but perhaps it was good that she was resting her ankle for a bit.

She leaned back in the chair and watched the people walking by the tent, as well as the dancers twirling and bobbing. Soon her mind wandered to her conversation with Richie from that morning.

Just as she'd feared, Richie had asked her whom she had dreamed of the night before.

"I would rather not say." Louisa wouldn't look at Richie but continued putting her things in her bags.

"Oh, then I shall guess!" She clapped her hands like a child awaiting a gift on Christmas. "It was Sir Charles, wasn't it? You dreamed of Sir Charles."

"I won't tell you." What if Richie told Sir Charles? She would be mortified for Sir Charles to know that she dreamed of him, especially on Midsummer Eve.

Richie clapped her hands again and laughed. "I knew it. And I feel I had a bit of a hand in it all by buying you those dresses and arranging your hair so prettily."

Louisa shook her head and sighed. She knew she shouldn't fall in love with Sir Charles. There were too many reasons why she shouldn't, and she'd gone over and over this in her mind already. At the very least, she couldn't let him think she had any inkling of their ever getting married. It would be too mortifying, for he would have to tell her that their union was impossible. And that would hurt more than anything had since her mother and father died.

FOURTEEN

CHARLES COULD STILL FEEL THE HEAT IN HIS CHEST FROM when he'd gazed into Louisa's eyes. Why did he react that way to her? He had thought himself in love with Lady Mirabella, but even she did not affect him like that.

Indeed, it was a very fortunate thing that he could not dance with her.

Even though he'd left her in the Cockayne family's pavilion, he didn't like leaving her unprotected for too long. They soon drew near Morten's booth, and what he saw made him feel as if a story were unfolding before his eyes.

Morten was sitting on a stool holding Elias on his lap while Sybil was standing next to them, gazing down at Morten with a small smile on her face. He'd not seen her smile before. Richie also stopped and stared at them, her eyes wide.

Morten dandled Elias on his knee, talking to the boy, who laughed at something Morten said. Charles started recalling other times when he'd seen Morten interacting with Sybil and Elias, how Morten had spoken patiently and gently to them.

What were Morten's intentions?

Sybil was under his protection, just as Louisa was, and the widowed mother had been mistreated enough. He would not allow Morten to take advantage of her. But Morten had come across as a meek and humble man, even though his family must be relatively wealthy, given that they owned a shoemaking business. Morten did not speak in a disrespectful manner about women, as so many men did, blustering about their conquests or making ribald jests.

Charles was only able to watch them for a moment longer, for Richie suddenly cried out, "There you are, Sybil! We have been searching for you and Elias. But I see you are with Morten, here at his stall." She raised an insinuating eyebrow at Morten.

Morten met her stare, his cheeks coloring slightly. "They are safe and sound with me."

"I shall go inform Louisa that Sybil and Elias have been found." Charles turned and left poor Morten and Sybil to Richie's sly looks and questions—they would have to fend for themselves—and went back to Louisa.

He found her where he'd left her. "We located them. They were with Morten at his booth."

"Oh, that is good news!"

"Have you been pleasantly occupied?"

"Oh yes. I love listening to the music, and I must confess, I enjoy seeing all the different people."

"People can be very interesting."

"Yes." She smiled. "I sometimes make up stories in my head about who they are and what they're doing and what their life is like."

"My brother David has a mind for story. He likes to tell stories to amuse our nieces and nephews. He's quite good at it. I like to hear his stories myself."

She quirked her head to one side with a thoughtful look.

"Perhaps you will tell me what you are thinking about the people walking by." He came to stand beside her to watch them.

"Well, do you see that woman dancing with that man, the woman with the red dress and the long blonde hair and the man with the green shirt?"

"Yes."

"I imagine that she is the baker's daughter, since she is dressed rather well, and has been hoping to dance with the man in the green shirt today. She even dreamed of him last night. He is the butcher's son, but he had not really thought much about her. She was just a young girl with messy hair who played with the other children in the streets—until today. He saw her in that dress, with her hair hanging down over her shoulders, and it stopped him midstride. She smiled at him, and he immediately asked her to dance. They've been dancing every dance for the last half hour."

Charles smiled and nodded. He felt a kinship with this imaginary butcher's son, as he'd felt the same way when he saw Louisa in a dress for the first time. Did she know that?

"Well, you have a talent for stories."

"I used to tell Margaret stories when we were children, about fairies and giants, kings and princesses. I also used to make up stories about how we would go get the Viking treasure in Yorkshire, traveling across the countryside and finding it using our wits."

She looked serious, a bit sad and worried, as she stared out across the marketplace. Was she questioning her goal of finding the treasure? But she soon sighed, and her demeanor changed.

"Do you see that girl there with the yellow dress? See the way that young man is looking at her and the way she smirks and tosses her head? I think he is in love with her, but she is just enjoying his attention and doesn't plan to marry him. In fact, I think she feels nothing for that poor man, but she wants him to think she does."

Charles was immediately reminded of how he had been duped in the same way by Lady Mirabella. Was he only a way for her to amuse herself and build up her pride at being able to break his heart?

He could see the smirk on the young woman's face as the man seemed to be pleading with her. She frowned on one side of her mouth, as if she was thinking, then shrugged her shoulders and walked with him toward the dancers.

Wake up, Charles wanted to say to him. *Find someone who will be proud to dance with you. Don't let her drag your heart over the hot coals only to kick you aside when she marries someone with more money.*

His next thought was that Louisa would never treat him that way. She wouldn't be flirtatious and then reject him when he fell in love with her. In fact, he'd never seen Louisa be flirtatious with anyone.

What would it be like if Louisa flirted with him? As unwise as it was, he really wanted to know.

Louisa was rattling on about her silly imaginings and Sir Charles looked as if he was thinking of something else.

"I'm talking too much. You probably want to get back to Morten and the others."

"No, you're not talking too much, and no, I do not."

Truthfully, she wanted to go. She was tired of sitting. "Do you mind if we walk around? I will take care not to hurt my ankle."

"I don't mind."

He took hold of her elbow and helped her up. But the chair was low, and as she was trying to place all her weight on her good foot, she lost her balance and pitched forward, her hands slamming against his chest.

He held on to her upper arms, steadying her. A wave of tenderness swept over her, followed by an intense longing to be closer to him.

He gazed into her eyes. Her heart beat hard against her chest. While they looked into each other's eyes, she grew even more off-balance.

She should feel embarrassed, but his intense blue eyes captured her, and she couldn't look away, couldn't even move. She wanted this moment to never end. But what if she misunderstood the look in his eyes? What if he was just trying to steady her and was wondering why she kept leaning on him?

"Forgive me," she whispered. Her voice was hoarse and breathy.

"There is nothing to forgive," he said in a low voice. His eyes were heavy-lidded as they moved to stare at her mouth.

Her stomach turned inside out at the thought of him kissing her. *Yes, please*, she thought, then felt her cheeks burn.

She looked down, breaking her gaze from his. She shouldn't want him to kiss her, shouldn't tempt him—if he was tempted. He was so kind and considerate; he was probably just trying to make sure she didn't fall. And now he was holding her away from him so that she was no longer pressed against his chest.

Her uncle would never allow her to marry anyone who couldn't pay a big price for her. And how could she bear to hurt him the way he'd been hurt by Lady Mirabella?

Had he been staring at her lips, thinking about kissing her? It was probably just her wild imagination. He couldn't marry her, and he was too noble to tempt her, or to let himself be tempted.

He still didn't speak. Finally, Louisa said, "Shall we go?"

"You are sure you're all right?"

"Yes, I am well."

How glad she was that he couldn't read her thoughts.

He let go of her and put out his arm so she could hold on to him as they left the pavilion, walking slowly.

"I'm sorry I'm such a bother," she said. The man was patient, but even his patience would run out eventually.

"You're not a bother." He looked down at her as if he was shocked by her words. "Why would you think that?"

"I am just sorry that you have to help me when you could be enjoying yourself, dancing, exploring the sellers' stalls, and—"

"I would rather be here with you. Besides, I can hear the music from here, and I'm looking at all the goods and the stalls with you. And you should realize by now that I enjoy your company."

Her heart did a strange leap.

"I enjoy your company as well." She barely stifled the nervous giggle before it escaped her throat.

As they walked around, Louisa couldn't help stopping to admire the embroidered belts and shawls at one of the booths. "They're so colorful."

She lingered the longest over one particular shawl that was embroidered with birds and flowers, so intricate and pretty in bright blues and purples, reds and yellows, the whole rainbow of colors. There was also one with a white unicorn and a pheasant but with more colors than any pheasant she had ever seen. If she had enough money she would buy it, but she still needed to be able to pay for food for the rest of their journey. Besides, it was the middle of summer, so it did not seem practical.

She forced herself to stop running her hand over the silk threads and take a step away from the stall.

Soon they reached Morten's booth. Morten was helping a customer try on some shoes and Sybil was sitting on a low stool with Elias. The three-year-old was playing with his tiny wooden horse, but his eyes were droopy and his movements sluggish. She noticed that both Elias and Sybil were wearing new leather shoes.

Sybil looked up and smiled at them. "How is your ankle?" she asked.

"A bit better."

"I am glad." Sybil glanced up at Morten but quickly looked down at Elias.

Louisa had begun to suspect that there was something between Morten and Sybil. Though she was probably imagining it. She was constantly putting people together in her mind, even strangers she knew nothing about.

While Sir Charles chatted with Morten, she asked Sybil, "Have you seen Richie?"

"She was here, but she left to visit some of the booths and find a gift for her daughter."

Elias rubbed his eyes with his little fist just before his eyelids fell closed and his hands went still.

Louisa suddenly had an idea. "You and Morten should go dance and enjoy yourselves. I can watch Elias."

"And I can watch your stall," Sir Charles said to Morten.

Morten had just finished selling a pair of shoes and turned to look at Sybil. "That is a very good idea. Would you like to?" He held out a hand to Sybil.

Sybil looked from Morten to her sleeping child, then up at Louisa. "Are you sure? He's quite heavy."

"Of course. I've cared for children before."

"Very well." Sybil stood and let Louisa sit on the stool and laid the sleeping boy in her lap.

Morten gave Sybil his arm, and the two of them walked

through the crowded marketplace while Sir Charles took his place behind the booth beside Louisa.

Louisa wrapped Elias in her arms, enjoying the little boy's warmth and softness, reminding her how much she missed Margaret's hugs.

She'd never been away from Margaret, not since she was born, and she missed her terribly, so much that thinking about her made tears well up in her eyes. But she didn't want to risk letting Sir Charles see her cry, so she took deep breaths and drove the tears away, forcing her thoughts off her sister and onto Morten and Sybil.

She wished she could see them dancing together. "Do you think they will marry?" Louisa asked.

"I don't know. We shall see."

Sir Charles kept glancing down at her with the sleeping boy in her lap. What was he thinking?

It was strange to see him minding the stall, greeting people who came to look at the shoes, answering their questions.

"Are you the owner?" one man asked.

"No, but he will be back later."

Sir Charles was not like the other people manning booths. He stood like a knight, bold and confident. His shoulders were broader, his chest more filled out with muscles from all his training. Even his legs were thicker and more muscular than the other men walking around. But of course, his muscular body was not what made him lovable. It was everything else about him—his gentleness, his chivalry, his fierce protection of her, and his self-sacrificial way of taking care of others.

What would it be like to be loved by such a man?

She needed to be glad that he was her friend and that he was taking her to Yorkshire to find the treasure. After all, most people would think her quest was ridiculous.

O Lord God, have I been horribly foolish in putting all my hopes in such a thing?

Sir Charles was gazing down at her again. "Is something wrong?"

"No, no." She didn't want him to know she was having doubts. He might want to talk her out of going, yet she couldn't give up now. She had to try, for Margaret's sake, if not for her own.

FIFTEEN

ABOUT AN HOUR AND A HALF LATER, MORTEN AND SYBIL returned to the stall, both with smiles on their faces and gleams in their eyes.

"We have something to tell you," Morten said.

Sybil blushed and stared down at Elias's sleeping form.

"We wish to be wed." Morten was still smiling, but he was looking at Charles.

"That is wonderful. Is there anything I can do to help?"

"There is. I wish to take Sybil and Elias back with me to Chesterfield, and I am leaving tomorrow, so I've asked the priest at the church—St. Oswald's—if he would marry us tomorrow morning, even though the banns have not been cried. He said he would, if we promise to have the banns cried at our home parishes, and if we have at least two witnesses who know us and can vouch for our character. So would you two be our witnesses?"

"Yes," Charles and Louisa both answered at the same time.

Louisa's face was brimming with joy. "We would love to do that."

Charles didn't mind that she was speaking for him.

Her excited tone must have awakened Elias, because he suddenly sat up, his eyes not even open yet, and said, "Mama."

Sybil was quick to take the boy in her arms. She held him close, a tear dripping from her eye. She wiped it quickly.

"Mama," the boy said, putting his hand on his mother's cheek. "Mama sad?"

"No, no, I'm very happy."

And indeed, she looked very happy.

Truly, Charles knew marriage to be a joyous thing, as all of his older siblings—Delia, Edwin, Gerard, Berenger, and Merek—were very happily married.

While Sybil and Louisa were discussing the particulars of where Sybil and Morten would live, Morten came around to the other side of the booth with an earnest look.

"I shall take good care of Sybil and Elias," he said quietly but intently. "I know she has been mistreated, and so has the boy, by the boy's father and by people who accused the boy of . . . well, you know. But my family will welcome them and be kind to them. You see, my own mother was born with an affliction that made it difficult for her to walk. I don't believe that hardships are a curse or justification to shun a person."

Charles nodded. "I agree, and I'm glad for you both. I think you will be very happy, and so will Elias."

"Thank you." Morten's eyes became watery, and he cleared

his throat, obviously choking back tears. Yes, they should be very happy.

Charles pushed away the thoughts he'd been having while Louisa was holding the sleeping Elias, thoughts that made his shirt feel too tight around his throat. They were similar to the thoughts he'd had when they were alone in the Cockayne family's pavilion, and he couldn't tear his eyes away from Louisa's lips or drive out the thought of kissing her.

He needed to sort this out or he might end up doing something he would regret. Or equally concerning, he might *not* do something he would later regret not doing.

He liked taking action. Doing was his forte, not thinking. But this was too important to rush into without thinking, praying, and using self-control.

He did rather admire Morten, however, for taking action and not delaying.

Louisa wiped away a tear as she, Sir Charles, and Richie witnessed Morten and Sybil's exchange of vows in the beautiful St. Oswald's Church.

Afterward, they all said their heartfelt farewells, and then the new family of three set out for Morten's hometown.

Sir Charles, Richie, and Louisa finished gathering supplies in Ashbourne. As they continued on their journey north, they were a bit quieter, with even Richie being less talkative than usual. Something about weddings made one ponder one's own life.

MELANIE DICKERSON

Soon they stopped to rest and eat a meal of bread and cheese.

Louisa wandered into the forest several yards away from where Richie and Sir Charles were sitting. She felt as if she were deep in the woods, even though she was not very far from the others. After she relieved herself, something large and white caught her eye a little farther away, toward a slight rise where the trees were less dense.

The large white thing was obviously an animal, probably a horse or mule. She moved closer to it, walking stealthily so as not to scare it or let it know she was there. When she was still fifty feet away, she saw the long, straight horn and realized it was . . . a unicorn.

Her heart beat wildly in her chest. Unicorns had been extinct for at least a hundred years, hadn't they? But there it was, clearly visible through the trees, a white horse with a straight, pointy horn, its head lowered as it grazed.

She turned and hurried as quietly as she could back the way she had come. She found Sir Charles alone with the horses. "Come quickly! I must show you something!"

"Show me what?" He grabbed his sword and started toward her.

"You won't believe me, but it was a unicorn, grazing in the woods. Come and see!"

She took hold of his arm to hurry him along.

She could hardly believe that a unicorn would choose to show itself to her. Was it some kind of sign from God that she should continue on with her journey? That God was planning to give her the treasure?

170

"I don't want to scare it," she whispered, slowing down as they drew near the hill where she'd spotted the unicorn.

O dear Lord God, please let it still be there.

Sir Charles was right behind her. She even felt the brush of his arm against hers as she moved forward.

Then she saw the broad, dirty-white side of the animal's body. It was still in the same place, still with its head down, still grazing.

But as she drew near, the animal raised its large head, and . . . the horn did not move with it. The "horn" was just a small light-colored branch.

Louisa gasped and covered her mouth with her hand. Her face started to burn. How could she have thought it was a unicorn?

They stepped into the small clearing where the animal was grazing, and it looked at them with big, bland eyes.

"It's just a horse. The horn was a tree branch." Louisa covered her face with her hands. "I can't believe I thought I'd found a unicorn." She laughed, then found she couldn't stop laughing. Sir Charles probably thought she was addlepated.

She was embarrassed, but she could already imagine how funny the story would be when she saw Margaret again and could tell her about the "unicorn."

Charles moved carefully toward the horse, which turned out to be quite gentle and tame, and started stroking its neck as he watched Louisa laugh at herself.

She was so adorable—the way she laughed, the tilt of her head, the way she started out looking shocked, then embarrassed, and then laughing so hard that she was wiping tears from the corners of her eyes.

She had been so excited to show him the unicorn. And instead of trying to capture the creature, she'd come back to fetch him and show him her amazing find.

"Hello!"

Richie was calling to them from a long way off. He didn't bother to call back to her because she could just follow the sound of Louisa's laughter.

"Louisa?"

"We're here!" Louisa called back.

When Richie came into view, she said, "I wasn't sure if you were laughing or crying. What happened?"

Louisa's laughter was finally subsiding. Her smile was so pretty and genuine, and she took a deep breath and let it out, wiping the last of the tears from her face.

"I thought I saw a unicorn."

"That horse?"

"I dragged Sir Charles here, telling him there was a unicorn in the woods." Louisa started laughing again. "But of course it was just a horse."

"What made you think it was a unicorn?"

"A branch was sticking out of a tree on the other side of its head. It looked exactly like a unicorn's horn."

"A branch? You couldn't tell a branch from a unicorn horn?" Richie started laughing too, but her laughter was more derisive.

LADY OF DISGUISE

Charles said, "Even I thought it was a unicorn for a moment when I first saw it."

"You thought a branch was a horn?"

"It very much resembled a horn from that distance."

"At least you got a good laugh from it," Richie said to Louisa. "I wish I had been here."

Charles was glad she wasn't, for he enjoyed seeing Louisa laugh so delightfully, and Richie probably would have made her feel more embarrassed.

"Should we try to find the owner of the horse?" Louisa asked. "She could get hurt out here by herself."

"She probably wandered away from somewhere nearby." Charles marveled at how quickly Louisa thought about the horse's predicament and had compassion for the animal.

He used a cloth belt that Richie was wearing to make a quick harness to lead the animal. Instinctually, he followed a path that looked more human-made than like a game trail, and soon he came to a farm. A man came running toward them.

"You found her! Glory to God!" The older man hurried to take the animal from him.

Charles untied Richie's belt from the animal's head. "It's a good thing she is so tame and was so easy to catch."

"Yes, she is forever wandering off at every open barn door," the man muttered as he shook his head. "Thank you, sir."

Charles was glad to have found the owner so easily. He walked back and saw Louisa lingering near where they'd found the horse.

She looked up and said, "You found the owner already?"

"I did."

Staring down at a leaf in her hand, she started smiling and shaking her head. "I can't believe I thought I'd seen a unicorn."

"It was an easy mistake to make."

"Did you really think it was a unicorn too? Or did you only say that to keep Richie from laughing at me?"

"No, I did think it was a unicorn, until the horse moved its head."

They began walking back toward the road together. He moved a branch out of Louisa's way, holding it until she was past so it wouldn't hit her in the face.

"Thank you."

"How is your ankle?"

"It only hurts a little bit now. Thank you for asking." She sent a quick glance at him over her shoulder, then kept walking.

Everything about her was beguiling—her smile, her eyes, her laugh, her gentle ways, her gratitude, compassion, and kindness. He even liked her short hair, but he could imagine how beautiful it would be when it grew out.

And she wasn't anything like Lady Mirabella, who'd been vain and prideful and oblivious to how anyone else might feel. She was immature and completely unaware of how her actions affected those around her.

A small part of him thought Louisa's belief in the Viking treasure and her ability to find it was rather immature. But she'd lost her parents at a young age, and she still held on to faith in things she couldn't see and had dreamed of the treasure for years. She had not been hardened by the harsh circumstances of life, and she was nothing like the spoiled Mirabella, whose parents had given her everything she wanted. Louisa was an orphan for whom life had never been very easy.

How could he ever let her go when this quest was over? What would happen to her? What would she do? He felt sick in his stomach when he thought of her marrying someone, anyone besides him.

He loved her. The reality of it had been coming on gradually, and he was only just now accepting it. And although the emotion scared him, bringing back the stinging pain of Mirabella's rejection, he might as well admit that he felt it, at least to himself.

He didn't want to speak to her of love, as it seemed unwise while they were still on their journey and unchaperoned. But once she realized there was no treasure to find, he would ask her to marry him. He would hopefully find a romantic way to tell her he loved her and that he wasn't exactly sure how, but he would provide for her and her sister, even if they had to live with his sister and her husband, Lord Strachleigh, for a while, or with one of his brothers. He would not rest until he could earn enough in service to the king for his own manor house.

He would do whatever it would take, and she and her sister never would have to go back to her uncle's guardianship. He would love and cherish her every moment.

Sixteen

Over the next several days, as they traveled closer to Richie's home in Yorkshire, Louisa wondered why she often caught Sir Charles staring at her. And when she did, he always looked away, as if to pretend he hadn't been looking at her.

"We should get to my home by this time tomorrow," Richie announced as the sun was sinking low and painting their faces with a warm glow.

Even though Richie sometimes made thinly veiled insinuations about her and Sir Charles, Louisa would miss her. She was a lively, interesting person who entertained them with singing or rhymes or stories that had happened to her on all her travels.

Louisa knew that once they left Richie behind, she and Sir Charles would be traveling alone. She felt a strange excitement every time she thought about it. But she shouldn't feel excited. It wasn't as if anything could happen between them. Still, she

looked forward to being able to talk to him without anyone
else around.

Brother Matthew's words did haunt her—his condemnation
of her as a young woman traveling on her own, his prediction
that she would ruin Sir Charles's reputation as a pure and noble
knight. Even though the thought made her feel a bit guilty, she
believed they would enjoy each other's company more without
Richie watching them for signs of affection.

As they stopped for the night and laid out their sleeping
bundles on the ground, Richie said the very thing Louisa had
been mulling over.

"You two will be all alone after tomorrow night. Personally,
I don't see why you don't do what Morten and Sybil did and
get married."

Sir Charles stopped what he was doing, freezing in the
middle of spreading out his blanket.

"Truly, Richie, you say the most inappropriate things." Louisa rolled her gaze heavenward and hoped she sounded only
mildly exasperated.

"Well, after you find the Viking treasure, you will have
plenty of money and can do as you please. You should marry."

Sir Charles never turned around or acknowledged her words.

Was he angry? Or just annoyed at Richie for suggesting they
should get married? Of course Richie was being sarcastic about
them finding the treasure and having a lot of money. But Louisa
said nothing.

A few minutes later, Richie excused herself to go into the
bushes for some privacy.

Sir Charles still had not said a word since Richie's bold, intrusive words. Louisa started brushing her horse, talking softly to her as she did so. A moment later, Sir Charles was coming up behind her. She turned around to face him.

"Richie can be so ridiculous," she said.

"Do you think so?" Sir Charles's demeanor was a bit cloudy. "I . . ." He ran his hand through his hair and turned away.

Louisa's heart sank. She must have said the wrong thing, for she could tell by the slump of Sir Charles's shoulders and the way he kept his hand on the back of his neck that he was perturbed. But why?

"I just meant that Richie says too much sometimes, I think, just to see what reaction she gets. But I know she is a good person, only a bit intrusive sometimes—"

Sir Charles turned toward her and held up his hand. "All is well and good. You have nothing to feel bad about or explain."

But he did not look as if all was well. Something was bothering him.

"If I said anything amiss—"

"You didn't." He walked away from her, saying, "I'll be back in a few minutes."

He walked in the opposite way that Richie had gone, and since Louisa had already taken her turn in the woods, she stayed with the horses, her thoughts spinning. Why was he upset about what Richie had said? Was he sorry he had agreed to accompany her on this quest? Richie had never been forthright enough to say she thought it was foolish, but she had declared it so in many snide comments and insinuations. And perhaps she was right.

O Lord God, please don't let Sir Charles abandon me.

It was her biggest fear, besides him deciding he didn't care for her.

They still had a long way to go, but more than her worry that he wouldn't help her, she deeply longed for his approval.

She also desperately wanted to know what he was thinking.

Some minutes later, Richie returned. "I can hardly wait for you to meet my daughter. She has been sick a long time, but this St. Thomas's Water should cure her, God willing. And you can stay a few days at my house and rest up for your journey to Yorkshire. I almost wish I could go with you and see all the adventures you will have."

Louisa couldn't imagine how Richie could want to keep traveling after such a long journey. Why would she not want to be relaxing in her own home?

The thought of having her own home, of peace and quiet, sitting beside her own fire and sleeping in her own bed . . . That was what Louisa had wanted for such a long time.

Richie obviously was not thinking about what she had said about Louisa and Sir Charles marrying. That was characteristic of Richie, only thinking of what was to come, not what happened in the past, even as recently as a few minutes ago. But perhaps that was better than the opposite—constantly dwelling on the past, which was Louisa's tendency.

Sir Charles came striding back to their little group. His expression was less clouded, thankfully. "I saw a pheasant."

He took his crossbow from where it was strapped to his saddle, loaded it with a bolt, and hurried back the way he had come.

"Some roast pheasant would be a wonderful meal for the last night of our journey," Richie said.

It would indeed. Louisa's stomach growled just thinking about it.

Sir Charles came back a few minutes later carrying a large pheasant. He quickly skinned it as Louisa and Richie started a fire. Sir Charles fashioned a spit, and in no time the bird was roasting, dripping and sizzling into the flames.

Later, as they sat around the smoldering fire eating the evening meal, Richie regaled them with stories her father had told her, some of which were very fantastical and involved fairies and elves and giants.

Louisa would miss Richie. She remembered how Sir Charles had looked earlier, troubled and tense, and she feared he wasn't looking forward to the two of them being alone together.

They stayed with Richie and her daughter, who was mostly bedridden, for two days. Then Louisa and Sir Charles parted ways with Richie with an enthusiastic farewell and promises to visit on their way back from Yorkshire—and the older woman's numerous sly smiles and hints about marriage.

Neither of them talked very much as they made their way out of Richie's town and headed northward toward the highlands of Yorkshire. The first night they were alone, Louisa watched for any signs of that tension Sir Charles had displayed when Richie had said they should get married. As they went about taking care of the horses, he was talking more than usual and even told a funny story about one of his brothers. She felt her own shoulders relax at seeing him in a good humor.

Later, as they were eating their evening meal, the conversation turned to the treasure. Louisa said, "It probably seems unlikely that I will actually find the treasure—I know Richie thought we wouldn't find it—but if I do, I want you to know that I plan to share it evenly with you."

Sir Charles's face was serious as he gazed back at her. "Truthfully, I admire you for going after the treasure. Instead of just wishing things were better for you and your sister, you did something. And who knows? Perhaps God put that dream and plan in your heart because He truly does intend for you to find that treasure. Or if not that treasure, then a different one."

Her lungs expanded as she took in his praise. Could he truly admire her? It was a heady thought. No one had ever told her they admired her, or anything akin to that.

"You are very kind," she said, trying not to let him know just how much his praise meant to her. "Sometimes I'm afraid this Viking treasure is going to turn out to be no more real than the unicorn I saw."

"Well, you never know until you try. After all, since we know Vikings came here and looted and pillaged, it's very possible they may have buried some of their treasure here for safekeeping until they could come back for it. And if it is God's will that you find it, then you will."

Louisa nodded, her breath catching in her throat at the thought that he believed she might find the treasure.

They covered a lot of distance the next three days, with the landscape becoming more rugged and hilly. Yorkshire was a vast county, but they must surely be nearing the Scottish border by now. Even though it was summer, the air was noticeably colder.

They came to a crossroads and stopped. The signpost bore several town names, each pointing in a different direction.

Louisa dismounted to look through her saddlebag for a blanket she could put over her shoulders. While she was searching through her bag, Sir Charles also started taking something out of his saddlebag.

Louisa finally fished out her blanket, and when she looked up, Sir Charles was holding out a familiar-looking silk shawl.

"It's the one from the Ashbourne market!" she cried as he placed the pretty one with the colorful embroidery in her hands. Her throat became clogged, and she had to stop speaking as she held the shawl against her chest. He had bought it for her secretly, just because she'd admired it. She had to blink furiously to keep the tears from falling.

"I could see you liked it and I thought you might need it."

She gazed up at him and smiled. "I love it. Thank you." She threw it over her shoulders and ran her hands over the silk embroidery.

"It has a clasp. Here, let me do it." His hands brushed hers as he took hold of the fabric that came together under her chin and fastened the clasp.

He was standing quite close now, staring into her eyes. "It has a hood too. I hope it keeps you warm."

"It will. Thank you."

She imagined throwing her arms around him and kissing him, or at least hugging him, but she was too afraid of making him uncomfortable or, even worse, causing him to push her away or otherwise reject her.

However . . . if he continued to stand so close to her, gazing into her eyes and tempting her, she might just kiss him anyway.

He took a step back and she sighed.

"It looks very pretty on you."

"Thank you."

He cleared his throat and turned toward the signpost. "So the place we are looking for is Kilwyn in Swaledale. Is that right?"

"Right. My father said Kilwyn is supposed to be the last town before we reach the mountain where the treasure is hidden."

"There's no Kilwyn on these signs."

"On my map of Yorkshire that I copied, Kilwyn is directly north of Stirling."

"The sign says Stirling is straight ahead. So we go straight."

They continued on for the rest of the day, the wind growing colder.

"It looks like we may be in for a storm." Sir Charles was staring up at the sky. "I shall make a shelter tonight to keep out the wind and rain."

The clouds were thick, so they ventured off the road so Sir Charles could look for a good place for a shelter.

"I will help you look," Louisa said. "What exactly are you looking for?"

"A rock outcropping, something that will provide at least one wall for us, and then I can enclose the rest."

They wandered over the rocky, hilly terrain. "We aren't getting lost, are we? I can't see the road."

"No, we're not lost. The road is over there." He pointed.

They came to a low place, a valley between two hills, and Sir Charles went straight toward a dark place in the thick of some juniper trees. He moved the branches back to reveal a large rock with a space between the trees and the rock.

"This will do very well." He led the horses into the sheltered space and tied them to the tree branch.

"We won't even have to build anything," Louisa said. "This place is perfect."

"I will still need to lash the limbs to something sturdy. Otherwise, if the storm is bad, it will push the branches around and expose us to the rain."

She couldn't imagine what he was going to do, but she was glad he seemed so knowledgeable.

"Stay with the horses. I'll be right back." He took his small axe with him.

While he was gone, Louisa collected sticks for a fire and brought them into the shelter, so if it did rain, they would have some dry firewood.

He came back with four sturdy trees, cut and trimmed, about the thickness of Louisa's leg and as tall as Sir Charles. He started digging in the ground with a tiny spade he produced from his saddlebag. He buried one end of each of the poles in the ground and used rope to lash the juniper branches to them. Then he took the sailcloth that he used to cover his bedding, lashed it against the tree limbs, and brought it over the top of their makeshift shelter. There was an opening just large enough for them to fit through next to the giant rock.

By the time he finished it was quite dark. He'd left an opening in the tree branches at the opposite end from the door flap for smoke to go through, and Louisa built a small fire just underneath the hole.

They sat side by side against the rock wall and ate a meal of dried beef, smoked fish, bread, cheese, and dried apricots. In their small pot, Louisa poured some water and put it over the fire.

"I bought these dried herbs at the Ashbourne market. My old nurse taught me how to make a drink from them that tastes good. It's even better if you have some honey to put in it. I'd forgotten all about them, but it will warm us up to drink something hot."

Her hands had grown quite cold, and she could only imagine how Sir Charles felt after working outside in the cold wind.

When the water was hot and the drink was ready, she poured some into each of their cups, and holding it warmed Louisa's fingers quite delightfully.

"Do you like it?" she asked him as he took his second sip.

"It is better than the medicinal tea the servants used to make me drink when I was a boy."

Louisa laughed. "I hope so. Feverfew tea is disgusting. That's what my nurse used to give me when I was sick."

"I bet you poured it out when she wasn't looking. That's what I did."

"You bad boy! I usually drank it."

"You were a good girl. I should have known." He nodded, a rueful smile on his lips as he stared into his cup.

"Were you always a bad boy?"

"I wasn't cruel, but I disobeyed when it suited me. I had to grow up when I became a squire. I realized I wanted to be a noble knight worthy of my title. I didn't want to be one of those knights for whom their vows meant nothing."

The wind was making the piece of sailcloth flap up and down from where it hung over the opening, so Sir Charles got up and staked it down with a piece of rope and a sturdy stick.

Suddenly the wind picked up even more, howling through the juniper tree above them, and rain began pelting their shelter. Soon the noise from the wind and rain was so loud they had to raise their voices to be heard, even though they were sitting right next to each other.

"We had better get our blankets down before the fire gets blown out."

The wind was already coming in through the smoke hole and blowing the smoke into their faces.

They hurried to pull out their blankets and lay them on the ground. Just about the time they finished, the wind blew out the fire.

The wood continued to smoke, burning her eyes and nose and making her cough. Sir Charles used his booted foot to shove the smoking wood out of the shelter.

"Will it catch the tree limbs on fire?" she asked.

"I don't think so, but even if it does, the rain will put it out."

There was nothing to do but lie down. And in the small

space, which they were sharing with the horses, they had to lay their blankets side by side.

"Forgive me," he said, his voice coming from the pitch-black dark. "I'm sorry I couldn't think of a way to give you your own shelter so you didn't have to share with me and the horses."

"We are safe and warm and out of the rain, so that is all we need."

"I hope it holds and doesn't fall down on our heads."

"You don't think it will, do you?"

He laughed. "It depends on how bad this storm gets."

It was a strange feeling being alone in the dark, lying next to Sir Charles, knowing he was there but unable to see him.

She'd slept near him for weeks now, sharing a fire, but it felt different now. It was so dark, and Richie was not there with them.

God, forgive me for wanting to kiss him.

What would happen if they did kiss?

Hadn't Sir Charles just said that she was a good girl? Now was the time for her to prove it. But she had to admit, her mind kept going to how close Sir Charles was to her, to how dark it was, to how much she wanted to kiss him.

O Lord God, help me. I don't want to embarrass myself, or worse.

SEVENTEEN

SWEAT FORMED UNDER CHARLES'S ARMS AND ON HIS forehead as he lay there thinking that, as much as he wanted to, he mustn't kiss Louisa.

He'd made a vow that he would never kiss another woman unless he was in a position to marry her, which included having the means to provide for her. But what did that truly mean anyway? He might not have a house, but as a knight he would be rewarded by the king someday, whenever he was able to distinguish himself. And he had good and kind family members, wealthy ones too, who would be happy to take in his wife in the meantime.

What kind of terrible person would he be if he tried to kiss her now?

She didn't know how beautiful she was, how beguiling her laugh, how delightful her company. Even when men noticed her, which happened frequently since she started wearing the dresses that Richie had bought for her, she didn't seem to realize it, or at least didn't realize it was because she was so pretty. And if he kissed her, she would wonder what his intentions were, and rightfully so.

He had to control himself.

The wind was no longer blowing so hard, though the rain was heavy, and he was fairly certain Louisa was asleep.

His heartbeat slowed and he let out a pent-up breath. He certainly wouldn't try to kiss her while she was sleeping. That would not be chivalrous, to say the least.

It had been a long day. His hands and shoulders were sore from building their little shelter, and he soon felt himself drifting off to sleep.

Louisa opened her eyes but could barely see anything, it was so dark. She was startled when she suddenly realized how close Sir Charles was. Then she remembered the storm and the shelter he had built for them.

The sun was probably up, from the bit of light coming through the cracks at the bottom of the shelter, but she hated to get out from under the warmth of her blanket. As she lay there, she watched Sir Charles's face while he slept.

How handsome he was, and how very dear he was too. He'd been her protector and her rescuer, and she knew him as a good man with a heart both gentle and fierce. He had such a strong chin, the way it was squared off, and the stubble on his jawline was so rugged and masculine. She imagined running her finger over it and letting it prickle her skin, imagined kissing his cheek and resting her head against his shoulder.

He opened his eyes and stared straight at her.

Her cheeks grew instantly warm. Did he know what she was thinking? Could he see her blushing and realize what she had just been imagining?

"It must be morning," he mumbled and turned over onto his back, stretching his arms over his head.

Thanks be to God, he didn't seem to notice that she was blushing.

"I believe it is," she answered.

She crawled out of her blankets and stood up in the cool morning air, which felt colder than the day before. She was still wearing all her clothes since it had been so cold, and she was too near to Sir Charles to take off her outer clothing before lying down the previous night.

Charles had stood up at the same time as Louisa, Louisa's shoulder brushing against Sir Charles's chest. Louisa stepped back, her heel colliding with the rock wall, and she flailed her arms to catch herself.

Sir Charles caught her arm at the same time she latched onto his. He pulled her upright and held on.

"Forgive me," he said. "I was crowding you."

"No, no. I just lost my footing."

They were staring into each other's eyes. How good he looked, how gentle and yet intense his eyes were.

They broke away from each other, but the moment left

Louisa thinking that something had changed between them. They were no longer the easy friends they were when she was Jack and he was a knight who had nothing better to do than accompany her on her journey. And they were no longer just traveling companions who were looking out for Sybil and Elias while being entertained by Richie.

There was something in his eyes that hadn't been there before, which both thrilled and frightened her. But she reminded herself, *Just get to the mountain. Just get to the treasure. Just get back to Margaret.*

She was on a quest, and although she did not know what would happen between her and Sir Charles, she would not veer from her mission. She had come too far to stop now, and she had to keep her mind on her goal.

Finally.

Charles stared down at the little village of Kilwyn in the glen below them.

It had been four days since the night in the shelter during the storm. After traversing hills and even mountains, they'd finally reached their destination, which was good. Now he could tell her that he loved her and would marry her and take care of her and Margaret.

But first they had to discover whether the treasure existed and if they could actually find it, and if and when that option was no longer a possibility, he could explain his plans and intentions more fully.

They started down the mountainside road that led to the village.

He'd imagined Louisa's excitement when she saw the village of Kilwyn, their last stop before making their way up the mountain, which he could already see in the distance. But after what they'd been told in the last village they'd gone through, he wasn't surprised that she looked more nervous than pleased.

They'd gone into the village to buy food and asked the baker how far they were from Kilwyn Mountain.

"Hunting treasure, are you?"

Charles didn't respond. It didn't matter because the middle-aged baker assumed the answer was yes.

"I wouldn't go there if I were you. No one escapes there without getting skinned."

"Skinned?"

"Taken for everything he has, even his life sometimes."

"Someone is robbing and murdering people in the village of Kilwyn?"

"Not someone. Some *thing*." He scrunched his face in an expression of disgust and horror.

"Come, now. You don't mean a giant."

"Of course I do. You've heard the rumors, same as everyone else, and they're true. How else do you explain all the people who come back from there with tales of losing everything but the shirt on their backs, talking of a giant, misshapen beast of a man. They went there seeking treasure and came away glad to have escaped with their lives."

Louisa was beside him, listening to it all.

They had procured their supplies and left that village, but not before asking another man for directions to Kilwyn. That person just shook his head and pointed. "Keep to this road. It will take you over a mountain, and on the other side in the glen is Kilwyn."

"Thank you."

He just raised his brows at them, frowned, and turned away.

And now they were here.

They proceeded carefully, as the mountain was slippery from the misting rain that had carried on all day.

He let Louisa go ahead of him. She'd tied her skirts in a knot to one side so that they would not get in the mud on the steep hillside, and because of the colder air, she was also wearing her men's hose underneath.

They reached the small village of Kilwyn and were met with smiling faces. Truly, he couldn't remember ever arriving in a friendlier place. Several people greeted them with a cheerful "Good morning." Yet the hair rose on the back of his neck, though he couldn't quite explain why.

When they went into the baker's shop, the woman behind the counter said, "You're new here, are you not?" in an overly enthusiastic voice.

"We're just passing through."

"You will be wanting supplies to climb Beinn Kilwyn, will you not?"

"A few things, yes."

"You'll be needing bread to keep up your strength, which I can supply, and then you'll be wanting to go to the shop next to mine to get the pickaxes and ropes and whatnot to help you get up our wee mountain."

She seemed deliberately slow about fetching their bread and taking their money.

"Where are you from, if I may ask? You look like a knight and his lady." She smiled and waggled her eyebrows the way Richie used to do.

He didn't want to answer her, but he couldn't seem to help himself, she was so welcoming. "I am a knight, and she is a lady." He left out their names.

"Just as I thought." She beamed as if she thought herself very clever. "I can always tell the noble folks from the villeins."

Charles's unease was growing by the minute. Though he didn't like thinking ill of the gregarious woman, there was something too friendly about all these people, something sinister in their eagerness. He could see the same thoughts on Louisa's face.

He paid for the bread and left the shop. He did not even have time to decide which adjacent shop the baker woman had meant when a man approached him, saying, "My shop has all the mountain climbing tools you need. Come this way."

These people might have evil intentions, but he had yet to see anyone who could pass for a giant. And he was confident he would have no trouble defending himself from these villagers should they try to attack and take their supplies, their money, or their lives.

Inside the shop, he did find what they needed for climbing— pickaxes and rope. The shopkeeper tried to sell them other things like saddlebags and water flasks, but he refused, as they already had those items.

"That was strange," Louisa said as they set out from the village.

They both looked over their shoulders. A group of people stood in the road watching them leave.

"Very strange."

They headed toward the mountain, and he could finally see a smile on Louisa's face. She was finally excited.

"I've waited for this for so many years. It hardly seems true."

"Stay on your guard."

"I will." Her expression changed as she pursed her lips together and stared hard at the mountain, which looked quite green and lush, with pointy ridges and a smooth, low place resembling a saddle. All along were bald rocks sticking up between areas of green grass, bushes, and moss. And one point at the very top showed a small area of white, a patch of snow that had not melted since winter.

Charles didn't believe there was a giant. Perhaps there was something sinister up there, but it was not a giant. But the villagers living below it had certainly prospered off the people who believed there was treasure on that mountain just waiting for someone to discover it.

Most likely there was no treasure either, but he was glad Louisa had made the trip to search for it. Otherwise he never would have met her.

Eighteen

Even though it was thrilling to have actually made it to the treasure mountain, the words *fool's errand* kept going through Louisa's mind over and over. Had she made a terrible mistake coming here?

Something was wrong with the way those villagers reacted to their presence, something in their faces that Louisa did not trust. She knew what it felt like to be used. Their expressions reminded her of the way her uncle looked at her when he was trying to marry her off, the way her cousin looked at her when he bossed her around and threatened to tell his father and mother that Louisa hit him if she didn't do something for him, the way he looked at her when she acquiesced just to avoid trouble.

She could see that those people in the village of Kilwyn were using her and Sir Charles, but how? They sold them goods for climbing, but she felt in her spirit that that wasn't what she was discerning about them. Something else was going on.

She could tell by the look on Sir Charles's face that he noticed it too. But there was nothing to do but keep going to the mountain, keep going on her *fool's errand*.

The intrusive words wouldn't leave her alone. But she couldn't stop now. They were so close.

She'd never climbed a mountain before. Indeed, all the little hills she'd ever seen before would seem like nothing to the people who had lived around these mountains all their lives. Louisa had never seen anything like them. This one was so high that it still had a bit of snow on the top. Truly, it was majestic, like the tall, beautiful church spire in Ashbourne. A wall of greenery and rocks loomed ahead of them, beckoning them to climb it and see what was at the top—if anything. Certainly, the view would be a sight to behold. She could hardly imagine it.

Her ankle had not pained her in several days, which was good since she would need it to be strong in order to make this climb.

Despite her misgivings, she felt her joy rising. She was here! She was finally here, and she would now see if she was on a fool's errand—or a glorious quest.

Many other people had come looking for the Viking treasure. If they hadn't found the treasure, why did she think she could? But Louisa had to put those thoughts aside for now. After dreaming about this since she was a young child, she was finally here, and with Sir Charles, the bravest and best knight in the kingdom, by her side.

She couldn't stop smiling. "I'm here," she said on a breath, staring up at the mountain. Suddenly tears sprang to her eyes and made her catch her breath.

Sir Charles put his arm around her shoulders and pulled her close in a side embrace. "You did it. You did what most others, man or woman, have never done. You left home all on your own, against the wishes of your guardians, and you made it all the way across the kingdom. That is something to be proud of."

"Do you really think so?" She ducked her head while she flicked away the tears that fell onto her cheeks. She took a deep breath to drive the rest away. When she'd overcome the urge to cry, she looked up at him.

"I do think so. You are very courageous. And I am honored that I was able to come on this journey with you."

"You are?"

"I am." He smiled. Then he pulled her into his chest in an embrace.

His arms were so strong, so warm, and his chest was so solid that it took her breath away. If only she could feel this good, this warm, this protected every day of her life.

At the thought that such a thing was not possible, that Sir Charles would soon have to part from her, the tears started to come again. She quickly forced them away by thinking how good and safe it felt to be held by someone she loved and trusted.

Loved. Yes. She loved him, and at this moment she felt he loved her too, but only as friends, of course. But even to be loved as a friend by someone as good and noble as Sir Charles was more than she had expected in her life.

The embrace ended. Sir Charles turned away without looking at her. "Let us go."

Her heart sank. Even though she knew she shouldn't be disappointed, shouldn't feel rejected or expect anything from him, she'd hoped in her heart that he might feel as deeply in love with her as she was with him. And she was—oh, how she was!—deeply, madly, forever in love with this man.

They started up the mountain with Sir Charles leading the horses after looping their reins around his arm. There was already a worn trail, but Sir Charles directed her to go ahead of him and to walk in the grass and moss beside the muddy trail, which was slick. "That way if you were to slip, I could catch you before you fell too far."

The clouds were parting overhead, revealing blue sky.

"If it's sunny by the time we get to the top, we should get a great view of the area around us." Sir Charles was following close behind her.

"I can hardly wait." Louisa could hear the excitement in her own voice.

Her foot slipped on a smooth rock and Sir Charles grabbed her on both sides of her waist to stop her from sliding backward. His hands on her sides sent pleasant sensations all through her. But she mustn't behave as if it affected her. He was only helping her.

"Thank you. I'm well. But I might need to slow down a bit." She hoped he wouldn't notice the slight tremble in her voice.

"Of course." He removed his hands from either side of her waist. "There is no reason to hurry. Take care and go slow."

Louisa nodded and kept climbing, choosing more carefully where she placed her feet.

"Who is that to the left there?"

Louisa turned her head in the direction Sir Charles was looking and caught a glimpse of a small, wiry man disappearing behind a rock as he climbed the mountain about a hundred feet to their left.

"He looks like one of the men from the village." Louisa's uneasy feeling returned.

"That is what I was thinking."

Sir Charles had his sword strapped to his back and his crossbow tied to his horse's saddle. She shouldn't be worried about the little man, but she couldn't shake the feeling that something bad was about to happen.

They'd been climbing for about two hours. The clouds had cleared, and the sun was directly overhead, causing Charles to shed his cloak and Louisa to put away her shawl.

They came to a place where a tiny stream trickled straight down from a rocky ledge and continued down the side of the mountain.

"Such a pretty little waterfall," Louisa said in a hushed voice, as if she was in awe.

It was a rather pretty spot, but what truly took his breath away was seeing her so enthralled.

They continued on for a few minutes, then Louisa stopped.

She was breathing hard, so he said, "Why don't we sit here and eat and let the horses graze?"

They sat down on a grassy knoll and started eating the bread and cheese they'd procured in the village.

"Here is the ale-soaked dried fruit that the woman gave me." Louisa showed him the wet fruit that was wrapped inside a small piece of leather. "She tried to sell it to me, and when I refused, she gave it to me. Rather suspicious, is it not?" She raised her brows at him. "She was so determined that I have it, it makes me think she may have put something in it."

"Like poison?"

"I hate to think the worst of people, but—"

"No, you are wise to be cautious and to trust your suspicions. I do not think you should eat it. Everything about that village was strange."

They ate their bread and cheese, looking at the shorter peaks around them, the bright-green plants growing on all of them, except where the bald rocks showed through. Nearby were several sheep grazing. It was so quiet that he could hear the sound of the sheep cutting the grass with their teeth and chewing, cutting and chewing, placidly ignoring them.

"It is a beautiful place," Louisa said, sighing. "Do you think we're about halfway to the top?"

"Perhaps more than halfway."

Louisa smiled, clasping her hands together.

"You won't be too disappointed if there's no treasure, will you?"

She seemed to think for a moment. "I know it's possible that there's nothing there, but I still believe there is. I know that seems daft."

"No, not daft. But I do worry that you will be disappointed."

She frowned and gazed up at the clouds. "I will be disappointed, but I will be all right." She suddenly smiled. "Let us keep going."

They got up and were soon on their way again.

They were nearly to the top. Louisa could feel a nervous energy in her limbs, driving her upward, making her not want to stop to rest. She took one step after another until she was only about five feet from the level place at the top.

A deep voice rang out from above them. "Fee-fie-foe-fum." Then the voice said, "I smell the blood of an Englishman. Be he alive or be he dead, I'll grind his bones to make my bread."

Her eyes met Sir Charles's, her heart thumping hard against her ribs. It couldn't actually be a giant, could it? Could the stories about him be true? He certainly had a deep voice.

Her hands trembled. But what kind of intrepid journeyer would she be if she got to the top of the mountain and then was too scared to go the rest of the way? She had to at least see who—or what—that voice belonged to.

Sir Charles leaned close to her ear and said, "Let me go first. You can stay here if you like."

"No, I'm coming too."

He unsheathed his sword and climbed two more steps, then

raised his head and looked around. Then he climbed the last few feet and scrambled over the top.

Louisa followed right behind him. Now that she was on the top, she could see a figure standing partially hidden behind a large rock about thirty feet away. He stepped out from behind the rock, a very large club in his very large hand.

In fact, his entire body was large. He was at least two feet taller than Sir Charles, who was over six feet tall.

And there was something a bit strange about his body proportions. His head was enormous and his skull slightly misshapen behind his huge ears. His head was also tilted to one side, as if he couldn't straighten it.

"Did you not hear me?" he said. "I will grind your bones to make my bread." He raised the club higher.

"We mean you no harm," Sir Charles said.

"You mean me no harm? Ha! I could crush you with one blow." He brought the club down into his own hand.

Louisa's heart jolted. Would he kill Sir Charles and then her? *O Lord God, why did I ever come here?*

NINETEEN

LOUISA'S HEART WAS IN HER THROAT AS SHE WAITED TO see what the large man would do next.

"I believe you could," Sir Charles answered calmly, holding out his hand as if to keep the giant from coming any closer.

This was real. This giant man was real. For even though he was very large, and he looked slightly different from other men, he was a man nevertheless.

"You all come here to find the Viking treasure. Do you not think if the Viking treasure existed that someone would have found it by now? But you keep coming, more and more of you, to take something that is not yours."

His abnormally deep voice also held a bit of a slur, and he spoke slowly, as if opening his mouth and talking was painful.

Louisa suddenly felt ashamed. What was she doing here? This was obviously this man's home, and he had undoubtedly been plagued with treasure seekers for quite some time. Was she no better than the greedy people who had come before her?

"You are right," Louisa said. "That is wrong. I am sorry." Indeed, she felt very sorry that she was one of those terrible people who kept invading this man's home, trying to steal something they thought he possessed. But in truth, she never imagined the "giant" was real.

"Is there anything we could do to help stop the people from coming here?"

The man stared, turning his whole body to get a better look at her, since he couldn't seem to turn his head.

"Why would you want to help me?"

"It seems wrong for us to come to your home and not offer to help now that we realize what has been happening here. This mountain is your home, is it not?"

"It is my home. And I defend it when I must." He raised his club again.

How awful for this poor man, to be so tormented by treasure seekers. But why was he here? Was he living on this mountain alone? He said the treasure was not here, but Louisa still had many questions. But most of all, she wanted to show him that they were not there to take anything from him or threaten his home. So she asked him again, "Is there anything you need, anything we can do for you?"

"I would like some shallots and peas for my stew, but all they ever bring me is cabbage. And I need another boiling pot."

"We can certainly get some shallots and peas for you, and another pot," Sir Charles said.

"Why would you do that for me?" He narrowed his eyes at them.

"Other people bring you food, don't they?" Louisa asked.

He grunted. "Not for nothing they don't. But I will not give you my treasure for shallots and peas."

His treasure? But she thought he said there was no treasure—no Viking treasure, anyway.

"Of course not. My name is Louisa and this is Sir Charles. What is your name?"

"My name?" Again he looked taken aback.

"Yes. What is your name?"

"No one has asked my name for a very long time."

"I would like to know your name." Her heart squeezed at the thought that this poor man was living all alone on top of a mountain and had no one to talk to. Did he have no family? And he must have suffered so much abuse by the people who came here in search of treasure.

"My name is Allistor."

"It is a pleasure to have met you, Allistor."

Sir Charles lowered his sword. "Is there anything else we can get for you? We will go down to the village tonight and be back tomorrow."

"Are you really going back down the mountain to get peas and shallots and a boiling pot for me?"

"Of course." Sir Charles gave him stare for stare. He was a trained knight, but he had such a kind, honest, earnest face that no one could possibly disbelieve him.

Allistor stood staring back at them, this giant of a man, now leaning on his club like it was a walking stick.

"The people from the village bring me most of what I need, but I would like to have a second pot for boiling the last of the medicinal leaves my mother gave me."

"Your mother?" Louisa asked.

"She's been dead these ten years. I make a drink from the leaves she gave me."

"A second pot is a good thing to have," she told him. "We shall bring you a pot as well as the vegetables."

She and Sir Charles turned to leave.

"Wait. Stay for a while," Allistor said. "Tell me your stories."

Sir Charles's expression was one of caution mixed with compassion.

"What stories would you like me to tell?" Louisa asked.

"Tell me about your journey here." Allistor, leaning on his club, lumbered toward them several steps. There was a slight grimace on his face, as if walking was painful.

Louisa could see Sir Charles's shoulders tense, his hand on the hilt of his sword. She wanted to tell him that she was sure their friendly giant didn't mean them any harm, at least not at the moment.

Allistor sat down about ten feet away on a rock, groaning. When he had sighed and propped his club against the side of the rock, he said, "Tell me something about yourselves."

Louisa sat down on the grass, prompting Sir Charles to do the same, and she started telling Allistor about how she had dressed herself in men's clothing and sneaked away from home, about that first night when she'd been afraid and alone, hearing wolves howling, cold and wet. She told how she was chased away from the barn where she was sleeping and then met Sir Charles and how grateful she was that he had agreed to accompany her on her quest.

She told him about Richie and Morten and Sybil and Elias, but she skipped over the part about Brother Matthew.

Allistor sat very still and kept his eyes on her the whole time, occasionally making a "Hmm" sound, or an "Ah!" or an "Oh."

"You are a good storyteller," Allistor said when she paused to get a drink of water.

"You are a good listener." Her experience had mostly been with people who didn't listen to her, and perhaps that was why she rarely told stories. But it felt really good when people listened to her.

"I especially like the part about Morten marrying Sybil and taking Elias as his son. Tell me more about them. What did they look like, and what did they say to each other?"

Louisa told him everything she could think of, with Sir Charles pitching in to add details here and there.

"Tell me about your family," Allistor said.

Louisa told him about her mother and father dying, and about Margaret and how they'd gone to live with their uncle and his wife and their son, Bertram. She told him about some of the adventures she and Margaret had had, playing with the animals around the manor house. As she talked she noticed how closely Sir Charles seemed to be listening to her, as closely as Allistor. He even asked a question or two.

All the time she was talking, she was noticing the sun moving closer and closer to the horizon. Unless the moon was very bright tonight, it would be too difficult to see well enough to descend the mountain after the sun went down.

Sir Charles did not show it, but he must have also been paying attention to how low the sun was getting as well. After all, it had taken them about four hours to climb the mountain. It would probably take them just as long to get down.

"Tell me about you," Allistor said to Sir Charles. "Who are your family? How did you become a knight?"

Louisa was very pleased to listen to Sir Charles talk about his family and his life of training to become a knight. She wanted to know everything about him, all his stories, his preferences and his dislikes, as many of his thoughts and feelings as possible. She learned a few things about his family that she had not known. It filled her heart with warmth to hear his voice and the way he revealed bits of his character and temperament in the manner in which he told his story.

When he was finished, he asked Allistor, "Will you tell us about yourself? About your family and how you came to be living on this mountain?"

Allistor leaned his head back slightly, staring at them. "Most people, if they ask me anything about myself, only want to know how the giant became a giant. They want to know if I made a deal with the devil, or if I was cursed by a witch or a demon to cause me to look like this."

Louisa could well imagine that people would say such things to him. She assured him, "We don't believe you are cursed. We just want to hear your story."

"I was born to ordinary parents," Allistor said. "My mother

was shorter than you." He nodded at Louisa. "And my father was of normal height, a bit shorter than you." He looked at Sir Charles. "But even as a young child, I grew much faster than the other children in the village. My father told my mother not to feed me so much, but when I didn't get enough food at home, I went into the woods and caught rabbits in snares and ate the wild berries and roots and mushrooms. I even raided birds' nests and ate their eggs.

"But I don't think it was because I ate so much that I grew so big. My grandmother told me I had a great-uncle who grew too much. He had pains in his legs and feet, his shoulders and ankles, and in his jaws, just as I do. My grandmother said she thought my giant size was like red hair, which sometimes skips a generation, or green eyes that are passed down to children and grandchildren.

"And now I will tell you something I've never told anyone else before." He crossed his enormous arms and rested them in his lap. "My mother died when I was twelve years old, and the people threatened to run me out of the village if I didn't do what they said. They make me do bad things, make me frighten people and . . . I don't want to do it anymore. And besides that . . ." He paused and stared out across the mountain where they were sitting. Finally, he sighed and said, "I don't think I will live very much longer, and I don't want to die doing something that God will not forgive me for."

"You shouldn't have to do anything you don't want to do," Louisa said.

"She is right," Sir Charles quickly agreed. "You are big and strong enough to defend yourself from them, surely."

"I have tried, but they know I can no longer make it down

the mountain. I am dependent on them to bring me things."
He sighed, a heavy sound. "But it is getting late. Soon it will be
dark." He stood, pushing himself up using his club.

"We should go." Sir Charles stood up too, and Louisa followed suit.

"No. Don't go," Allistor said.

"We will return tomorrow morning with your pot and your
peas and shallots, just as we promised," Sir Charles said.

"For your sakes, you must not go."

"But it looks like we will have a full moon tonight," Sir
Charles said.

"Listen to me," the mountain man said in his deep, drawling
voice. "If you go now, the villagers might kill you. At the very
least, they won't let you leave with your horses and your money.
They are expecting me to capture you both and hold you for
ransom."

"Why would they expect that?" Louisa's heart was in her
throat.

"Because that is what they make me do. For years they demanded that I take everyone's horse and other belongings. Most
people are too frightened to fight me, so it's easy to take anything
I want. But now the villagers have thought of a new plan. They
want me to capture people and hold them in cages while they
ransom them."

Sir Charles frowned. "So that is what those villagers were
scheming."

"They've made me do it twice. The first man was cruel but
cowardly, so it wasn't hard to put him in a cage, but I didn't like

it. He cried and yelled all day long. But they got a big ransom from his family to let him go, so then they forced me to seize two other men, young men from noble families. They were terrified the first night in the cage, and they begged me to let them go, so I did. Later I found out that they killed those two men, and they blamed me. Now they want me to capture you two."

Louisa felt sick. If her uncle received a demand for ransom for her return, he would never pay it, and then everyone would know that even her own uncle did not care for her. The only person who cared was her poor sister. Margaret would be horrified, thinking of her being held in a cage by a giant.

"They thought it was likely you two had families who would pay a ransom. I am supposed to put you in my cage, and then someone will come and find out who your families are and send letters demanding a ransom for your release."

Louisa hated to admit that she was frightened, but she was more afraid of the villagers than of Allistor.

Sir Charles spoke up. "Who was the man we saw climbing up the mountain earlier?"

"That was Johnne Craig. He was coming to tell me to capture you and take your horses. But I didn't want to hit you both over the head and drag you to the cage. He told me I had to do it, but I didn't want to. And then you asked me what I needed and said you would go and fetch it for me. You asked me my name and treated me like a human being." He wiped his eyes with his sleeve. "I don't want to hurt you, but they will. I know they will."

"You shouldn't worry about the villagers harming us," Sir Charles said. "I am very good with a sword."

"I have seen them shoot arrows at people as they climbed down the mountain. That's how they killed those two men. They will kill you as you're climbing, when you can't defend yourselves."

Sir Charles met Louisa's gaze, but there was no fear in his eyes. Then he asked Allistor, "What do you suggest we do?"

"Spend the night here on the mountain. I will hide you, and in the morning you can go down another way that I will show you."

"But what will they do to you if we get away?" Louisa asked.

"They will be angry and might refuse to bring me supplies. Because of the pain in my joints, I can no longer get up and down the mountain. They know I depend on them for anything I can't find up here. But I am tired of doing this for them. They give me a share of the money they are getting from the people and from selling their horses, but what do I care for money when I cannot even leave this mountain?"

Louisa's heart constricted. The poor man. At the same time, her knees were weak at the thought of the people he had harmed and held against their will. Still, she couldn't judge him for doing what he thought he had to do to survive. And now he wanted to help her and Sir Charles escape the cruel villagers.

"I am so sorry they have done this to you," she said softly.

He wiped his eyes again. This time she could see, even in the waning light, the tears wetting his cheeks. "I never should have done it. I could have run away from here years ago, but I was afraid. People always scream the first time they see me, or they assume I am an evil spirit and try to chase me away."

The tears were falling faster than he could wipe them away. His chin trembled as he talked.

"I don't want to hurt people anymore, and I've started having pains in my chest. I think that means I don't have much longer to live. My grandmother said chest pains were the last thing my great-uncle complained about before he died." He wiped his face once more and sniffed. "Do you think it's too late for me to be forgiven?"

"No, of course not," Louisa said.

"It's never too late to change," Sir Charles said. "You can pray and tell God you are sorry and you won't hurt anyone again."

"Will you pray with me?" the large man asked. "Tell me what to say, I mean?"

Sir Charles's eyes went wide. "Louisa might be better at that."

"I will pray with you," Louisa said.

They both knelt on the grass, with Sir Charles joining them, and Louisa began aloud.

"Our Father in heaven, we beseech You to forgive us of our sins. We all sin and fall short of perfection, and we trust that You are faithful to forgive us, by the power of the blood of Jesus and by our faith in You and in Your Son. Allistor comes now asking for forgiveness for hurting people and holding them for ransom. He repents and will never do it again, not for money, nor to please the villagers, nor for food or for any other reason, for now he has Sir Charles and me to be his friends and to help him.

"Thank You, God, for Your mercy, grace, and compassion and for Your forgiveness and salvation. We pray in the name of Jesus who is God, the Son. Amen."

"Amen," Sir Charles and Allistor both intoned.

"How do you feel?" Louisa asked Allistor.

He raised his brows, a small smile spreading over his face. "I feel lighter, as if the big stone that was sitting on my shoulders has lifted."

"I'm so glad." Louisa felt herself beaming at her new friend.

"I can never thank you enough for your kindness. Please, will you come and share my stew? It is probably not what a knight and lady eat, but it will fill you up."

Sir Charles's eyes were watery, but he blinked and the tears were gone.

They led their horses and walked with the slow-moving Allistor as he made his way toward the other side of the relatively flat peak, which was shaded by tall rocks at the east end of the knoll where they had been sitting and talking.

"The villagers would expect me to put you in here." The huge man walked around the rocks and they saw the metal cage built into the broad side of the mountain.

"Those villagers must be making a lot of money with this scheme," Sir Charles said. "They will not let you stop filling their pockets without a fight."

Allistor sighed. "What can they do to me? They have already controlled my life since I was twelve years old. If they kill me, they kill me."

Now that Louisa thought about it, everyone in the village was wearing fine clothing, and she saw several horses, which was unusual in such a small village. Normally villagers just had mules and donkeys; only the lord of the manor owned horses.

"I won't let anyone harm you," Sir Charles declared, resting a hand on Allistor's arm.

Allistor gazed down at Sir Charles. "Thank you, but if you try to defend me, they will kill you too."

"We shall see." Sir Charles's jaw was set in a hard line.

"You may tie your horses there." He pointed to a sheltered spot and a horizontal pole set in the ground beside a watering trough. "I have my own well," he said. "Come, I will show you."

TWENTY

ALLISTOR ROLLED ASIDE A LARGE ROUND ROCK, WHICH revealed a hollow space and a lantern hanging from a hook inside the rock. He took the lantern and started walking down, as if he were descending into the mountain itself. Then he turned and handed the lantern to Sir Charles.

"I don't want you to miss your step," he said.

Sir Charles grabbed the lantern and Louisa took hold of his arm. Where were they going? Her heart fluttered.

Sir Charles went first, following right behind Allistor, who had to lean down as he went.

Louisa entered the cave behind Sir Charles, now clutching the back of his shirt.

The light from the lantern showed wide, uneven steps carved into the rock floor. Allistor moved slowly, bracing himself with one hand on the rock wall as he made his way down. If it was difficult for him to walk across level ground, how much more painful must it be to go up and down these steps?

They didn't go down far. Allistor stopped and stepped aside to reveal a large cave room, as big as two bedrooms in her uncle's manor house. A lamp was burning near the middle of the room, showing a rudimentary bed. Against the wall on either side of the bed were two large wooden chests.

He pointed to a hole in the rock floor where water bubbled up and disappeared with a trickling sound off a rock ledge. "I call it my well. It's really a spring."

He sat on a stool next to it, dipped a small metal bucket into it, and handed it to Louisa. She raised it to her lips and drank the cool water.

"It is very good water," she said.

Sir Charles also took a drink from the bucket and agreed.

"I beg you not to try to go down the mountain tonight," Allistor said. "They watch the mountain very carefully in the evenings."

Allistor had a clever fireplace against the wall of the cave, with a small hole at the back where the smoke went out. He went to the fire, dished up three bowls of stew, and handed a bowl to Louisa and one to Sir Charles.

The mutton stew was not bad. Her bowl contained several chunks of meat, more meat than her aunt and uncle allowed in their own stews. There was also garlic, wild onion, parsnips, and several familiar-tasting herbs, with a generous amount of salt. But with all the money the villagers were bringing in because of him, they could afford to give him anything he wanted.

"It is very good," Sir Charles said.

"I suppose Lessie gave you some of her ale-soaked dried fruit."

"Yes, a woman did."

"I take it you didn't eat it," Allistor said between bites. "She puts herbs in it that make a person go to sleep."

Louisa met Sir Charles's eyes as he raised his brows at her. "I told you she was much too eager to give it to me."

Allistor shook his head. "It seems to me that all people must be cruel and selfish."

"Not all people," Sir Charles said quietly. "Though I understand why it must appear that way to you. You have seen more than your share of cruel, selfish people."

"I do not know if there is anything left for me now. This place, these things, are all I know. But now I have peace knowing that I shall die forgiven and free. Thank you both. You have been very kind, nothing like the people who come here to steal treasure. I have no doubt that the villagers encouraged them to believe that I have no conscience, that I'm a terrible beast, once they come back down the mountain. But I have hope that it is almost over now."

"We will take you with us tomorrow," Sir Charles said.

"Yes! You must come with us when we leave," Louisa insisted.

"I told you, I cannot leave. It is too far to climb. My knees are bad. My ankles, my hips, they won't allow me to go so far. I tried to climb down once a few years ago."

"Then we will make a litter and the horses will help haul you down the mountain."

"It is too much trouble to go to for me. And the villagers will never let me leave."

"But if you don't get away from here, eventually someone will arrive with a small army of soldiers to capture you or kill you."

"I have done a lot of bad things. Perhaps I deserve whatever happens to me."

"None of us get what we deserve," Louisa was quick to say, "because God is merciful and forgiving, and He has forgiven you."

"I believe that is true. But I am too old to start over somewhere else. This mountain is my home."

Sir Charles said, "Very well, if you are determined to stay, I will petition some of the nobles I know to send their knights and guards to force the villagers to stop robbing people. And we will force them to stop harassing you."

"That's the best I could ever hope for. If you do that, I would be very grateful."

They ate the rest of their stew while Louisa marveled at how warm it was in the cave.

"Do you have any friends who visit you?" she asked.

"No. I don't have anyone since my mother died, only an elderly aunt who sometimes sends me small gifts through the villagers, when they allow it."

She felt sad that he didn't have friends or family besides his aunt, but if Allistor didn't have to worry about people coming to steal from him, or the villagers forcing him to rob and capture people, then he could live peacefully here on the mountain, warm all year round in his cave.

Allistor offered to let them spend the night in the cave,

but Sir Charles said they needed to stay with the horses in case someone tried to steal them.

Once they were outside, Louisa and Sir Charles began discussing what to do next.

"I don't like leaving him here," Louisa said.

"He won't leave, and there are multiple reasons it would be too difficult to get him down the mountain. I think he will be happy here, where he grew up. Besides, when all is said and done, we may be able to find some sympathetic villagers who will take care of him. But I must go to Strachleigh. The duke will give me at least a dozen knights, and I can get a dozen more from my brother Edwin. Then we can come back here and make sure those villagers never steal from anyone again."

Night had fallen, and though the moon was full and bright, because they were lying on the sheltered side of the large rocks, she could barely see his face. Her heart was full as she recalled his behavior earlier in the day.

"You were so very forbearing and kind to Allistor," she said. "You could have defended us and our horses, but you chose to listen to him instead. Thank you for that."

"You were the most forbearing and kind," he said in a low voice. "You are the most compassionate, humble, beautiful woman I have ever known."

Her breath caught in her throat. Had he really said what she thought he had? She stared hard into the darkness. He wasn't laughing. Or even smiling.

"What . . . did you say?" She didn't want to embarrass him. "That is, I admire you very much too."

Oh dear. She sounded patronizing. That was even worse.

"I think very highly of you, Louisa. How could I not? You are an amazing woman."

Her face was burning. She didn't know what to say and wished he would continue.

"We can talk more in the morning. Good night, Louisa."

Was it her imagination that his voice had sounded more intimate, like a man speaking to the woman he loved?

Her hand lay outside her blanket on the ground between them. He reached out and squeezed it, then brought it to his lips and kissed the back of her hand. He let go, then rolled over so that he was facing away from her.

Her heart was pounding against her chest. Sir Charles, whose friendship was all she ever thought she could hope for, had just kissed her hand after telling her she was the most humble, compassionate, beautiful woman he had ever known. That was what he had said, wasn't it?

Could life truly be so wonderful as this? Could Sir Charles be in love with her? But why had he turned away from her?

Surely being loved by Sir Charles was too good to be true. Oh, why couldn't morning come faster?

There it was, the first gray light of dawn beginning to illuminate the sky. Was it too soon to wake up Louisa?

Charles listened to her steady breathing, still with his back to her.

He had lain awake a long time. He hadn't planned to say what he'd said. Did she feel the same?

He knew without any doubt that Louisa was the good sort of person he'd always thought her to be. She had traveled all this way to reach this mountain, had gone through many trials, and found out that the Viking treasure she'd put so much hope in was not only out of her reach but didn't even exist, which meant that all her plans to save herself and Margaret had come to nothing. And yet she was worried about a man they had just met rather than about herself.

Perhaps he shouldn't have said anything to her when it was so late, or kissed her hand. Perhaps he should have waited until morning to tell her anything about his feelings, but a wave of love for her had swept over him and he couldn't resist. Then he had to turn away to stop himself from kissing her lovely lips.

"Are you awake?"

Louisa's voice startled him.

"Yes." He rolled over and was lying face-to-face with her.

She stared back at him with those lovely blue eyes and those lips that had haunted his dreams the night before. He tried to draw in a deep breath, but his throat was too tight.

She rubbed her face. "Did you want to go before the sun comes up?"

"We probably should. Louisa?"

"Yes?" She sounded a bit breathless as she gazed at him, her lips slightly parted.

"I meant what I said last night. I know you must be disappointed about not finding the treasure, but I want you to know that I will always take care of you and Margaret."

She seemed to be waiting for something more.

He was ruining this. There was no halfway now. He sat up,

taking both of her hands in his as she sat up too. "I love you, Louisa, and I want to marry you."

"You . . . love me?"

"I do."

She threw her arms around him, pressing her face into his chest.

He wasted no time encircling her in his arms and pulling her close.

They had both slept in their clothes, but the morning air was cold. He hardly felt it, though, as he held her.

"So does this mean you will marry me?" he asked.

"Yes." She laughed against his shirt. "Yes, I will marry you."

He stood and helped her to her feet, embracing her and burying his lips in her hair.

"Perhaps I should have waited to ask you in a more romantic and thoughtful way." He had never been very smooth in the way he addressed a beautiful woman. "I promise I shall make up for it."

"Good morning."

Allistor's unmistakable voice came from the cave entrance behind him.

Charles quickly placed a kiss on Louisa's forehead before stepping aside and turning around, one arm still around Louisa.

"Good morning," they both said back to him.

"I know how this must look," Charles said, sounding awkward again, "but I have just asked Louisa to marry me, and she has said yes."

Louisa laughed, no less adorable for how nervous she sounded. In fact, she was the most adorable creature in the world, and he could finally allow himself to say so.

"That is very happy news. Let us celebrate with some breakfast," Allistor said with his crooked smile.

Charles took her smaller, softer hand in his as they followed the man, ducking, into his cave. He couldn't resist bringing her hand to his lips once again and kissing it.

She sighed, such a happy sound that it filled up his chest and made him wonder for the hundredth time what it would be like to kiss her.

"You must eat quickly," Allistor was saying. "The villagers are lazy people, especially now that they are so wealthy, but when they roll out of their beds, they will be coming here to get your horses—and your names so they may send their ransom letters."

Allistor had packed them some food, including bread that he had made in his little fireplace. It was covered with ash, but it was fresh and would taste good with the butter he had wrapped in cheesecloth.

They ate the eggs and toasted bread he had prepared for them. Allistor gave them some instructions on which path to take, and then he hurried them out and on their way.

"We shall return as soon as we can," Louisa assured their new friend, then hugged him. He patted her on the shoulder with his enormous hand, and as he blinked back tears, Charles could see Louisa blinking rapidly as well, probably realizing she might never see the large bear of a man again.

Soon they were on their way down the mountain.

Charles reminded himself to stay alert. He was thinking so much about Louisa that he was in danger of forgetting where he was, and that was a mistake that could get them killed.

Twenty-One

LOUISA COULD HARDLY BELIEVE THAT AFTER FEELING SO resistant to marriage, thinking she'd never want to give up her freedom to a man, how happy she was now about getting married. But it was Sir Charles! And Sir Charles had specifically said that he would take care of her and Margaret. It was truly wonderful to be marrying a good man, even if he was not so very wealthy.

Goodness and integrity had never factored into her uncle's desire for a husband for her. And her aunt had preached to her and Margaret over and over again about how marriage was their duty, to the point that Louisa longed only for freedom.

A niggling of fear and doubt still lingered at the back of her thoughts. Was she falling into the same trap that her uncle and aunt had set for her—marriage and a life of having babies until her body was so worn down that it gave up?

That was her fear talking, fear and the loathing she had for her uncle's greedy desire to marry her off, as well as her aunt's constant lecturing about marriage, like the incessant hammering of nails when the servants were building a new barn. And the more her aunt lectured, the more Louisa just wanted to rebel against anything and everything her aunt told her.

But Sir Charles was a man of her own choosing, a man who was not wealthy enough to enrich her uncle's coffers, and yet she knew they would need at least a bit of wealth and their own place to live. Otherwise, how could they ensure that Margaret was taken care of? Her uncle never would release his claim on her without some form of payment.

She didn't know where they would live or how he would provide for them, but that was what he had promised, and she believed him. He'd never lied to her, and he'd proven his character and courage over and over.

Now, as they made their way down the mountain with their horses, riding when the way was not too steep, going on foot when it was, she couldn't stop glancing at Sir Charles. And more often than not, he was glancing her way too, and smiling.

How good it felt to be loved and wanted. She'd never felt this way before. It was as if the part of her heart that had been missing ever since her mother and father had died was being brought to life again.

Her foot slipped in a particularly steep spot. Sir Charles grabbed her arm, although she'd already stopped sliding.

"Going down is even harder than going up," Louisa said, "although I wouldn't have thought so yesterday."

"I'll catch you if you fall." He wrapped his arm around her.

"Thank you." She smiled, gazing up at him. What would he

do if she just stood on her toes and kissed him? She was a bit dizzy just thinking about it.

"There is a place just ahead that Allistor told me about. I want to show it to you. Come this way."

Now that he mentioned it, she had noticed Allistor and him talking quietly when she returned from a few moments of privacy in the bushes.

Sir Charles moved diagonally, instead of straight down, veering off the path that was barely visible in the grass. He seemed to be heading toward a large outcropping of rocks on the side of the mountain. As they drew nearer the rocks, Louisa heard the sound of rushing water. And when they came around the side of the huge boulders, she saw a waterfall, much bigger than the one they'd seen the day before.

"It's beautiful!" Louisa cried, clasping her hands and letting out a little giggle. "My whole life I've never seen such a large waterfall." She couldn't seem to stop sighing over the way the water looked and sounded—powerful and yet peaceful at the same time.

"I'm glad you like it so much."

She noticed out of the corner of her eye that Sir Charles had dropped to one knee on the ground beside her.

"My lady, Louisa," he was saying, his hands outstretched toward her.

She gasped, tears flooding her eyes.

"I want you to know that I love you. And beside this waterfall, and on the side of this mountain, I declare my love for you, Louisa Lenton, and my intention to marry you as soon as may be, if you will have me."

He actually had a sheen of tears in his eyes, which made them even bluer and sent a thrill of love straight into her heart.

Louisa couldn't speak as she struggled to stop her own tears from falling. Sir Charles took her hands in his as she gazed into his handsome face. His expression was achingly earnest.

This was too good to be true, but it was true nevertheless.

"I will! I love you too."

He seemed to expel a breath he'd been holding, and with one movement, he stood, pulled her into his arms, and kissed her lips.

She no longer felt the crisp, cool morning air as her heart pounded. His lips were like a revelation, the way they moved over hers. It was a feeling she'd never experienced before, unnerving and yet thrilling. She leaned into him, her heart crying, *I love you, I love you*, over and over.

They stood beside the waterfall kissing, thoughts flitting, half-formed, through her mind as her spirit silently confessed her love.

When the kiss ended, Louisa leaned her forehead against his shoulder, her cheeks flushing hot.

He stroked her hair and said softly, "I wanted you to have a special memory of me asking you to marry me."

"It is wonderful," she said. "You are wonderful . . . so thoughtful." She looked up into his eyes. And just as she'd hoped, he kissed her again, this time even more intensely than before. It took her breath away.

When he ended the kiss, she suddenly realized she was stroking his jawline with her fingertips. He gazed into her eyes long enough to make her stomach flip, and then he kissed her again.

How enjoyable kissing was. She'd never imagined it would be this way. Did married people kiss every moment they were able? They must, surely.

They were both breathing hard when the kissing stopped.

Sir Charles brushed her cheek with his fingertips. "We should go before the villagers find us."

"I suppose we must," Louisa said.

He was smiling at her. "You are delightful . . . delightful and lovely." He kissed her cheek again. "But yes, we must go."

The horses had wandered a few feet away, and he went and caught hold of their reins.

"This is the most beautiful place," Louisa said, sighing with one last look at the waterfall. She would never forget this mountain waterfall or how loved she felt at this moment.

Two hours later, they were nearly down the mountain and Charles's chest was still full, as was his heart, as he remembered how Louisa reacted first to the waterfall and then to his declarations of love. She was truly the most delightful woman in the world, with her authentic reactions of awe and wonder. And he believed her when she said she loved him. He knew her well enough to know that if she didn't feel love for him, she would never say she did.

His heart was comforted after the blows to his pride wrought by Lady Mirabella and her fakery. But this was way beyond a salve to his wounded heart. He was truly, irrevocably in love with Louisa. He couldn't imagine a more perfect woman, and he would cherish her for the rest of his life.

230

An arrow whooshed past his head. Then he saw them—two men at the base of the mountain, shooting at him and Louisa.

"Get behind the horses!" Charles yelled to Louisa.

The horses were too valuable. They surely wouldn't shoot them—unless it was unintentional.

He put his body between her and the shooters as she scrambled behind the animals.

Charles grabbed his crossbow, which was already loaded with a bolt, and took aim at the closest archer. He shot the bolt straight into the man's shoulder. The man cried out and dropped his bow.

Charles quickly loaded the next bolt, took aim, and called out, "Leave us alone and I won't shoot you."

The second archer appeared undecided, holding his longbow and arrow at the ready. He looked back at his friend, who was sitting on the ground, clutching his shoulder, then at Charles. Finally, he slowly pointed the arrow at the ground and released the string.

Charles used his hand to motion Louisa forward. "Take the horses and keep going."

"You're coming too, are you not?" Her voice was high, the only indication she was afraid.

"I am right behind you. Don't worry."

He kept his crossbow trained on the men in case they changed their minds about shooting at them again. He picked up one of their arrows as he went, tucking it under his arm. Thankfully, they weren't the best shots and were only villagers, not trained warriors. They went the other way, with the injured man leaning on the other one.

Louisa was moving fast, pulling the horses along.

"I think we can ride now," he said as he caught up with her.

They mounted their horses and rode the rest of the way, letting the horses go at their own pace, which was faster than walking. The mountain was less steep on this side, and they were riding at an angle toward the western side of the mountain, the way Allistor had instructed them, to avoid going through the village.

When they were at the bottom of the mountain, they urged their horses to go faster, riding through a valley where sheep were grazing.

Soon they were galloping toward a road they could see in the distance that looked hardly traveled, so grown up as it was with weeds and grass. When their horses turned onto the road, they pushed them to go faster as they wound around the hills and valleys just west of the village.

When they came to the crossroads Allistor had told him about, they turned south and rode until Charles was sure they were south of the village.

"We will stay on this path for several more miles," Charles told Louisa, now that they had slowed the horses to a trot. "It will lead us back to the more traveled road, and we can stay on it all the way through Yorkshire."

She nodded. "Poor Allistor will have to suffer for our escaping, especially since we took our horses. What do you think they will do to him?"

"I don't know." To reassure her, he said, "They will be angry with him, but they won't harm him, since they need him to make money. We will be back soon with a small army, and they will never threaten him or withhold anything from him again."

"I am glad. Is that where we're going now? To gather an army of men to save Allistor and all the treasure seekers they might try to take captive or rob in the future?"

"Yes. It should take about seven days to get to my brother Edwin in Bedfordshire. He will have some guards he can spare, and from there we can go to the Duke of Strachleigh, and he will give us enough knights to round out our army. They can both send word to King Richard about what we're doing and why."

"That sounds like an excellent plan." She was smiling at him and looking so beautiful she just might stop his heart from beating.

"You may stay with my brother and his wife, Lady Audrey. They will love you. And then I shall return to you as soon as I can, which should only be two weeks, or three at the most."

"Can I not go with you?"

He didn't want to hurt her feelings, but she must understand that the other men would not look favorably upon a woman coming with them on such a mission.

She must have read the look on his face, for she said, "It is all right. But I shall miss you terribly."

"And I shall miss you, but I'll sleep better knowing you're safe with Edwin and Audrey."

They rode on, and he was grateful she didn't cry, for he might have shed a tear or two himself if he had seen her tears.

The day was drawing to a close, the sun dipping low, and Charles could see that Louisa's head and shoulders were drooping. He began to be afraid she might fall from the saddle.

"Let us stop for the night," he said.

"It's early yet, but I am tired," she said.

"I had hoped we might come to a town where we could find an inn."

"You know I don't mind sleeping on the ground." She smiled at him, even though she had dark circles under her eyes. She must have slept very little the night before.

She was so brave.

Before he could turn his horse off the road, he heard people coming their way. Soon a group of men rode toward them from the south.

He and Louisa had slowed to a walk when Louisa suddenly gasped.

"It's my uncle. I have to hide."

But it was too late. They had already seen her.

"Stop them!" the man in the lead shouted. "That's my niece! Stop!"

There was no use trying to outrun them. Besides, he didn't want to risk Louisa's safety.

"Don't let them take me away." Louisa turned to him with pleading eyes.

Two of the men with her uncle unsheathed their swords. Charles drew his, moving his horse to stand between Louisa and them.

He recognized the men as Sir Gilbert and Sir Henry, a couple of mercenary knights who hired themselves out, whom he had met when he was sent to serve in Lady Mirabella's father's guard. He knew them to be unscrupulous and brutal. And while one was headed straight toward Charles, the other was trying to flank him and come around behind Louisa.

Charles backed up his horse until he was alongside Louisa's.

"If you touch a hair of her head," Charles said, looking first at Sir Gilbert and then at Sir Henry, "I shall kill you."

Neither of them were excellent swordsmen, but if they attacked him at once, he would be hard-pressed to defeat them both.

"It isn't you we want." Sir Gilbert grinned and his teeth were just as black as Charles remembered.

"Like I said," Charles told him, pushing back all emotion, "if you harm her, or even touch her, you are dead."

"I demand to know your name," the pompous man in the lead said. His beard was untrimmed and he spoke like someone who was used to being obeyed, even though he was surly and unkempt.

"You are Louisa's uncle, I presume," Charles said. "I am Sir Charles Raynsford of Dericott. My brother is the Earl of Dericott." He loathed using his brother's status to get himself out of trouble, but he would gladly do so if it would save Louisa from being taken from him.

"I am Lord Reedbrake, and you are traveling with an unmarried maiden, alone. What do you have to say for yourself?"

"The lady and I are pledged to be married. We are on our way to my brother's home in Bedfordshire to have the banns cried in my home parish as well as hers."

"Not without my permission!" he sputtered. The man was

posturing in the saddle, raising himself up, frothy spit getting in his beard with every word. "I am her guardian, and she is under my authority."

"The lady is of age. She can decide for herself."

"How dare you! She will marry whomever I say she shall marry. If you are not prepared to pay handsomely for the privilege, you will hand her over now, or my men will take her by force. What is your fortune?"

Charles felt the heat rising, his hand gripping his sword hilt. But he had to be calm and act in a manner that would ensure Louisa's safety and well-being.

"Perhaps I have no fortune at present, but I will care for the lady and provide for her. As I said, I am taking her to Dericott Castle in Bedford—"

"You will do no such thing! Guards, take her—"

"Stop!" Charles's voice rang out. No one moved. "These men will not touch her. Do you understand?"

"You do not give orders to me! Attack him! What do I pay you for?"

Charles did his best to move away from Louisa and her horse as Sir Gilbert brought his sword down, obviously aiming for his head. Charles blocked it with his own blade.

Louisa screamed.

Twenty-Two

Both knights came at Charles at once. He fought them, angling his body toward first one knight, then the other, keeping his horse moving from side to side to throw his opponents off-balance.

"Stop! Stop this!" Louisa tried to ride her horse in between them.

Sir Gilbert and Sir Henry backed their horses away. No doubt they were thinking that they would get paid whether they injured Charles or not, and they did not want Charles's seven brothers, including his brother-in-law, hunting them down and demanding an eye for an eye.

Then he realized Louisa's uncle had also been shouting at them to stop.

"You lackwits!" Her uncle yelled at the two mercenaries. "You incompetent swine herders. You could have injured my niece."

Louisa had moved her horse close to Charles's. She reached out and grabbed his shirt, leaning over in her saddle, forcing her horse to stay close to Charles's.

"Louisa! Come away from that man!"

"No!" she yelled back. "I will not leave him."

"You must and you will!" her uncle said. He trotted his horse over to her and grabbed her shoulder.

She yelped in pain, and Charles saw that he was pinching her between her neck and her shoulder.

Charles shoved the man's arm, forcing him to let go. He maneuvered his horse closer to Louisa's uncle and said between clenched teeth, "You will not hurt her, or as God is my witness, I will come and find you and do exactly to you as you have done to her—and worse."

The man backed his horse away from Charles and looked at Louisa. "If you do not come with me, I shall have my men follow you, and while you are both asleep, they will slit Sir Charles's throat and bury his body where no one will find him."

The uncle was cleverer—and more malicious—than he'd given him credit for. "Perhaps you will, and perhaps I will get to you first." Charles at least had the satisfaction of seeing the fear on her uncle's face.

Big tears were sliding down Louisa's cheeks. "Very well, I will come with you."

Charles's heart sank to the pit of his stomach. But perhaps it was safer for her to go with her uncle. He wouldn't harm her, for she was too valuable to him, but it made Charles sick to think of her at the mercy of that man.

"But you must let me say farewell to Sir Charles," she quickly added.

The uncle motioned to his henchmen, and they moved away about ten feet.

Still mounted on their horses, Louisa held on to Charles's arm while he held his sword to one side and cupped her face in his other hand.

"I couldn't let them hurt you," she said. "They would keep coming for you, and you wouldn't be safe." She started to sob.

He kissed her trembling lips. "I don't like letting you go with them. I will fight them if you want me to."

"No, please don't. I can't bear it if—" Her voice was choked off by a sob.

"Do you think they will harm you? If you do, I will—"

"No, they won't hurt me. You go and get help for Allistor. I'll be all right." Tears were running down her cheeks, but at least she wasn't sobbing.

"I'm so sorry they found us, but I will come for you. You just have to wait for me."

"I will," she said in a watery voice. "Follow your plan, raise your army, and after you save Allistor, then you can come and get me."

"I will. We will be married very soon. Nothing has changed."

"That's enough!" her uncle called out. "You've said your farewells. Now let us go."

"If you try to marry her to anyone else," Charles said to him, "I shall make you wish you had never been born."

Lord Reedbrake's expression faltered. He cleared his throat

and said, "I shall give you a week, perhaps two, to come up with the bride price."

"Remember my words," Charles said. "You will rue the day."

Louisa moved away from him. "I love you," she said softly, her eyes trained on his.

"I love you, my soon-to-be wife."

He watched her leave with her uncle and the other men, thinking over how he might follow them and take her away after they were all asleep. But Edwin's castle was probably six days away, and it seemed unwise to assume he would be able to keep Louisa and himself safe from Sir Gilbert and Sir Henry for that long.

Charles watched until she was out of sight, then put away his sword and sat in the saddle, clenching his fists.

He should have stopped them from taking her. She was safer with him! He could have fought Sir Henry and Sir Gilbert. They were mediocre swordsmen at best. He should have told her uncle what he thought of him—that he was a greedy, selfish man unworthy of the privilege of being the guardian for Louisa and her sister.

But that would have served no purpose except to vent his feelings.

If that uncle of hers did anything to hurt her, Charles would make good on his promise and make him sorry he was ever born.

His head ached and he wanted to tear something apart and beat it to a pulp. But there was one thing he could do, the only thing that would have any positive effect, and that was pray. So he started praying fervently, letting his horse walk down the road toward Dericott Castle.

Louisa kept her head down, letting the tears track down her face as long as no one could see. They were as much tears of fury as sadness. How dare her uncle tell Sir Charles he couldn't marry her unless he could pay?

How was it that a woman could not even control her own life and had no right to decide whom she would marry, or even whether she would marry? Even Jesus had women followers who went where they pleased and supported Him out of their own means. More than a thousand years later, women had no more power, even less than in Jesus' lifetime.

Sir Charles was so brave, and when he told her, "I will come for you. You just have to wait for me," he had looked so incredibly noble and handsome, she felt as if her heart was breaking. When would she see him again?

Traveling with her uncle and his disgusting men was arduous, but most nights they slept at a manor house or castle, where her uncle could pretend to be someone important to the lord of the manor or the noble castle owner.

Once, she caught one of her uncle's men staring at her with a disgusting grin, and instead of looking away, he'd looked her up and down. She said to him, loud enough for everyone to hear, "Keep leering at me, toad, and Sir Charles will cut out your liver when he returns for me."

The man's leer instantly disappeared from his face, and he

took a step back. She never caught him staring at her again. Indeed, she made sure to glare anytime she caught one of them looking her way.

Heartless, odious men. Sir Charles was better in every way when compared to her uncle and his men. Good, kind, loving Sir Charles. And he wanted to marry *her*.

She could hardly wait to tell Margaret all about him. But in the meantime, she would pray for him, every single day, for his safety and favor and success. And that he would come back and marry her.

Louisa was so happy to see Margaret running across the yard toward her, she practically leapt from her horse. She hugged her sister and kissed her cheeks and cried.

"Louisa! You look different. Did you find the treasure? What was it?"

"Yes and no. I'll tell you all about it when we are alone."

Her uncle had not spoken three words to her in the eight days it had taken them to reach home. He was more furious with her than she had ever seen him. Much of his fury must have come from the fact that her running away—and his wish to get her back so he could sell her off—had forced him to get up off his cushioned chair and do something.

She was even glad to see Aunt Celestria and Hanilda, even though they were both giving her withering looks, standing in the doorway with their hands on their hips. Even though her aunt lectured her often on her duty as a woman and a wife, Louisa still loved her. And Hanilda only pretended to scold and be grumpy with her when her aunt and uncle were around.

She walked toward them with her arm around Margaret.

Margaret whispered, "Do you have the treasure? I need to know because two men are coming here tomorrow."

"That's ridiculous. We have not been home . . . Uncle has not been home."

"Aunt Celestria arranged it."

A feeling of dread settled on Louisa's shoulders, but she had to say something reassuring to Margaret.

"We don't have to marry anyone. I am already pledged to be married—to a knight—and he is coming to fetch us soon."

"You are?" Margaret was now speaking loudly. "Who is he? Is he handsome? Can I come live with you?"

"His name is Sir Charles, and yes, he is handsome, and yes, you will come and live with us. He has already said so."

"What is this?" Aunt Celestria asked. "The prodigal daughter returns and she thinks she's betrothed?"

"To a knight!" Margaret jumped up and down and squealed.

"I have pledged to marry him. He must rescue our friend in the north, in Yorkshire, and then he will return for me."

"How long will that take?" Margaret was asking as her aunt was also talking.

"Ah, sure he will return for you. Sure he has to rescue someone first. You never should have left home, Louisa. You've been taken advantage of."

"Shut your mouth, Celestria," her uncle said in a hushed

voice. "He is a knight from a noble family, the man who asked to marry her, but he is poor, and therefore I cannot give him permission." He leaned closer to his wife and whispered harshly, "Do you want word to get around that she is no longer a pure maiden?"

Celestria scowled at him and then at Louisa. "It hardly matters."

"Of course it matters."

"The merchant, Scarcliff, and his friend, Lord Wingfield, are coming here tomorrow to meet them," she told her husband with an air of pride.

"You didn't know when we would be back. Why did you invite them?"

"Well, you are back now, are you not?" She crossed her arms over her chest and went inside the house.

Her uncle scowled darkly at Louisa. But then his scowl turned into an ugly smirk. "You are fortunate I found you when I did. Now you shall meet a man wealthy enough to marry you."

"I will not marry the man who is coming here tomorrow, nor any man but Sir Charles Raynsford of Dericott."

"You will marry whomever I tell you to." Her uncle was bending toward her, his finger in her face, his teeth showing in a menacing sneer.

Margaret leaned away from him, but Louisa stood her ground. "I will not marry anyone but Sir Charles, and when he comes for me, he will not look favorably upon you for threatening me or trying to force me to marry someone else."

Her uncle drew back his hand, as if to slap her across the face.

"I believe his words were, 'I will do exactly to you as you have done to Louisa—and worse.'"

"Empty threats!" her uncle shouted, but he lowered his hand and yelled in her face. "He is never coming to get you. And why should you want him to? He is poor. I have asked around. The man has no fortune, no land. He's an obscure knight with nothing."

"He has a powerful family and powerful friends, and he will distinguish himself and win favor with the king, and then he shall have whatever he wishes, much more than you or any of the men you try to force on me."

"Dreams! That's all you ever do is dream. Your head is in the clouds now, but if you and your sister do not marry well, you shall both be put out. I shall not continue to feed and clothe you. Not I! You can starve for all I care."

"You feed us with the money and tenants you got from my father and mother when they died."

A stinging slap across her mouth made her ears roar and her eyes water. She covered her mouth and took a step back.

Margaret started crying.

Hanilda came running and put her arms around Louisa and Margaret, pulling them away from her master.

"You will obey me," her uncle said, pointing at her, but his voice was quieter, and he was no longer snarling. He stomped away.

"Child," Hanilda said, turning Louisa to face her, "you mustn't goad the master. He was angry fit to die when you left. And defying him to his face will do you no good. Promise me you won't talk to him like that again."

"He isn't worth fighting with," Louisa said quietly. Her face was still burning from where he slapped her, and she tasted blood on her front teeth.

She thought of how Sir Charles would have reacted to her uncle's slap, feeling soothed by imagining him slapping him exactly as he had slapped her, but harder.

She would never stop defying her uncle, not as long as he tried to force her to marry someone besides Sir Charles.

Lord God, please bring Sir Charles back to me quickly.

TWENTY-THREE

THE NEXT DAY LOUISA AND MARGARET WATCHED OUT THE window as the wealthy merchant, Godwyn Scarcliff, and his friend, Lord Wingfield, arrived about an hour before nightfall.

"You are to call him Master Scarcliff," her aunt had told her. "He is the one your uncle intends for you. He owns five ships and has two motherless children, since his wife died from birthing a third that was stillborn. And Lord Wingfield is for Margaret. He has a manor house three times the size of this one not far from London."

Louisa felt sick. She would not marry Master Scarcliff, but the very thought of it was horrifying, and even more horrifying was the thought of Margaret marrying anyone. She was still a child who liked to run and play and catch butterflies. Lord Wingfield would surely agree to a betrothal period of a few years. But then again, he might want to marry her immediately. And her aunt and uncle would agree to it.

"That Scarcliff fellow looks very old indeed," Margaret said. "Lord Wingfield looks much younger, but I don't want to marry him." She looked at Louisa with nervous eyes.

"Don't worry. I won't let Uncle force you."

"But what will you do?"

"I don't know yet. But no one can force us to marry. The Church protects us. Church law says we must be willing."

"They're here." Hanilda came bustling into the room. "Come, girls. Let me fix your hair."

She tucked the ends of Louisa's hair under her veil, no doubt so Scarcliff wouldn't notice that it was quite short. Next, she straightened Margaret's belt and smiled.

"Such lovely ladies," she said. "Now, make me proud of you. Be respectful and attentive, and don't make your uncle wrathful again. He has been angry all day." Hanilda aimed a pointed look at Louisa.

"We shall be good, Hanny," Margaret said, looking like the saint she was.

"Let us go, then."

Louisa planned to tell Scarcliff, as soon as she could do so without other people hearing, that she was pledged to marry a knight who was due to come and fetch her in a few weeks. She would tell him, politely, that she was sorry her uncle and aunt had wasted his time. And furthermore, her sister could not marry his friend because she and Sir Charles would soon be making her their ward, and they would never give their approval for him to marry one so young as Margaret.

Their guests were already seated at the large trestle table in the manor house's dining hall, and her uncle was in full charm mode, smiling and speaking warmly, inviting his guests to drink his ale and to expect a fine meal.

"And here are my lovely nieces." He extended his arm toward Louisa and Margaret as they entered the room and made their way to the table.

"Louisa, you sit here beside Master Scarcliff. And, Margaret, you sit here beside Lord Wingfield."

Louisa had to admit that Lord Wingfield was not disgusting-looking or old, but Master Scarcliff's face was pockmarked, which was not his fault, but his eyes were sallow and turned down at the corners, like a hound dog's. The worst part was the way he looked at her—with narrowing eyes that appraised her as if she were a horse he was considering purchasing.

The man gave her a slight frown, his droopy face almost making her laugh. But this was no laughing matter. How would Sir Charles feel if he could see what was happening? She could not allow this man to wed her, for in her heart she was already wed to Sir Charles.

She desperately wished he would hurry back for her.

Poor Margaret looked conflicted—afraid of displeasing their uncle while also afraid of being friendly, or even civil, to Lord Wingfield, which Louisa had warned her not to do. Perhaps she shouldn't have told her that. But it was their uncle's fault for putting them in this position.

Louisa watched Lord Wingfield carefully, making sure he did not do anything to make Margaret uncomfortable. But on the contrary, he looked very polite as he stood and offered his arm to her while she stepped over the long bench to seat herself between Aunt Celestria and Lord Wingfield.

Lord Wingfield had a pleasant face and did not seem unkind. Still, what kind of man considered marrying a twelve-year-old? It seemed indecent and uncouth.

Thankfully, Scarcliff spent most of his time talking to her uncle instead of her, which also had the added benefit of preventing her uncle from glaring at her.

Louisa kept a wary eye on Lord Wingfield and Margaret while she thought of Sir Charles, of his laugh, his voice, his face. She remembered how he'd seemed ready to kiss her in the Cockayne family's pavilion. She also remembered how he'd chased away the robbers who tried to steal from her, and how he'd put himself between her and just about every disaster she'd encountered.

But right now Allistor needed him, as well as all the people who might be tricked, robbed, or otherwise harmed by the villagers of Kilwyn.

Images of Sir Charles fighting those villagers were making tears well up in her eyes. She had to think of something else. She blinked furiously while reminding herself of how glad Margaret had been to see her. She'd been counting off the days by making notches in a stick she kept by her bed.

"I thought you would be home after two weeks," Margaret said. "It seemed to be taking you so long, and I thought of all kinds of things that might have caused you to tarry—terrible things."

Louisa had assured her that they would never be apart again.

And she meant it. Whatever she had to do, she was not letting her uncle marry off either of them.

The meal had lasted for almost three hours, during which time the servants had refilled Scarcliff's cup with ale several times. His cheeks were flushed when he turned to her uncle and said, "Shall we discuss the terms now of my marriage to your niece?"

Louisa's stomach churned.

Her uncle quickly said, "Yes, yes, of course. You may come with me."

Her uncle and Scarcliff both stood abruptly.

"Pardon me, but I cannot marry you." Her face heated as she spoke, staring hard at the man. "I am very sorry, Master Scarcliff, but I am pledged to marry a knight, Sir Charles of Dericott."

"No, that is not true," her uncle said, pointing at Louisa. "She is not pledged to marry. I have not given her my permission." He shook his head. "No."

"It is true. Sir Charles shall come for me soon. And he is not a man to be crossed."

Her words had the desired effect on Scarcliff, for he looked positively appalled.

"You did not tell me of a prior commitment," he said, turning toward her uncle.

"It only just happened," Louisa said before her uncle could respond, "and my aunt did not know about it until yesterday."

The old merchant huffed out a breath. "Well, then. It looks as if you have wasted my time."

"Do not leave just yet," her uncle said.

"Oh, I have no intention of leaving until morning. Do you expect me to travel in the dark?"

"Our time has not been wasted," Lord Wingfield said. "We have enjoyed your company"—he nodded at her uncle—"and that of your wife and nieces, as well as enjoying the good food and drink you have provided."

At least Lord Wingfield knew how to be courteous.

"I thank you," her uncle said, looking quite flustered. Then his eye landed on Louisa. "Go. You and your sister are dismissed."

Louisa happily obeyed, stepping away from the table and waiting for Margaret to scurry around to her side.

As they turned to go to their bedroom, she noticed Lord Wingfield staring after them with an amused look on his face.

Louisa was awakened the next morning by Hanilda whispering, "The master says you are not to have any food today because of what you did last night, and that you're not allowed to leave your room. He will punish me, too, if you do leave."

"Don't worry, Hanilda. I won't leave the room."

"Thank you, sweet Louisa." Hanilda slipped a bread roll into Louisa's hand.

Louisa stifled the laugh in case her uncle was near enough to her door to hear her.

"I'll bring you some food," Margaret whispered, smiling conspiratorially. "But I'm sorry you won't be able to go outside. It's a warm, sunny day."

"I'm glad I can't go outside," Louisa said. "I'm still tired from all the traveling I did. You can't imagine how exhausting it is to ride on a horse all day long. Besides, I don't want to see Uncle, especially right now." She winked at Margaret, trying to look playful and unworried.

"He isn't bad all of the time, Louisa. Priest says we should pray for those who make us angry and do bad things to us."

"I guess I'll be praying all day then." Louisa tickled Margaret's side, making her giggle.

"Stop that laughing," Hanilda whispered. "Do you want the master to hear you? He wants you to show remorse."

"Me too?" Margaret asked with wide eyes. "I didn't do anything, did I?"

"I suppose not, but you don't want to raise his suspicions, do you?"

Margaret shook her head.

"Well, then, come on to the kitchen with me and get your breakfast. Mercy, mercy, but I have more work to do than a body has time for," she muttered as she left the room with Margaret, closing the door after her.

Louisa spent the day sleeping and daydreaming about Sir Charles and all the adventures he must be having with his brothers, as he should have rounded up some guards and knights by now and be on his way back to Kilwyn and Allistor.

Would she ever see her new friend again? Was Allistor right in thinking that the pains in his chest were an indication that his life was near its end? The poor man.

Louisa had stayed up late the first night she was home,

telling Margaret all about her experiences. Her sister had a lot of questions about Allistor. Louisa even told her that she'd seen two large chests inside his cave, one of which surely contained Allistor's share of the stolen goods the villagers had taken and sold.

When Louisa told her about Sir Charles's proposal next to the waterfall, Margaret put her hand up to her forehead and pretended to swoon.

"I hope my future husband tells me he loves me and wants to marry me beside a beautiful waterfall, or maybe in a field of wildflowers, or during a beautiful sunset—or all three!"

Louisa laughed. "The man had better start hunting now for that special place."

Margaret turned thoughtful and quiet for a few moments, then said, "Uncle said some terrible things when the first group of men came back. They had spoken with Maury. Remember the little boy who sneaked into our room? He told them you were talking to him about the Viking treasure and he thought you were on your way to Yorkshire to find it. I was very upset to hear Uncle say what he did. I told him to stop saying such things about you."

"What things?"

"I don't want to tell you."

"It's all right. You can tell me. I won't be upset."

"He said you were the biggest fool in the world, thinking there was a treasure and that you could just go and take it."

"Well, Allistor did have a treasure, but it wasn't the Viking treasure we thought would be there."

Margaret looked sad. "But you are not a fool. Uncle was wrong about that."

"Yes, I was trying to save us both from bad marriages, and that was not foolish."

"He also said that because you are a woman, bad things would happen to you. That if he didn't find you soon, you would be with child and then you would be no good to him anymore."

"Our uncle has a depraved mind, and a greedy one, for all he cares about is the wealth he will gain from marrying us off." Louisa took a deep breath. She'd promised Margaret she wouldn't get upset at the things their uncle had said about her, so she forced the anger down before continuing.

"The truth is, it was dangerous for me to leave and go on a journey alone. Bad things certainly could have happened to me, and probably would have, if I had not found good people to travel with. I needed help to find good places to bed down for the night and to find food, and those who could keep me company and help me stay safe. What I'm trying to say is that I found a good person and I asked for his help. It is good to ask for help. We need other people to help us sometimes."

"You found Sir Charles, so it all turned out well."

"Yes, it did." Louisa smiled and let out a sigh. "It did indeed." The true treasure had been love . . . Sir Charles and their love for each other. It was better than money, because she didn't think money would make her nearly as happy as Sir Charles's love had made her.

Now she just had to wait and trust that Sir Charles would come for her and Margaret.

TWENTY-FOUR

AFTER FIVE DAYS, LOUISA'S UNCLE LET HER LEAVE HER room. Then he summoned her to the dining hall, where he sat in his chair like a king on his throne, slumped back into the cushion and frowning at her.

"So are you with child?"

"No, I am not." Her cheeks grew warm, more out of anger than embarrassment. "Are you with child?"

"That would be impossible."

"It is the same with me."

He just stared at her. Finally, he said, "How long before it is reasonable to expect Sir Charles will come for you? Two weeks? Three weeks? Four?"

"As it has already been two weeks since we parted, I would think it should be about two weeks from now."

"Very well. In two weeks, if he has not come for you, you will accept a marriage proposal from the man of my choosing. That is very reasonable of me, is it not?"

How could she agree to such a thing?

"I said, that is very reasonable of me, is it not?"

"I can see how you might think it is reasonable," Louisa said, forcing down her emotions, "but you must also see that if something prevents Sir Charles from executing his duties in a timely manner, and in the event that something should go wrong, it may take him a bit longer than two weeks."

"No." He sat up and leaned forward, his jaw twitching. "You said two weeks. He should be here in two weeks, and I am holding you to that. In the meantime, you will meet whomever I wish you to meet and you will not mention that you are pledged to marry someone else. Is that understood?"

She did not want to answer him, but she also knew he would keep badgering her if she didn't. "Very well. I trust Sir Charles, and I know he is capable and determined. I believe he will be here in two weeks."

"And in the meantime, you will be expected to meet with any suitors I present to you, and you may not tell them you are betrothed to someone else. If you do not follow my wishes, I shall force Margaret to marry the first man who asks for her."

He knew just how to threaten and manipulate her. But no matter what, she would not allow Margaret to marry anyone who was cold or cruel. She would do whatever she had to do for her sister, even if it meant running away again and taking Margaret with her.

MELANIE DICKERSON

"Very well."

"Remember this conversation," he said, pointing his finger at her.

"Oh, I shall." And he would regret being so onerous and demanding when Sir Charles came for her. Indeed, she hoped he quaked in fear when Sir Charles asked him why he was such a cruel, greedy guardian.

Knowing that the sooner he finished what he had to do, the sooner he could be reunited with Louisa, Charles had pushed himself and his horse to ride harder and longer than he normally would.

He ended up gathering knights and soldiers from his brother Edwin, his brother-in-law, Strachleigh, and his brother Merek. Berenger's castle was along the eastern coast and too far out of the way, but Merek's was practically on the way, and it was just the sort of mission Merek would relish.

As Charles had expected, Merek agreed to accompany him and their group of thirty knights and ten longbowmen.

He chafed at how long it was taking, as he hadn't factored in the delays at each stop while the knights and soldiers were rounded up and made ready. Also, a letter had to be written to the king, signed by each of them, explaining their mission.

It was even suggested by Strachleigh that they wait until they had heard from the king, to ensure he approved their mission.

"No. I promised Allistor I would return as soon as possible. It is the right thing to do, and I do not want to tarry." Besides, Louisa was waiting for him.

"As long as we don't massacre the villagers," Merek said, "which I know we don't plan to do, I don't see why the king would object to our stopping the thievery."

Merek was never one to back down from a fight. And since their brother David was visiting him at the moment, he was also eager to go with them.

David said, "I agree. Furthermore, I'm tired of doing nothing but training and sitting around. I'm ready to right some wrongs and see new places while I'm doing it."

Merek shook his head and ruffled David's hair, causing him to sidestep and slap his hand away.

Merek was so different from the way he was before he married. He used to be so angry all the time, always ready for a fight. It made Charles wonder how marriage might change him. Which made him think about Louisa having to live with that awful uncle of hers. Which made him want to get on with the mission.

Thankfully, his brothers agreed, and they were soon on their way to Yorkshire.

Louisa was surprised at how many men her uncle was able to get to come to their manor house to look over her and Margaret. She was also amazed at how unacceptable most of them were.

"The only good one was the one we had dinner with right after you came home," Margaret said. "Lord Wingfield."

"What did he say to you?" Louisa hoped her sister wasn't set on someone who would agree to marry a twelve-year-old. "And how old was he?"

"He told me he was twenty-eight. And he said he didn't know I was only twelve when he agreed to come, and he thought I was a bit too young to marry."

"At least he had that much decency."

Their uncle, on the other hand, didn't seem to have any decency at all. He paraded them before men of every age, from sixteen to sixty, sometimes several of them in one day.

Another week and a half had gone by when her uncle met her in the yard outside as he was coming back from the privy.

"Any word from Sir Charles?"

"No, not yet." She crossed her arms and met his gaze.

"Only four more days." He raised his brows at her.

She said nothing.

Her uncle smiled his snakelike smile and went into the house.

Louisa went to her room to pray.

Charles had been away from Louisa for four long weeks, and he rode his horse hard toward the little village of Maydestone, the location of Louisa's family's manor house. But when he arrived, the house was closed up and there was a lock on the door. He soon found a tenant family living nearby and asked about Louisa and her uncle.

"Oh, you must be looking for Eluard, Lord Reedbrake. He is Lord of the Manor of Maydestone."

"Where does he live?"

"Reedbrake, about ten miles east of here," they told him.

"And he is the uncle of Louisa Lenton?"

"Louisa is the oldest of his nieces, I believe. Yes, you will find Louisa there, I daresay."

"Thank you."

He should have remembered that even though Louisa often talked of her childhood home, she'd been forced to move to the manor house where her uncle lived.

He rode for two or three miles before the disappointed ache in his chest left him and he started anticipating seeing Louisa again. It would not be long now.

"I'm sorry, old boy," he said apologetically to his horse. "But we shall be there soon."

He finally arrived in the village, asked for directions to Reedbrake Manor, and pushed his horse on. "Less than half a mile now," he assured himself and the horse.

Finally, the house came into view, a rather run-down looking place, with an ugly wattle fence around the front yard.

Suddenly he saw Louisa burst out of the house through the front door, her uncle holding her arm as he was yelling at her.

A younger girl, about a foot shorter than Louisa, ran out of the door behind them, shouting, "Stop! Don't hurt my sister!"

Charles galloped up the lane, drawing the attention of Louisa, then her uncle a moment later. He let go of her arm.

"Sir Charles!" Louisa cried, a smile breaking over her face.

He dismounted and strode to Louisa, who met him halfway, throwing her arms around him.

Holding her close to his chest with one arm, he turned to her uncle. "I saw you holding her arm and practically dragging her, and I heard you yelling at her. What else have you done to her? You remember that I promised to do exactly to you what you did to her."

His face blanched white.

"I-I didn't do anything—She . . . That is, she is very well, as you see."

"Are you well?" He turned to Louisa as she lifted her face to look into his eyes.

"Yes, but I am so glad to see you."

She was staring at his lips, and he leaned down and kissed her, his heart soaring.

When he ended the kiss, she was staring up at him with a dreamy-eyed smile, an expression that made his lungs fill with air. But the next moment he was wondering what she had been through the last few weeks.

"Hey, you can't kiss her," her uncle said, although he had backed away a few feet. "I have promised her to someone else, someone who will pay the bride price to marry her, and unless you can pay the same price . . ."

Charles glared at the man. "How dare you try to marry her to someone else when I told you she was pledged to marry me."

The man opened his mouth but didn't speak.

"Furthermore, she has been summoned by the king. King Richard wishes to speak to her."

"That's preposterous. Why would the king want to talk to Louisa?"

"I don't have to tell you anything." Charles pushed past the man and went into the house, holding Louisa close to his side. "Go and get all your things, and tell Margaret to get hers."

"I'm here!" Margaret cried from behind him, a huge smile on her face. "I'm getting my things!" She ran past him.

Louisa kept hold of his hand and led him in the same direction.

He watched as she and Margaret threw their clothing and other scant belongings into three drawstring bags.

"Was I really summoned by the king?" Louisa asked in a quiet voice.

"Yes, you were. We sent a letter to the king explaining what we were about to do in Kilwyn, and now he wants to hear a report about the giant and the money the villagers stole and how we convinced the villagers to stop robbing and capturing treasure seekers."

"But I wasn't there when you dealt with the villagers."

"I know, but that is King Richard's way. He wants to hear the whole story from many witnesses."

She looked a bit worried, but she was probably too eager to leave to ask any more questions. And a moment later, they were finished packing.

Charles took the bags and threw them over his shoulder. "Shall we go?"

"We should say farewell to Hanilda and Aunt Celestria," Margaret said, an anxious look on her face.

"Let us find them, then."

They hadn't gone far, with Louisa and Margaret leading

the way, before they encountered a middle-aged woman in an apron. Margaret exclaimed, "Hanilda! We are going. Fare well, dearest Hanilda."

She wrapped her arms around the rather rotund servant woman, who embraced her back.

"Your knight has come for you, then?"

"Yes, Hanilda. It's Sir Charles."

"He is so handsome. Oh, dear." The woman started sniffing, rapidly blinking her eyes. "I will miss my two best girls in the whole world."

"We will miss you too, Hanilda." Margaret sounded too excited to be sincere.

Louisa squeezed the woman's arms. "I will send for you if you wish it," she said quietly.

"Oh, saints above. Mayhap, I don't know." The woman was crying in earnest now.

"Who is this?" A lady came into the house, waving her hands.

"Aunt Celestria," Margaret said, "it's Sir Charles. He's come to marry Louisa."

"Sir Charles." The lady greeted him with a small bow. "Louisa has told us so much about you. Your brother Edwin is an earl, I believe."

"Good morning to you . . . Lady Celestria, is it?"

"I am Louisa's aunt. Her uncle and I have taken care of Louisa and her sister since my poor sister died."

"Your service and sacrifice are most appreciated," he said, just in case there really was any service or sacrifice to speak of, which, from Louisa's accounts, he doubted.

A half smile graced Louisa's lips as she looked askance at him, probably wondering if his words were sincere.

The uncle came in behind his wife—hiding behind her, as it seemed—and said, "You didn't say how much you were willing to pay to marry her."

"No, I didn't." Charles pushed past the aunt and uncle, pulling Louisa alongside him, with Margaret hopping along in front.

He saw the look on Louisa's face. Was she worried about him not being willing to pay for her? He didn't want her to think that he didn't value her more than any other man might.

"If all you care about is money, Lord Reedbrake, I shall give you money, every penny you were asking for her, but Louisa is worth far more than mere coins, silver and gold. And besides that, she is not yours to sell."

The uncle blustered while they went out the front door, following them out.

"No one said anything about selling . . . That is preposterous. But it is customary to offer a bride price to the parents."

He used restraint and didn't say what he was thinking. "You will hear from me very soon," Charles said and started loading his horse with the bags.

"I'll go and get my horse," Louisa said.

"You're welcome to take my horse," her uncle said to her, "but I expect to be paid for it."

"Louisa's horse was paid for by me," Charles told him. "But since you offered, Margaret will take a horse and I shall reimburse you for it." Charles dug in his saddlebag for his coin pouch.

"Margaret? Margaret is not leaving," the man said, looking alarmed. "Margaret cannot go with you. She must stay here."

"Margaret and Louisa are sisters. Margaret goes where Louisa goes."

The man cursed under his breath, turning away. "I shall expect payment for—"

Charles approached the man from behind and held out a handful of nobles, enough to pay for the finest of horses. The man held out his hand and Charles dropped the coins in his palm.

"Margaret is coming with us." Charles led his horse to the stable to find Louisa and Margaret, who were helping the servant boy saddle two horses. Charles tied his horse to a post and assisted.

Soon they were all mounted. The two sisters waved and called, "Fare well!" to the servants standing outside the house, some of them crying.

Finally. He drew in a deep breath as his eyes met Louisa's. He held out his hand to her. She grasped it and he squeezed. They were finally together again.

TWENTY-FIVE

LOUISA'S HEART WAS FULL AS THEY ENTERED LONDON AND headed to the alehouse called the Swan. It was at this alehouse that she would meet two of Charles's brothers, Merek and David, and his brother-in-law, whom he called Strachleigh.

She glanced at Margaret. Her eyes were wide as she repeatedly gasped and exclaimed about the buildings of London, whispering to Louisa about the hosts of people on the streets. Thankfully, the long hours on horseback the last two days had not dimmed her enthusiasm for new sights.

Even though Louisa had seen many villages and a few towns on her travels, nothing had prepared her for the enormity that was London. She'd seen some pretty churches, but the cathedral in London was bigger, taller, and much more detailed and elaborate than any other church she'd ever seen, and it was breathtaking. From anywhere in the town, one could see the White Tower of the Tower of London rising above everything surrounding it.

"Stay close to me," Charles said as the street became more and more crowded with people, carts, donkeys, mules, and horses.

Louisa kept her eye on Margaret, who was too busy looking at everything to pay attention to where she was going. Thankfully, Charles stayed close beside Louisa, who stayed close beside Margaret.

Charles seemed to know where he was going. Moving slowly through the streets, they made their way toward the White Tower. When they were probably half a mile from it, she saw the wooden sign ahead, with a freshly painted white swan and the words *The Swan*.

They dismounted and left their horses at a nearby livery stable. Then they walked to the Swan with Margaret chattering away like a magpie.

"Did you see the enormous church and the colored windows? And the statues on the outside? It was my favorite. Do you think we can go to the Tower of London and see the menagerie—the lion and the bear and the wildcats?"

Louisa looked to Charles. He was smiling.

"We can go see the king's menagerie," he said, "but first we must find my brothers."

Louisa loved the way Margaret's eyes were shining. How good it was for her to get away from Reedbrake and to see a bit of the world.

The Swan was a very charming alehouse, well-lit and better furnished than any of the inns she had seen. All the furniture looked new, and the men and women working there were cheerful and well-dressed. Even the glass in the windows was clean.

They had just walked inside when someone shouted, "Charles is here!"

A young man who slightly resembled Charles was waving at them from across the room.

They made their way toward a group, weaving their way around the tables.

Three men, all of them handsome, stood up when she, Margaret, and Charles approached.

"Louisa and Margaret, this is the Duke of Strachleigh and my brothers: Merek, who is the Viscount Burwelle, and Sir David, who is newly knighted. Brothers, this is my soon-to-be wife, Louisa Lenton of Maydestone, and her sister, Margaret."

They were all polite and warm as they greeted her and Margaret.

Immediately a young woman came and brought them tankards of ale and bowls of stew, with a large loaf of bread and some fresh butter.

"And this is Ro," Merek said, gesturing to the woman who was busy setting down their food and drink. "She is the very good friend of our brother Berenger's wife, Mazy."

Louisa smiled and greeted the young woman. She remembered the story Charles had told her about Mazy finding herself alone in London and selling goods in the market, then starting a business with a woman named Ro whose father owned an alehouse.

"I am honored to meet you," Louisa said.

"You will be very blessed being a part of this family," Ro said, winking at her. Then she rushed away to get the rest of their food.

The Duke of Strachleigh said, "We told her about you and Charles and how he wouldn't stop talking about you."

Louisa felt her cheeks flush. How strange it was to talk to men who were dukes and earls, and for them to talk to her as if she were an equal. And it was gratifying to know that Charles had told them about her. She glanced at him and saw that he was smiling down at her, not embarrassed at all.

"Allistor is very fond of you as well, Louisa," the brother called Merek said. He looked at Charles and asked, "Have you told her yet?"

"Not yet."

"Told me what?" She looked back and forth between Merek and Charles.

"Forget I said anything." Merek pinched his lips closed.

"I'll tell you later, when we have a chance to speak privately," Charles whispered next to her ear.

"What is it about?"

"Something Allistor wanted you to have. But don't worry about it now."

They ate their meal and laughed and talked, but mostly they listened to Charles's three brothers tell them stories. Her heart warmed at hearing tales about Charles when he was a boy, enjoying time with his brothers, roaming the woods, and even rescuing a baby bird that had fallen from its nest as it was being stalked by a wildcat.

As soon as they finished eating, he covertly gave her hand a gentle squeeze under the table, then held it while they talked.

"So when are we to meet the king?" Charles asked. "Tomorrow?"

"Day after tomorrow," David said.

"At the Tower?"

They nodded. "At the king's apartments."

Louisa felt her stomach do a nervous flip at the thought of meeting the king. Would she even be able to speak? Would he be frightening?

"The king just wants to hear about the treasure," David said.

Merek fluffed the hair on the back of David's head.

"Watch what you're doing to my hair," David said, smoothing it down.

Merek shook his head. "Always so vain."

"I am not. I just don't want to be walking around with my hair sticking every which way like a drunken man who's been asleep in a ditch."

They good-naturedly teased their younger brother, who must have been around eighteen years old.

"What are you thinking?" Charles asked Louisa while no one was paying attention to them.

She shook her head, then shrugged her shoulders.

"You're probably wondering where you and Margaret will

sleep tonight. I will go and talk with Ro and see if she has a good recommendation."

"Thank you."

He kissed her, just a peck on the cheek, but it made her happy, and she watched him go, admiring the way he walked—straight and tall but comfortable with himself.

When he came back during a lull in the conversation, he said, "Ro says she has a couple of rooms here, above her sleeping quarters, where the ladies and I can sleep." He turned to Louisa. "Not in the same room, obviously, but in the room next to you and Margaret. Is that satisfactory?"

"Yes, of course." She was glad he would be close to her and Margaret in this big, strange town.

They stayed and talked until night fell and the brothers left to go to their inn. Then Ro showed them to their rooms.

"This is where Mazy, Sir Berenger's wife, stayed for two years. But I rent it by the night now."

Ro pushed her unruly red hair behind her ear as she unlocked the door.

"There is this room, which has the bed you see there, and a second bedroom through that door there."

Charles went and opened the door to the second room. The bed in it was a bit larger. "You ladies can sleep in this second room, if that suits you, and I will sleep in the first room."

Louisa and Margaret both nodded.

"I had some water brought up for bathing and a foot tub. Let me know if you need anything else."

"Thank you so much, Ro," Louisa said, clasping the woman's hands. "We are very grateful."

"I'm more tired than I thought," Margaret said, starting to yawn.

"You go and take the first bath," Louisa said, having seen the buckets of water and the little foot tub in the second room.

"Very well." Margaret went into the other room and shut the door.

Charles wrapped Louisa in his arms and said, "How much I have missed you."

She buried her face in his chest, feeling shy now that they were alone for the first time. With all the riding and Margaret's questions, they hadn't even had a chance to talk. When she lifted her head, he was looking questioningly at her.

"Are you well? What was your uncle yelling at you about when I arrived?"

"He was trying to force me to agree to marry someone, a wine merchant from London."

"Forgive me for taking so long to get there. I came as quickly as I could."

"I know. It's not your fault my uncle is greedy."

"Did he hurt you?"

"Not really. He slapped me once, but . . ." She shrugged.

She could see by the way Charles's jaw twitched that he was clenching his teeth. "I should have asked you when we were there. I told him I would do to him what he did to you."

"I was so very happy to see you that I didn't care to tell you any of that. I'd rather just forgive him than see you slap him, to be honest."

"What else did he do?"

"Nothing, really. He made me stay in my room and said I wasn't allowed to eat, but Margaret and Hanilda brought me food anyway."

"I'm so sorry." He was touching her temple, gently stroking her skin in a way that made her weak in the knees.

Louisa wished he would kiss her. If he didn't kiss her soon, she would stand on her toes and kiss him. Finally, he was bending toward her, pressing his lips to hers, pulling her closer, then kissing her in a way that made her dizzy. When he lifted his head, she tottered slightly to one side.

"Steady," he said, pulling her close. "Do you need to sit down?"

"Just a bit dizzy. Your kisses are very powerful." She smiled flirtatiously.

"Well, I'm glad to hear that," he said in a deep, almost ragged voice, "but I don't want you to fall." He bent and lifted her up in his arms before she knew what he was about to do. Then he went to the bench that was set against the wall, sat down, and held her close to his side.

"What if Margaret sees us?" she said.

"We aren't doing anything wrong."

He started kissing her neck, making her weak and breathless. His kisses made her lose all thought besides how he made her feel . . . tingly and loved and pretty.

"We should stop before Margaret comes back." She sounded breathless.

"I'm not making you uncomfortable, am I?" he asked, his lips still on her neck, his breath sending pleasurable goose bumps across her shoulders and down her arms.

"No . . . not uncomfortable."

He leaned back and looked into her eyes. "I asked the priest at your parish church to cry the banns, and my priest as well."

"In three weeks we can be married?"

"Yes." He started on her neck and kissed his way up to her jawline, across to her chin, then his lips found hers and he kissed her passionately.

When he finally pulled away, they were both breathing hard. "You're right. I'd better be a bit more restrained until we're married and alone with a lock on the door."

His words surprised her. She stared up at him, then started to laugh. "Yes, that might be best."

TWENTY-SIX

THE NEXT MORNING THEY WERE ON THEIR WAY TO THE Tower of London to see the menagerie when Louisa suddenly remembered something.

"You forgot to tell me what Allistor wanted to give me. In fact, you haven't told me much of anything about what happened when you and the other men went to the village."

"It all went well." He was staring at the moat they were about to cross. "The villagers gave up the ransom they had taken from the first man they held captive and my brothers returned it to the man here in London. They also agreed to give up ten thousand nobles, plus some gold and silver coins. They said that was all they had taken from the people who came there to climb Allistor's mountain, besides what they had already spent."

"Ten thousand nobles? I can hardly imagine so much!" Truly, it was an enormous sum. A noble was a coin much more valuable than pennies, which was the most valuable coin most of the common people ever saw in a lifetime.

"My brothers have brought it here, to give to the king to decide how to distribute it, since we didn't know who to return it to."

"Oh my. And when you left Allistor, was he well?"

"Not so well." Charles grimaced. "He was having a lot of pain in his chest and was getting weaker. He thinks he doesn't have much time left."

"Oh. I wish I could see him one last time. But I know that we shall see him in heaven." She wished she could go and visit him, but it was so far, she hated to mention it. Charles had already made the difficult journey twice in a month's time.

"As I said, he sent you a gift," Charles said softly while they walked across the drawbridge toward the Lion Tower inside the Tower of London complex.

Margaret was exclaiming over a swan she saw swimming in the water of the moat, hardly noticing Charles and Louisa.

"What is it?"

"He didn't want you and your sister to have to live with your uncle, or to be married off and separated, so he sent you enough money to pay your way out of your uncle's debt—the bride price, in effect."

"Oh my. That is so very kind of him." She clasped her hands, her heart pounding. "So very kind."

She had wondered how Charles, a knight with no living as yet, would be able to pay a bride price that her uncle would accept.

"So Allistor gave his money to me?"

"We decided to let Allistor do as he wished with the

money, even though it was ill-gotten. He had suffered as much as anyone at the hands of the villagers, so we allowed it."

"Oh. Poor Allistor." She felt so sad that he was probably close to death and would never know the joy that Louisa had felt since she fell in love with Charles.

"He was happy that he no longer had to help the villagers steal from people. He seemed content and talked a great deal about heaven and being with Jesus. He had a small crucifix that he kept with him."

Charles was gazing at her with such compassion in his eyes. It was amazing to be the object of that kind of devotion from a man with such goodness, but who also possessed such fierceness and strength of will as he did.

Her heart missed a beat as she also remembered how good he was at kissing.

Truly, she could hardly ask for anything else. Except, perhaps, for a house.

The next day Louisa headed out with Charles and his brothers for their meeting with the king, leaving Margaret with Ro, who promised to put her to work and show her how to make bread.

"With what I learn today, I can run an alehouse or an inn someday." Margaret was grinning as she went back to watching Ro knead the bread dough.

Louisa had dressed carefully in the best dress that Richie had bought for her. She'd also enlisted Margaret's help with her hair, as Margaret was quite good at it and was able to attach her veil and disguise how unfashionably short her hair was.

She held on to Charles's arm while he walked close to her. Her heart beat hard as she thought about meeting the king and being forced to talk to him. Would she lose her breath? Would she even be able to speak?

"Don't be afraid," Charles said. "I'll be right beside you. The king is very favorably disposed toward my family. Besides that, he will be happy about the money we're bringing him."

The brothers led a horse-drawn cart with a large trunk full of coins, which they had covered with a blanket. They had also been joined by two other knights who had helped them in Kilwyn, no doubt to help guard such a large sum of money.

Louisa was amazed at the buildings inside the walls of the Tower of London and couldn't take her eyes off them. The White Tower was the most magnificent, but there were many other towers and buildings, most of which were built right into the walls. A guard led them toward one of the towers along the wall that ran alongside the River Thames.

They entered the stone tower and walked up a set of stairs. Next they were ushered into a room that was much smaller than she'd expected. It was rather modest but lovely in its decoration, with colored tiles on the floor and frescoes painted on the walls.

Soldiers brought in the heavy trunk and set it in the middle of the floor in front of Louisa, Charles, and his brothers. A guard opened a door at the other end of the room and King Richard entered.

Louisa knew he was the king because of his youth and

his sandy-blond beard, and also because he was dressed in an elaborately detailed robe and belt, embroidered with gold and silver thread. He made his way toward them, passing the large, cushioned armchair.

"Your Grace," a well-dressed man standing near the door said, "these are the men—the Duke of Strachleigh, the Viscount Burwelle, Sir David Raynsford of Dericott, Sir Charles Raynsford of Dericott—and with them, Louisa Lenton of Maydestone."

They all bowed low before the king.

"Rise," the king said. "Does anyone have a key to open this trunk?"

"Yes, Your Grace." Strachleigh went forward and unlocked it, then lifted the lid. "Here you will see approximately ten thousand nobles, along with a bag of gold and silver coins. There are also some other coins, mostly pennies and German marks."

The man who had announced their names to the king had taken a seat at a tiny table against the wall and was bent over, his quill scraping quietly on the parchment as he wrote.

"That is a lot of money for one village to have taken." The king was stroking his chin. "But I understand these villagers have been defrauding people in this manner for almost twenty years." He paused, looking into each of their faces before continuing. "I had heard of this scheming and thievery before you wrote to me about it, as well as about the famed giant who was supposed to be guarding the rumored Viking treasure."

Louisa did her best to listen to what he was saying, trying to forget her awe at being in the presence of a king.

"As a matter of fact, the man they captured and ransomed

was my Lord Chamberlain's nephew. He told me of the giant who kept him in a cage on top of a mountain and the villagers whose idea it was to ransom him. But if I am honest, I was reluctant to believe him. I even thought he was inventing the entire thing in a scheme to benefit himself. But after I read the letter signed by you, Strachleigh, and the brothers Raynsford, I realized it must be true."

Louisa's heart was beating a bit less hard, her breathing more normal, the longer the king spoke. But then he fixed his gaze on her and her heart started pounding again.

"I believe it was you, Louisa Lenton, who tamed the giant. Is that right?"

"Your Grace," Louisa began but had to stop to take a breath. "Allistor is very tall and large, perhaps, and some might say fearsome to look at." She paused, her throat so dry that she had to swallow in order to go on. "But he is a man and no monster. He told us that he did not like what the villagers were forcing him to do, but he was dependent on them for food."

"I see." The king nodded at her. "Go on. Tell me what happened."

"Allistor said he had grown exceptionally more than other children his age right from birth, and that he'd had a great-uncle who had also grown abnormally large and had died young, probably from his heart failing, as he'd had a lot of pains in his chest before he died. And Allistor was also having those kinds of pains and believed his time on earth would soon be ending.

"He showed us his home, which was a cave on the mountain, and he asked us to do as Sir Charles had suggested and bring some knights to stop the villagers from stealing from those who came in search of the Viking treasure."

Her voice was finally sounding stronger and less breathless, as the king was a good listener, keeping eye contact with her and nodding and raising his brows at different points in her narrative.

"And how were you and Sir Charles able to escape from the villagers?"

"Allistor told us where to go down the mountain where we'd be least likely to be seen. Two men did see us as we were nearly to the bottom and shot at us with arrows, but God protected us. Sir Charles shot one of them in the shoulder and they ran away, thankfully."

The king nodded, his gaze moving to Charles.

Louisa breathed a sigh of relief. Although her voice had sounded halting and breathless, she'd managed to get through answering his questions.

Now she had only to pray that God would cause the king to show favor to Charles for his loyalty, bravery, and honesty in bringing back the stolen money.

Charles smiled proudly at Louisa. Even though she was obviously frightened and nervous, she had done very well.

The king turned to him. "I believe it is you, Sir Charles, and this lady to whom my gratitude is due, for uncovering this thievery and unlawful activity against English citizens. And best of all, you took it upon yourselves to right this wrong, while I was untroubled and did not even need to send any of my own guards.

"Also, you have returned my chamberlain's money to him. For that I am personally grateful, and for all of these acts of valor and chivalry, I wish to reward each of you."

"That is very kind and generous of you, my king," Charles said, bowing his head.

"Each knight who went with you should get two hundred and fifty nobles, including Strachleigh and the Raynsford brothers, and for Sir Charles Raynsford, I would like to grant the right and the means to build a castle, a strong fortress that will be a defense against invaders and those who would wish to attack the monarchy when we are residing in London.

"This castle should be within forty miles of London, although I have not yet chosen a location. I would be open to suggestions. And I also wish to reward the courageous young lady. Louisa, what is it you wish for me to do for you?"

Louisa obviously had not expected to be asked that question. She looked rather wide-eyed, glancing at Charles before saying, "Your Grace, if it pleases you, I should very much like to offer my father's manor house and lands for your castle, if Your Grace would grant that the ownership of this manor house and lands be given to Sir Charles."

"You are getting married, I presume?"

"Yes, Your Grace, we are pledged to be married," Charles spoke up, feeling even prouder of his clever wife-to-be. "The lands attached to her father's manor house in Maydestone went to her uncle when her father died, but if you could transfer ownership of those to Louisa and her heirs . . ."

The king was motioning to his clerk. "Fetch me a map."

The man jumped from his seat, found what he was looking for on the shelf beside him, then spread it out on the writing table as the king walked toward it.

The king motioned to Charles. "Show me."

Charles walked forward and quickly found Maydestone, the demesne that Louisa's father had owned before his death, and pointed it out.

"This looks like a very good place for the castle," the king said, stroking his beard. "Just the sort of location I was looking for. You can see that there are no other castles in the vicinity."

Castle symbols were all over the map, but indeed, there was no castle near the place where the king was pointing.

"Then that is where you will build it. And since this area adjacent to it is a deer park where my father used to hunt, I shall give it over to you. The land belongs to you and your heirs, for hunting and farming or whatever you like. And you shall build a castle, and I shall provide whatever you need to build it, as well as reward you for your time. I shall send my master mason Harwell to help oversee the building of it.

"And since the village is called Maydestone, shall I name you the first Earl of Maydestone?"

"I like the sound of that, Your Grace. I am very grateful to you."

"Do you approve, young lady?" the king asked Louisa.

Louisa had tears in her eyes, but she was smiling. "Yes, Your Grace."

EPILOGUE

LOUISA AND CHARLES WERE MARRIED THREE WEEKS LATER in her parish church, surrounded by Charles's family, Hanilda, and Aunt Celestria. Uncle Eluard did not attend.

Charles had already decided the exact spot where the castle was to be built, and the workmen had already broken ground on it.

While Charles enjoyed everything to do with the castle—making decisions about the structure of it and helping Harwell supervise the work—Louisa was enjoying being back in her childhood home with Margaret. Serving as its mistress was quite pleasant. She reacquainted herself with her father's old tenants and rehired old servants. She went for walks next to familiar streams and on familiar trails. And she hired a tutor for Margaret. "To force you to learn and study and read," Louisa told her.

Margaret scowled her best scowl.

Louisa just laughed. "You will thank me someday."

"I doubt that." But her scowl was already turning into a smile.

Best of all was being in her childhood home with the man who was her best friend, the one who loved her and the one to whom she could tell everything.

They hoped and dreamed and prayed together, and their future seemed as bright as the early morning sun.

ACKNOWLEDGMENTS

A SPECIAL THANK YOU TO MY PUBLISHER AND THE ENTIRE team at Thomas Nelson. I'm so thankful for the past nine years that we have worked together. It has been a dream come true to have you always supporting me and blessing my books with amazing covers, inspired editing, and great sales and marketing. I will always be grateful for the experience of being published with HarperCollins Christian Publishing.

I particularly want to thank my editors, Lizzie Poteet and Julie Breihan. Thanks for everything.

Thanks to Amanda Bostic for allowing me to give life to the Dericott Tales. Thanks to Caitlin and Taylor and Kerri for all your help.

And for the best agent I know, Natasha Kern, thank you for being amazing. May you have the best retirement anyone could ever ask for! You deserve it.

As always, thank you to my wonderful readers. I could not do this without you, and I want you to know that I'm not finished yet. Lord willing, I will write many more stories for us! Keep believing and loving and giving grace every day you're alive, because you are the only you God ever made, and He calls you Beloved.

Discussion Questions

1. Why did Louisa not wish to get married, ever? How does her decision seem especially daring, given the time and culture in which she lived?

2. What did Louisa plan to do with the Viking treasure if she was able to find it? Does this sound like a good idea? What role did her desperation play in her plans?

3. Why did Louisa disguise herself as a boy? Why do you think the disguise didn't fool Charles?

4. Why was Charles not eager to fall in love again? What do you think of Lady Mirabella's behavior? How was she different from Louisa?

5. What was it about Louisa that made Charles fall in love with her? What qualities did Charles have that made her fall in love with him?

6. What did you think of Brother Matthew's reaction to the beggar child? What would you do if you encountered a child alone and begging? What did Jesus teach about the poor?

7. Why did Charles and Louisa feel a new nervousness in each other's company after Richie dressed Louisa as a woman and fixed her hair? Do you find it difficult to talk to someone you find attractive? Why or why not?

8. Why did Allistor do as the villagers said when they first told him to capture a treasure seeker and hold him for ransom? Why did he not do the same to Charles and Louisa?

9. Louisa and Margaret had lost their parents and had to go live with their aunt and uncle, who weren't very loving. How do you think this influenced their relationship with each other?

10. What was the real treasure that Louisa found on the mountain? What treasure did Allistor find when he met Charles and Louisa?

LOOKING FOR MORE GREAT READS? LOOK NO FURTHER!

THOMAS NELSON
Since 1798

From the Publisher

GREAT BOOKS

ARE EVEN BETTER WHEN THEY'RE SHARED!

Help other readers find this one:

- Post a review at your favorite online bookseller

- Post a picture on a social media account and share why you enjoyed it

- Send a note to a friend who would also love it—or better yet, give them a copy

Thanks for reading!

Don't miss any of Melanie Dickerson's *Dericott Tales*

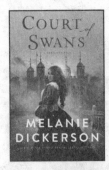

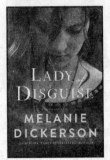

Available in print, e-book, and audio

ABOUT THE AUTHOR

Melanie Dickerson is a *New York Times* bestselling author and two-time Christy Award winner. Melanie spends her time daydreaming, researching the most fascinating historical time periods, and writing and editing her happily-ever-afters.

Visit her online at MelanieDickerson.com
Facebook: @MelanieDickersonBooks
Twitter: @MelanieAuthor
Instagram: @melaniedickerson123